'Atmospheric . . . extraordinary . . . delicate and detailed . . . *A Passage North* is an immersive experience' *Asian Review of Books*

'A timely, and timeless, mediation of collective memory . . . War, death and loss are so exquisitely rendered' John Self, *Critic*

'While [Anuk Arudpragasam's] first book examines how people live and die with war and violence all around them, this one looks at how we live and die in the aftermath . . . Arudpragasam unpacks exactly how our inner circuitry is forever rewired during instances, war-driven or otherwise, that enable closeness or disconnection, that lead to absences or ruptures . . . The novel is a tender elegy . . . [a] wholehearted and necessary act of preservation by its author' NPR

'In sentences of unusual beauty and clarity, Arudpragasam observes even the most mundane of actions – smoking a cigarette, waiting for a train, making eye contact with a stranger – with an attention so absolute it feels devotional. He is equally gifted at atmospheric, sensory description that transports the reader to Sri Lanka and India and at examining the emotions – elation, fear, impatience, satisfaction, shame – that simmer below the surface of our everyday lives . . . *A Passage North* is full of melancholy, but because it takes love and desire as seriously as it does grief and loss, it avoids despair' *New York Times*

'I strongly recommend both of Mr. Arudpragasam's novels . . . Arudpragasam's calibrated, carefully observed prose gives the novel, with all its tangents, its sense of perfect wholeness . . . So gracefully rendered are the long, balanced sentences that they envelop you – bring you to focused attention – without making a show of themselves' *Wall Street Journal*

ALSO BY ANUK ARUDPRAGASAM

The Story of a Brief Marriage

A
PASSAGE
NORTH

ANUK
ARUDPRAGASAM

GRANTA

Granta Publications, 12 Addison Avenue, London W11 4QR

First published in Great Britain by Granta Books, 2021
This paperback edition published by Granta Books, 2022
Originally published in the United States in 2021 by Hogarth, an imprint of the
Random House Publishing Group, a division of Penguin Random House LLC,
New York

A Passage North is a work of fiction. Names, characters, places, and incidents
either are the product of the author's imagination or are used fictitiously. Any
resemblance to actual persons, living or dead, events, or locales is entirely
coincidental.

A CIP catalogue record for this book is available from the British Library.

1 3 5 7 9 10 8 6 4 2

ISBN 978 1 78378 696 1
eISBN 978 1 78378 695 4

Book design by Jo Anne Metsch
Offset by Avon DataSet Ltd, Arden Court, Alcester, Warwickshire B49 6HN
Printed and bound by CPI Group (UK) Ltd, Croydon, CR0 4YY
www.granta.com

MIX
Paper from
responsible sources
FSC® C171272
FSC
www.fsc.org

A
PASSAGE
NORTH

MESSAGE

1

THE PRESENT, WE assume, is eternally before us, one of the few things in life from which we cannot be parted. It overwhelms us in the painful first moments of entry into the world, when it is still too new to be managed or negotiated, remains by our side during childhood and adolescence, in those years before the weight of memory and expectation, and so it is sad and a little unsettling to see that we become, as we grow older, much less capable of touching, grazing, or even glimpsing it, that the closest we seem to get to the present are those brief moments we stop to consider the spaces our bodies are occupying, the intimate warmth of the sheets in which we wake, the scratched surface of the window on a train taking us somewhere else, as if the only way we can hold time still is by trying physically to prevent the objects around us from moving. The present, we realize, eludes us more and more as the years go by, showing itself for fleeting moments before losing us in the world's incessant movement, fleeing the second we look away and leaving scarcely a trace of its passing, or this at least is how it usually seems in retrospect, when in the next brief moment of consciousness, the next occasion we are able to hold things still, we realize how much time has passed since we were last aware of ourselves, when we realize how many days, weeks, and months have slipped by without our consent. Events take place, moods ebb and flow, people and situations come and go, but looking back during these rare junctures in which we are, for whatever reason, lifted up from the circular daydream of everyday life, we are slightly surprised to find ourselves in the places we are, as though we were absent while everything was happening, as though we were somewhere else during the time that is usually referred to as our life. Waking up each morning we follow by circuitous routes the thread of habit, out of our homes, into the world, and back to our beds at night, move unseeingly through familiar paths, one day giving way to another and one week to the next, so that when in the midst of this daydream something happens and the thread is finally cut, when, in a moment of strong desire or unexpected loss, the rhythms of life are interrupted, we look around and are quietly surprised to see that the world is vaster than we thought, as if we'd been tricked or cheated out of all that time, time that in retrospect appears to have contained nothing of substance, no change and no duration, time that has come and gone but left us somehow untouched.

Standing there before the window of his room, looking out through the dust-coated pane of glass at the empty lot next door, at the ground overrun by grasses and weeds, the empty bottles of arrack scattered near the gate, it was this strange sense of being cast outside time that held Krishan still as he tried to make sense of the call he'd just received, the call that had put an end to all his plans for the evening, the call informing him that Rani, his grandmother's former caretaker, had died. He'd come home not long before from the office of the NGO at which he worked, had taken off his shoes and come upstairs to find, as usual, his grandmother standing outside his room, waiting impatiently to share all the thoughts she'd saved up over the course of the day. His grandmother knew he left work between five and half past five on most days, that if he came straight home, depending on whether he took a three-wheeler, bus, or walked, he could be expected at home between a quarter past five and a quarter past six. His timely arrival was an axiom in the organization of her day, and she held him to it with such severity that she would, if there was ever any deviation from the norm, be appeased only by a detailed explanation, that an urgent meeting or deadline had kept him at work longer than usual, that the roads had been blocked because of some rally or procession, when she'd become convinced, in other words, that the deviation was exceptional and that the laws she'd laid down in her room for the operation of the world outside were still in motion. He'd listened as she talked about the clothes she needed to wash, about her conjectures on what his mother was making for dinner, about her plans to shampoo her hair the next morning, and when at last there was a pause in her speech he'd begun to shuffle away, saying he was going out with friends later and wanted to rest a while in his room. She would be hurt by his unexpected desertion, he knew, but he'd been waiting all afternoon for some time alone, had been waiting for peace and quiet so he could think about the email he'd received earlier in the day, the first communication he'd received from Anjum in so long, the first attempt she'd made since the end of their relationship to find out what he was doing and what his life now was like. He'd closed the browser as soon as he finished reading the message, had suppressed his desire to pore over and scrutinize every word, knowing he'd be unable to finish his work if he let himself reflect on the email, that it was best to wait till he was home and could think about everything undisturbed. He'd talked with his grandmother a little more—it was her habit to ask more questions when she knew he wanted to leave, as a way of postponing or prolonging his departure—then watched as she turned reluctantly into her room and closed the door behind her. He'd remained in the vestibule a moment longer, had then gone to his room, closed the door, and turned the key twice in the lock, as if double-bolting the door would guarantee him the solitude he sought. He'd turned on the fan, peeled off his clothes, then changed into a fresh T-shirt and pair of shorts, and it was just as he'd lain down on his bed and stretched out his limbs, just as he'd prepared himself to consider the email and the images it brought to the surface of his mind, that the phone in the hall began to ring, its insistent, high-pitched tone invading his room through the door. He'd sat up on the bed and waited a few seconds in the hope it would stop, but the ringing had continued without pause and slightly annoyed, deciding to deal with the call as quickly as possible, brusquely if necessary, he'd gotten up and made his way to the hall.

The caller had introduced herself, somewhat hesitantly, as Rani's eldest daughter, an introduction whose meaning it had taken him a few seconds to register, not only because he'd been distracted by the email but also because it had been some time since the thought of his grandmother's caretaker Rani had crossed his mind. The last time he'd seen her had been seven or eight months before, when she had left to go on what was supposed to have been just a four- or five-day trip to her village in the north. She had gone to make arrangements for the five-year death anniversary of her youngest son, who'd been killed by shelling on the penultimate day of the war, then to attend the small remembrance that would be held the day after by survivors at the site of the final battle, which was only a few hours by bus from where she lived. She'd called a week later to say she would need a little more time, that there were some urgent matters she needed to attend to before returning—they'd spent more money than planned on the anniversary, apparently, and she needed to go to her son-in-law's village to discuss finances with her daughter and son-in-law in person, which wouldn't take more than a day or two. It was two weeks before they heard back from her again, when she called to say she'd gotten sick, it had been raining and she'd caught some kind of flu, she'd told them, would need just a few more days to recover before making the long journey back. It had been hard to imagine Rani seriously affected by flu, for despite the fact that she was in her late fifties, her large frame and substantial build gave the impression of someone exceptionally robust, not the kind of person it was easy to imagine laid low by a common virus. Krishan could still remember how on New Year's Day the year before, when they'd been boiling milk rice in the garden early in the morning, one of the three bricks that propped up the fully laden steel pot had given way, causing the pot to tip, how Rani had without any hesitation bent down and held the burning pot steady with her bare hands, waiting, without any sign of urgency, for him to reposition the brick so she could set the pot back down. If she hadn't yet returned it couldn't have been that she was too weak or too sick for the ride back home, he and his mother had felt, the delay had its source, more likely, in the strain of the anniversary and the remembrance on her already fragile mental state. Not wanting to put unnecessary pressure on her they'd told her not to worry, to take her time, to come back only when she was feeling better. Appamma's condition had improved dramatically since she'd come to stay with them and she no longer needed to be watched every hour of the day and night, the two of them would be able to manage without help for a few more days. Another three weeks passed without any news, and after calling several times and getting no response, Krishan and his mother had been forced to conclude that they were wrong, that Rani simply didn't want to come back. It was surprising that she hadn't bothered to call and tell them, since she was usually meticulous about matters of that kind, but most likely she'd just gotten so sick of spending all her time alone with Appamma that it didn't even occur to her that she should let them know. Confined to a small room in a house on the other side of the country, forced to tolerate the endless drone of Appamma's voice every day and night, unable to go outside the house for significant periods of time, since she didn't know anyone and couldn't speak Sinhalese, it made sense, they'd agreed between themselves, if Rani had decided after almost two years in Colombo that it was time finally to leave.

Krishan had told Rani's daughter that his mother wasn't at home, that it would be a couple of hours before she would return, had asked whether there was any message he could pass on, and after pausing for a moment she'd told him, without any particular emotion in her voice, that Rani, her mother, had died. He hadn't responded at first, the words he'd heard strangely devoid of meaning in his head, then after a few seconds had managed to ask how, what had happened, when. It had happened the previous night, she told him, after dinner, her mother had gone to get water from the well and had fallen in, nobody knew exactly how. They'd begun looking for her about twenty minutes after she'd disappeared, had searched all over for three quarters of an hour till her eldest child, Rani's granddaughter, had gone right up to the well, leaned over the wall to look inside, and begun to scream. She'd fallen headfirst and broken her neck, either by striking the wall on the way down or the floor of the well, which contained no more than a foot or two of water. Krishan asked how she'd fallen, whether it had been an accident, not knowing whether this was a foolish or insensitive question, and Rani's daughter replied that of course it was an accident, it was dark and there was no light, her mother must have tripped on the elevated concrete platform that surrounded the well, or perhaps she'd fainted while drawing water and fallen, she'd been complaining about headache and dizziness earlier in the day. She said all this in a somewhat mechanical tone, as if nothing about what had happened was shocking or surprising to her, and had then fallen silent, as if there was nothing more to say on the matter. Krishan wanted to know more, and wanting perhaps to ward off more questions Rani's daughter added that the funeral, if he and his mother could make it, would be on Sunday afternoon. Krishan said he would let his mother know and that they would certainly come if they could, a statement that immediately felt absurd, not only because he was unsure whether the suggestion that they attend was something Rani's daughter actually desired or merely a formality, but also because he realized as he gave his answer that he still didn't quite believe what he had been told. He felt an urge to ask more questions, to ask who else had been present the night before, whether there'd been any other signs earlier in the day, had Rani said or done anything odd or unusual, had she been having headaches or dizziness regularly, had she finished dinner, what had they been eating, to ask for any detail really, however trivial, for there is always a need at such times to seek out more information, not because the information itself is important but because without it the event cannot be believed, as though you needed to hear all the circumstantial details that connected the unlikely death to the so-called real world before you could accept that its occurrence was not in opposition to the laws of nature. It was the fact, above all, that sudden or violent deaths could occur not merely in a war zone or during race riots but during the slow, unremarkable course of everyday life that made them so disturbing and so difficult to accept, as though the possibility of death was contained in even the most routine of actions, in even the ordinary, unnoticed moments of life. Suddenly the small details that are glossed over in your usual accounting of life took on an almost cosmic significance, as though your fate could be determined by whether or not you remembered to draw water before it became dark, by whether you hurried to catch the bus or decided to take your time, by whether or not you said yes or no to any of the countless trivial decisions that come only in retrospect, once the event has occurred and nothing can be changed, to take on greater significance. Krishan couldn't think of anything to ask without seeming insensitive or overly inquisitive, and wanting to extend the conversation however he could he'd asked how far their village was from Kilinochchi town, what the best way was to get there. His mother would know, Rani's daughter said, once they got to town they would have to take two buses, after which they would have to walk or take a three-wheeler to the village. There was another pause, and unable to think of anything else to ask, seeing that Rani's daughter was unwilling to say or add anything more, Krishan was forced to say goodbye.

He'd remained standing there in the hall for some time, long after he heard the click on the other end of the line, and it was only when the phone began to make a continuous and disconcertingly shrill beep that he put it back down on the hook and drifted back to his room. He locked the door, walked slowly back to his bed, and sat down where he'd been sitting earlier. He picked up his cellphone, thinking to tell his mother the news, then remembered she was teaching and wouldn't be able to answer till classes were over at seven-thirty. Putting the phone aside he looked around the room restlessly, at the miscellanea of things on the dressing table opposite, at his work clothes inside-out on the floor in front of him, the books and clothes and DVDs strewn on his brother's unused bed. He picked up his trousers and turned them the right way around, folded them and placed them neatly on the bed. He did the same for his shirt, then looking around the room once more, got up and went to the window. Leaning upon the sill with both hands, forehead pressed lightly against the grille, he gazed out at the balcony of the house on the other side of the empty lot, at the clothes strung out on the line and the small TV satellite on the darkened terra-cotta roof. He tried to think about the phone call and what he had learned, of Rani's death and how it had occurred, but the news still felt unreal to him, like something he couldn't yet appreciate or understand. He felt not so much sadness as a kind of embarrassment for the way the news had caught him, in the midst of his self-involved thoughts about Anjum's email and his impatience in dealing with his grandmother, as if by jarring him out of his ordinary consciousness the call had compelled him to think, paradoxically, not about Rani but himself, to look at himself from the outside and to see from a distance the life in which he'd been immersed. He thought of the way he'd responded to the arrival of the email that afternoon, the way he'd leaned up close to his laptop and stared at the screen without moving, the quiet surprise he'd felt as he read the message and the quiet anticipation that had followed, an anticipation he'd done his best to stifle, knowing it couldn't be justified by the content of the message itself. The email had been fairly short, consisting of three or four carefully rendered sentences, deliberate and yet quietly lyrical, sentences that were intended to divulge no more and no less than Anjum wanted. They told very little of her life and asked very little of his too, this of course being Anjum's way, her way not just of writing but of being also, though perhaps, he thought to himself, she'd written so little only because she hadn't wanted to impose on him without permission, because she'd wanted to offer him the possibility of communication without obliging a substantial response. She'd been in Bombay for a couple of weeks, she'd written, where she'd taken a short break from the work she was doing in Jharkhand, the first time she'd returned to that city after the two of them had gone there four years before. She'd gone for a walk along the coast and had been reminded of the walk they'd taken there on the last day of their trip, had wondered how he was doing, whether his time since returning to Sri Lanka had given him everything he sought. She thought of him from time to time and hoped he was doing well, that he'd managed to find in his new home, with the passage of time, a solution to all his yearning, concluding the body of the email by attaching to that very specific word, yearning, the almost paradoxical idea of a solution, then signing off with only her first initial.

The message revealed nothing of the nature of Anjum's occasional thoughts of him, Krishan had noted almost immediately, and made no mention either of how Anjum's own life in the previous years had been, whether the home she'd set up in rural Jharkhand with her activist friends had given her what she wanted, whether she was fulfilled or disenchanted, satisfied or disappointed with what life had brought. It was unclear whether her decision to write now was related to some process of taking stock, of reflecting on other paths she might have taken or might still take, or whether on the other hand it was a matter only of disinterested curiosity, of the ordinary, passing interest that people often had in the lives of their former lovers. She'd written, too, as though their parting of ways had been mutual, as though each of them had been moved in their own directions by their own separate desires and histories, attributing a kind of agency to him that, he knew, he hadn't actually possessed in the relationship. Anjum had decided to leave Delhi long before she met him, had been planning for some time to make a base in Jharkhand with her friends and other activists she knew, with her comrades as she often put it without irony. The limited nature of their time together in Delhi had been decided therefore from the very beginning, and already from the beginning their future separation was something he'd known he'd have to plan for and expect. He himself had loosely considered the possibility of leaving Delhi before meeting Anjum, of abandoning the life he'd built there over several years and the PhD program he'd recently begun, of returning to Sri Lanka to contribute somehow to the efforts to rebuild and recover after the war. He'd become obsessed, in the years since the end of the fighting, with the massacres that had taken place in the northeast, become more and more possessed by guilt for having been spared, coming to long for the kind of life he might lead if he left the inert spaces of academia he'd become sequestered in and went to live and work in a place that actually meant something to him. This abstract longing to be in his imagined homeland had receded to the periphery of his mind soon after meeting Anjum, for whom, he realized very quickly, he was willing to abandon all his other hopes and plans, so unparalleled was their time together, so unlike anything that had come before or since. He'd hoped as they became closer that Anjum would consider rethinking her own plans, that she would consider including him in her new life or at least giving him access to her once she moved away, but she seldom took up any of the allusions he made to the possibility of a shared future together, implying with a combination of silences and stray remarks that the project she was beginning signified a complete break from her life in Delhi, a break that would be compromised if she remained with him after she moved.

It was their relationship, ironically, that had given content to his abstract earlier notion of return, not so much through conversations they had, since Anjum seemed reluctant to discuss her work in much detail with him, as through the example she herself embodied of what a life organized around a social or political vision could be. She didn't look down on his academic pursuits exactly, but he could tell she gave them little importance, and the longer he spent in her presence the more respectable his earlier ideas of abandoning academia seemed, the more earnestly he began to wonder whether a life governed by some ideal of collective action was possible for him as well. Anjum's unwavering dedication to the women's and labor movements she worked for in Delhi had already been making him feel, almost as a kind of self-defense, that he too needed to devote himself to a cause larger and more encompassing than himself, and knowing that he'd be unable to remain in Delhi once she left, driven by a need to prove both to himself and to her that he had a cause of his own, an independent destiny that would lead him somewhere with or without her, he'd actively begun redirecting his thoughts of the future toward the idea of a life in the northeast of Sri Lanka. It was a naïve idea in a way, since he had no notion what social work in the former war zone would entail, had none of the specific skills or experiences that would help him in this kind of vocation, but unable to bear the thought of waiting impassively as Anjum's impending departure drew nearer he'd begun to cultivate once more his sense of having a destiny in that place he'd never actually lived, fantasizing about what it would be like to walk over the same land his forebears had, to help create out of near annihilation the possibility of

some new and compelling future, as though living a life simpli-
fied in the way that only war can simplify he too would be able
to find something worth surrendering to.

It was strange to think how much had changed between
then and now, Krishan thought as he stood there in front of the
window, not in any sudden or decisive way but simply with the
decision to move back and the slow accumulation of time, how
what had once seemed like a distant, inaccessible, almost mysti-
cal place was now such an integral part of him. The predomi-
nant associations he'd had of the northeast for most of his life
had been formed during short trips to Trincomalee and Vavuniya when he was a child and a longer trip to Jaffna during
the cease-fire, when he was seventeen or eighteen, from the
painfully nostalgic accounts he'd always heard from older relatives living abroad about how idyllic their childhoods in the village had been. For most of his life he'd visualized, when he
thought of the northeast, wide landscapes of salt flats and palmyra trees, the copper-colored dirt roads of the Vanni and the
tracts of hard, dry earth that made up most of the peninsula,
the piercing, lilting rhythms of devotional music rising up from
temples during festival season, the sound of people speaking
their untainted Tamil loudly and musically, without restraint.
These images had filled him with a sense of freedom, with the
possibility of living a life radically different from his own, but
they'd been suffused at the same time with a dreamlike quality
that made it hard to think about them in any concrete way, just
as the news that arrived each day in the newspapers about shell-
ings and skirmishes, about advances, retreats, and cease-fires,
had always been of importance and concern but rarely dis-
rupted the flow of events in his own life in the south of the

country, part of the white noise of life that he'd learned since childhood to take for granted.

It was only much later that events in the northeast began to penetrate more deeply into the pattern of his everyday life, toward the end of the war in 2008 and 2009 when it was beginning to seem, for the first time, that the Tigers might be defeated, and with them the idea of a Tamil-speaking state in the northeast. He'd been in the final year of his undergraduate course in Delhi at the time, in the midst of applying for graduate programs in political science, and he could remember spending days trying without success to work in the blissfully ignorant silence of his college library, anxiously refreshing the news websites he kept permanently open on his computer at the time. There were rumors of vast numbers of civilians being killed by the army, and he'd known very well that the government's account of a humanitarian rescue mission in the northeast was a falsification, that nothing he read in the newspapers could be trusted. He'd spent hours poring through the internet in English and Tamil, going page by page through blogs, forums, and news sites that shared images and videos taken during the last months of fighting, most of these sites set up by diasporic Tamils who posted material that survivors had taken on cellphones and cameras and managed somehow to send abroad. The internet, he realized, was rife with the civilian photographic archives of recent wars around the world, each one a seemingly endless maze of nameless violence, and in the months following the war's end he'd spent much of his time exploring these archives at leisure, gazing blankly at images of bloated bodies and severed limbs, of molested corpses, burning tents, and screaming children, many of which remained imprinted in his mind with disturbing clarity. It was impossible to forget these images once they'd been glimpsed, not just because of the violence they showed but also because of their strikingly amateur quality, for unlike the highly aestheticized, almost tasteful shots of war one often came across in books and magazines, the images he found online were of jarringly poor composition. The images were grainy and blurred, carelessly framed and focused—a ruptured tube of toothpaste on the ground beside a corpse, a stunned old woman swatting flies from her wounded leg—as though taken on the run or as though the individuals taking them didn't want to look at what they were capturing. They were images, he couldn't help feeling, that he wasn't supposed to see, depicting people in positions they would sooner die than be discovered in, the fear in their eyes due less to the terror of the situation than the terror of being captured in states of such intimate agony, their gazes filling him with shame even as he was unable to turn away.

For a long time the horror these images elicited remained buried inside him, a morbid reality that he was constantly feeding and yet unable to express, as though unable to fully believe or understand what they depicted. It was only when the Channel Four documentary came out in 2011, accusing the government of war crimes and genocide, when later that year the UN published its report giving an estimate of how many civilians had died, that he was finally able to speak about what had happened, to accept that the images he'd become obsessed with were not some strange, perverted creation of his subconscious life, that they represented things that had really happened in the country he was from. Even now he felt ashamed thinking about his initial reluctance to acknowledge the magnitude of what had happened at the end of the war, as though he'd been hesitant to believe the evidence on his computer screen because his own poor, violated, stateless people were the ones alleging it, as though he'd been unable to take the suffering of his own people seriously till it was validated by the authority of a panel of foreign experts, legitimized by a documentary narrated by a clean-shaven white man standing in front of a camera in suit and tie. Like most Tamils his age living outside the war zone, whether Colombo or Chennai or Paris or Toronto, he'd watched the documentary and read the report several times, had continued trying to find out everything he could afterward, reading every article and essay that came out in both English and Tamil, watching all the interviews he could find with survivors on YouTube. His initial disbelief gave way first to shock, then to anger, and then to shame at his own easy existence, this shame giving rise, over the months that followed, to an uncanny sense of unreality, as though the world he was inhabiting in Delhi was somehow illusory, his courses at university and future academic plans, the protests and demonstrations he went to almost as a pastime, the various friends, lovers, and crushes who made up his social life. Nothing around him seemed to register the extent of what had happened—even on the final day of the war life in college went on more or less as usual, everyone immersed in studying for their end-of-term exams—and this incongruity between his environment and what was going on inside him—his growing sense that the world as he understood it had come to an end—led him to feel that the spaces he inhabited lacked some vital dimension of reality, that his life in Delhi was a kind of dream or hallucination. It was probably some dissonance of this kind, it occurred to

him now, that had led so many Tamils living in foreign countries to such acts of desperation, that led that boy whose name
he could no longer remember to travel from London to Ge-
neva so he could set himself on fire in front of the UN building
in February 2009, that led tens of thousands of protesters, most
of them refugees, to spontaneously gather three months later
on one of Toronto's major highways and bring the entire city's
traffic to a standstill—as if these exiled Tamils were willing to
go to any length to force the alien environments in which they
now lived, so far from the northeast of Sri Lanka, to come at
least briefly to a stop, to reflect or register in some way the cessation of life that they knew was occurring in their place of
birth.

Perhaps because he'd grasped the enormity of what had
happened only after everything was already over, when there
was no longer anything that could be done, perhaps because
he'd had no Tamil friends in Delhi with whom he could talk or
process his feelings, his own response to the end of the war had
taken a more inward direction. Thinking of that period now he
was slightly taken aback by the quiet intensity of his reaction,
by the unhealthy fervor with which he immersed himself in all
the images and videos he found, the diligence with which he
tried to reconstruct that situation from which he'd been spared.
He'd begun making mental timelines of the displacement of
civilians from their villages across the northeast, of the locations of the various hospitals that had come under attack by the
government, of the sites of the no-fire zones at which the worst
massacres had occurred, studying all the maps of the war zone
he could find and learning everything he could about these different places. He did his best to obtain every little piece of infor-

mation he could, noting the different kinds of shell the army had used and the different kinds of sounds they made as they fell, the weather conditions and soil composition at all the different sites of killing, guessing or inventing all the details he couldn't verify, re-creating those sites of violence in his mind so meticulously that his intention could only have been to personally inhabit them somehow. There was an element of self-hatred in these labors, he knew, a desire to punish himself for what he'd escaped by exposing himself to it as violently as he could, but it struck him now that perhaps there was also something religious in his devotion to understanding the circumstances under which so many people had been erased from the world, as though he was trying to construct, through this act of imagination, a kind of private shrine to the memory of all those anonymous lives.

Looking out through the window at the empty, endless sky, still golden yellow but streaked now by long, ribbonlike clouds of rose, Krishan thought of a poem he'd read many years before in the *Periya Purānam,* parts of which they'd had to study in some detail for literature at school. He'd had little interest in old Tamil literature at the time, had spent most classes gazing out through the window at the cricket ground next door, but the story of Poosal had, for some reason, always stayed with him. Poosal, according to the poem, was an impoverished man from a far-flung village who was possessed of unusually intense religiosity. From a young age his thoughts and feelings had always been lovingly directed toward Siva, and his entire adult life had been spent nurturing this instinctive love and trying to make it stronger. For a long time he'd been seeking a way by which he could honor his lord, the poem explained, and deciding after much reflection that the most fitting tribute would be to build a temple for Siva to live in, Poosal had energetically begun searching for all the necessary land and materials. For several months he looked into every possibility, going to every town and village in the area and meeting every important personage he knew, but gradually, after many failed attempts, it began to dawn on him that he'd never be able to obtain the resources needed to build his temple, that he was simply too poor to serve his lord the way he wished. Devastated, he sank into a state of deep despair, a condition of hopelessness he remained submerged in for some time, apparently, till reflecting on his situation one day it occurred to him that he could, instead of building a physical temple for Siva, simply build a temple for him in his mind. Stunned by the obviousness of this idea, Poosal had set to work at once. He found first a perfect plot of land in his mind, then began acquiring in his imagination all the materials that would be needed for his labor, from the smallest, most finely made tools to the heaviest slabs of stone. He solicited, mentally, all the best carpenters, masons, craftsmen, and artists, and then on an auspicious date, lovingly and attentively, laid the imaginary foundation stone deep in the center of the plot of land, following all of the stipulations set down in the relevant texts. With great care and studious rigor he began to work on the structure of the temple, refusing to sleep even at night, first completing the foundation, then adding layer upon layer to the edifice, so that over a period of several days the temple took form in his mind, from the halls and columns to the molding above the portals and the plinths. When all the towers and subsidiary shrines were completed, when the tank was dug and filled and the outer walls at last raised, he put the finial into place, saw to all the necessary details, then finally, exhausted but satisfied by his labor, chose an auspicious time for the consecration of the temple to Siva.

According to the text the king of the realm had, at the same time, been putting the final touches to a temple that he himself had been building in honor of Siva, and had happened to choose for the consecration of his temple the very same auspicious day and time that Poosal had. The royal temple was of unprecedented scale, built over many years and at vast expenditure, but the night before Siva's image was to be installed there, according to the poem, Siva appeared in the king's dreams to inform him that he wouldn't be able to attend the ceremony, that it would have to be postponed, since he'd decided instead to attend the consecration of a grand temple constructed in his honor by a man called Poosal, a loving devotee of his from the faraway village of Ninravur. Waking up the next morning, the king was stunned that a common man had built a temple that Siva preferred to the one he himself had built. He set off with his retinue for Ninravur, and when after many days of traveling they at last approached the lush groves of the village, the king ordered the locals to take him so he could see what Poosal had built. They knew who Poosal was, he was told in response, but he was a poor man, and he hadn't built any temple. The king was nonplussed on hearing this but ordered to be taken to Poosal regardless, and dismounting from his horse out of respect for the devotee he went to his modest dwelling place by foot, where he found an emaciated man sitting cross-legged on the ground, eyes closed and blissfully unaware of anything around him. The king called out to the man and asked him where his temple was, the one that everyone in the world was praising—

he'd come to see it because Lord Siva himself had said he was going to be installed there that day. Bewildered by the regal voice, Poosal opened his eyes with surprise and looked up at the man speaking to him, whom he recognized at once to be the king. He recounted humbly how he'd lacked the means to build a physical temple for Siva, how he'd painstakingly thought a temple into existence in his mind instead, and amazed by the devotion of this man who'd lacked any resources and nevertheless managed to honor his lord, the king had fallen to the ground in praise of Poosal, his fragrant garlands mingling with the earth.

Krishan would not have been able to say, as he stood there in his room, to what extent this poem he'd read so long ago had influenced his reaction to the events of the war, but it occurred to him now that the structure Poosal had constructed so meticulously in his mind was not so different, in a way, from the one he himself had constructed in the months and years after the war's end. He too had more or less abandoned the world around him to cultivate a kind of alternative space in his mind, and even if the time he'd spent dwelling in this site had been painful rather than joyful, driven as much by shame as by love, he too had in some way hoped that the object of his thoughts, the suffering of his partly real, partly virtual community, might receive through his labor a recognition it hadn't received in the real world. Thinking of his first months working in the northeast after his return to the island, Krishan could still remember the distinct sense he'd had of physically entering a place he'd imagined into existence, the feeling he was moving not so much across solid earth as across some region in the outskirts of his mind. He'd begun working for a small, local, underfunded NGO in Jaffna, earning little more than he needed to survive, and traveling on broken roads between bombed-out villages that glimmered with the corrugated steel and aluminum of makeshift homes, past the resentful glances of men who could no longer protect, the tired eyes of women who now bore all responsibility for the continuation of life, it was as though the scenes of prior violence he'd re-created in his mind were superimposed over everything he saw. The last shells had long since fallen, the last bodies been long since cleared, but the mood and texture of this violence suffused the places he went to such an extent that even his way of walking changed while he was in the northeast, his gait acquiring the same quiet reverence of someone moving in a cemetery or cremation ground. There were glimpses occasionally of a simplicity and beauty hearkening back to another kind of life—the joyful laughter of two girls sharing a bicycle on their way to school in the morning, the careless splashing of an old man filling up buckets of water at a well in the gathering dusk—and seeing the violence of the final years of war everywhere around him but also, at such moments, visions of possible futures, he'd given himself up to the work before him with vigorous, single-minded discipline.

He'd become, during his time in the northeast, less abstract and more grounded, more connected to the land and people that till then he'd seen mainly on screens, gradually internalizing the cyclical rhythms of rural life, where time never seemed to be heading anywhere but was always circling, returning, and repeating, bringing the self back to itself. He'd envisioned participating in some kind of dramatic change, in some kind of sudden rising or flourishing after all the pain and grief, but as the months turned into a year and as one year turned into two he began to realize that these visions would never be achieved, that some forms of violence could penetrate so deeply into the psyche that there was simply no question of fully recovering. Recovery was something that would take decades, which even then would be partial and ambiguous, and if he wanted to help in a meaningful way it would have to be in a way that was sustainable for him in the long term, without having to abandon all his needs for its sake. As his initial urgency and unity of purpose wore away, he began spending more of his weekends in Colombo, making the seven-hour journey back home two, sometimes even three times a month. The city had transformed dramatically in the years since the end of the war, its widened roads brightly lit by shop signs and electronic billboards, its skyline populated by sleek hotels and luxury apartment buildings, its new cafés, bars, and restaurants teeming with people he didn't know and couldn't place. Krishan registered these changes with resentment, as if the city's sudden modernity was in direct relation to the evisceration of the northeast, but he couldn't help being drawn to the easy distractions this urban life seemed to offer, and when a position opened up at one of the large foreign NGOs in Colombo—highly bureaucratic, well-compensated, and concerned mainly with applications and reports—he'd decided it was time to return, not for very long, he told himself, just until he'd saved up some money and had a better sense of what his next steps were. He'd settled back into life at home with his mother and grandmother after the better part of a decade away, old habits and routines returning but mingled with the freedoms of adulthood, his free time spent meeting old friends and new acquaintances, seeing the occasional or potential lover, reading and watching films at home. These small but varied pleasures had distracted him for a while, but there was a difference between pleasure that soothed and lulled one to sleep and pleasure that drew the self more widely and vividly into the world, and thinking of his return to Colombo now it seemed to him, as he stood there in front of the window, that something vital had been lost over the course of the previous year, the sense, so strong for most of his twenties, that his life could be part of some larger thing, part of some movement or vision to which he could give himself up.

Krishan turned from the window and looked around at the room in front of him, the room he'd grown up in with his younger brother and which, in the last few years, since his brother moved abroad, he'd had mostly to himself. The room was still suspended in the warm glow of early evening, but the shaft of light that fell from the window had moved along the floor, indicating that he'd been standing there for a considerable amount of time. He remembered the call from Rani's daughter and realized that he'd been thinking only about himself since returning to his room, that he'd failed to bring himself any closer to the fact of Rani's death, as though he was trying, somehow, to evade the significance of what he'd learned. He went to the dressing table, picked up his phone, and after hesitating a moment, dialed his mother's number. There was still time before her class ended but he hoped she would pick up, that in communicating the news to her he himself might better understand its meaning. The phone rang for a while before playing the network's automated message, informing him that the number he was calling was not available, and putting the phone down Krishan thought of his grandmother, who was probably sitting in her room with nothing to do. He hadn't yet told her about the call, and he could perhaps go to her room now and let her know. The news would sadden her, no doubt, but his grandmother wasn't the kind of person who was easily affected by the deaths of other people, in a way would even be grateful to learn what happened to Rani, obtaining from it the urgency and excitement that even a painful happening can generate in the life of someone without much to do. Relieved there was someone he could talk to, the one person ironically who always wanted to talk to him, he went to the door, turned the key in the lock, and took the four short steps across the vestibule that separated their rooms. It was only when he put his hand on the doorknob that he began to have doubts, realized that informing his grandmother right away might not actually be the wisest way to proceed. It was Appamma after all who would be most affected by Rani's death, Appamma who'd shared a room with Rani for more than a year and a half, and perhaps the best course of action was to keep the news from reaching her altogether, to let her go about her life with no notion that Rani had died alone in a well the night before. He remained in front of his grandmother's door, wanting to go in and talk but unsure whether it was a good idea, till feeling at last an urge to glance into her room, as if by getting a glimpse of her he would know what to do, he let go of the doorknob and knelt down in front of the door, closing his left eye and squinting in through the keyhole with his right.

2

APPAMMA'S DOOR WAS in line with the chair by the window, and peering into her room Krishan could make out her figure from behind, her body slumped forward on the chair, her arms placed along the armrests, and her legs stretched out on the stool in front of her, in accordance with her belief that keeping them horizontal was beneficial for her circulation. Her head was tilted to the side and hanging forward slightly, as if she were staring down at her lap, and from time to time it jerked up like something had startled her before sinking back down. His grandmother, Krishan realized as he stared through the keyhole, had accidentally fallen asleep. It was not an occurrence that was rare, given her difficulty sleeping during the nights, when she sometimes got up to go to the bathroom four or five times before dawn, but it wasn't something he could have counted on or expected either, especially not in the evenings when she was generally most on her guard. It happened usually only in the early afternoons, when she was lying in bed with the afternoon movie playing on the TV, very occasionally in the late mornings too, when she was sitting in her chair waiting for lunch to be brought up to her room. His grandmother didn't like being caught sleeping in the daytime, he knew, especially if it was obvious that she hadn't fallen asleep intentionally. Accidentally falling asleep indicated that she wasn't in complete control of her body, that sometimes her body acted of its own accord, independently of her own wishes, which wasn't something she could let other people think. If she ever woke up after a nap and discovered that someone had come into her room she would strenuously deny that she'd been sleeping, even if she hadn't been asked or challenged, would claim to have been resting with her eyes closed, enjoying the breeze, even if just a moment before her mouth had been hanging wide open and her snoring audible through the door. Seeing no reason to hurt her pride Krishan always avoided going near his grandmother at such times, had learned, over the years, if for some reason he did need to wake her up, to make a loud noise from afar before entering her room, to bang a door or pretend to sneeze so she would have time to compose herself before he was in front of her. He took these measures in part so she wouldn't feel anxious or embarrassed, so she wouldn't feel the need to persuade him she'd been awake and not asleep, but even more than this because it bothered him that his grandmother was willing to tell such obvious lies to convince him she was in good health. Almost everyone told falsehoods, it was true, in order to maintain in their minds a certain image of themselves, but whereas everyone else told these lies skillfully, without exposing the insecurities at their source, his grandmother's lies revealed that she was capable now of only the most transparent attempts at maintaining her preferred self-image, betraying herself far more in uttering them than if she'd simply kept silent.

Krishan moved back a little from the keyhole. He didn't want to wake his grandmother up, and was sure now that he shouldn't inform her about Rani's death, that for the time being at least it was best to let her continue existing in her state of ignorance. He didn't want to return to the stillness of his room either, and feeling an urge suddenly to put as much distance as possible between himself and the house, it occurred to him that he could leave to go for a walk, that being out in the open for a while, smoking a cigarette in his usual spot, he would be able to collect his thoughts. He went to his room, changed quickly into a pair of trousers, and put his pack of cigarettes and lighter into his pocket, left his phone on the desk and went downstairs. Stepping out of the house he saw with a little relief that it was still relatively bright outside, the sky still a pale, weightless blue, and closing the gate behind him he made his way up the lane with quick, determined strides. He passed the neighboring houses, the construction site where the workers were finishing up for the day, the sound of trickling water audible from their makeshift shower on the ground floor, turned left at the end of the lane and headed in the direction of Marine Drive. An un-broken stream of cars and vans was rushing past in both direc-tions, the vastness of the sea glimmering beyond them, and crossing the road as soon as a break emerged in the traffic he began to head south, keeping to the pavement between the road and railway tracks except for occasional stretches where the pavement seemed to disappear. Taking his lighter out and sparking it with his thumb he looked around distractedly as he walked, at a parked three-wheeler with an icon of the Buddha attached to its rear window, concentric circles of colored LED lights creating the illusion of a halo revolving around his head, at an elderly Muslim woman doing her best to keep up with a young girl and boy, her grandchildren most likely, who were tugging at her hands. Cars, vans, and three-wheelers continued to rush past in both directions, as though keen to avoid the twi-light, and the people passing him seemed fully absorbed in their various destinations too, tired commuters hurrying to the sta-tion to catch the next train home, aging men and women tak-ing their evening exercise in T-shirts and tracksuits, swinging their arms with exaggerated motion as they power walked toward some imaginary goal. It took a while to fall into a rhythm after the quiet of his room, to assimilate the sound and movement of the city into a workable state of equilibrium, but putting more distance from their house he began to feel calmer, to relax into a more even pace as he made his way along his habitual route.

His walks had become an unexpected routine in the previ-ous few months, one of the few effective strategies he'd found for escaping the restlessness that had begun taking hold when he returned in the evenings from work. In his first months of being in Colombo he'd still been engrossed by all the possibili-ties of life in the city, by the prospect of going out in the eve-nings, drinking and smoking weed, being obnoxious or lighthearted with friends, meeting attractive people with whom he could flirt. These activities had given movement and struc-ture to his time, a sense of something to look forward to, the possibility of an encounter that could change the course of his life, but perhaps because he'd met so few people in Colombo who really moved him, whether intellectually or politically or romantically, perhaps because he was less easily sustained by the things that had attracted and stimulated him when he was younger, the desires that led him to move back and the short-lived satisfactions they offered soon came to feel misleading, like distractions or diversions from a more basic absence. Solitude in the past had always been a pleasurable way to pass time, a kind of consolation for the demands and disappointments of the world, a tender solicitousness he could obtain simply by withdrawing into himself, but a quiet restlessness began to surface whenever he found himself alone at home in the evenings, as he moved here and there in his room, wasted time on the internet, tried to read books he'd been meaning to read. He tried to cope in whatever way he could, even if it meant going to his grandmother's room and listening to her discuss how mosquitoes were managing to enter the room despite her precautions, but the unease continued to lurk just below the surface, growing continuously over the course of the afternoons and evenings and reaching a peak during the last, dying moments of the day, when the sun was setting and the golden yellow light giving way, suddenly and dramatically, first to pink, then to violet, and finally to the lighter and darker blues of night. There was something about twilight that heightened his anxiety, which brought it to the surface of his consciousness and made it palpable, as though with the gradual disappearance of the horizon the last hopes and promises of the day too were disappearing from view, another day coming and going with nothing to show for itself.

He would set off well before the sky began darkening, moving with an intentionally slow, steady pace meant to calm him down, taking long, meandering routes through different parts of the city at first, out of a desire to familiarize himself with its significantly altered topography. No matter how many different paths he took he continued feeling out of place amid all the new signs and façades, markers of a new trajectory of development that he could find no way of relating to, and gradually he began circumscribing his walks to the residential areas closer to home, to the numerous small, scraggy lanes and byways of Wellawatta and Dehiwala, areas he'd rarely explored when he was younger on account of the war, the army checkpoints put up every hundred meters and the omnipresent risk of being interrogated and detained. He passed the small, old houses, most of them with people living in them, some of them converted into small offices and showrooms, passed the newer apartment buildings occupied mostly by Tamil and Muslim families, and thinking as he walked of the weight of life that all these structures contained he would begin to feel less burdened, as if with every step he took from his own house he was leaving behind some heavy and unnecessary part of himself. He was still full witness to the dramatic changes occurring in the sky above, but something about being outside and in the direct presence of these changes made them easier to bear, as if being out in the open, unbound by four walls, a floor, and a ceiling, whatever was weighing him down in his chest was free to spread out and dissipate. Listening to the sounds of the waves breaking gently against the rocks, the birds flapping their wings against the push of the warm breeze, he gradually became less restive, the present ceasing to be a void and becoming instead, for a short period of time, a place he could inhabit comfortably and securely. There were few moods that could persist after all when one was in full view of earth and sky, and even the more deep-seated moods one carried through the course of the day—those moods that maintained themselves in the chest against all the conflicting feelings that came one's way while out in the world—even these moods thinned slowly into nothingness when confronted by the immensity of the horizon, so that one could feel, at such moments, if not satisfaction or contentment then the peace at least of a brief inner extinction. When he returned to the enclosed spaces of his house and room after these walks he was usually too tired to feel the unease that had led him to leave, and getting on his bed, salty from perspiration and the breeze of the sea, a pleasant ache in his calves and thighs, he would lie there in the cocoon of his exhaustion, getting up only when it was time at half past eight to go downstairs and bring dinner up to his grandmother, when it was already dark and the most difficult part of the day, the transition from evening to night, was over and done with.

It was during these walks that he'd once more begun smoking, at first if only because smoking a cigarette at the halfway point allowed him to justify his otherwise purposeless walks, to feel he wasn't just walking because he had nothing to do or nowhere to be. He'd smoked casually since going to India for college, where most of his friends smoked too, but it had only become a serious habit later, when he started spending time with Anjum, who smoked frequently and with an elegance he found himself wanting to emulate. He'd given the habit up on moving to the northeast, mostly because of how harshly smoking was viewed in the environments in which he worked, though perhaps, it occurred to him now, his disavowal also had to do with Anjum, with the more general attempt he'd made to distance himself from her after they parted ways, to eliminate not only the various traces of their relationship that remained on his phone and computer but also the various gestures and phrases he'd picked up during their time together, most of which continued displaying themselves in his body despite his efforts to discard them. He hadn't felt the need to resume smoking upon returning to Colombo, not wanting to deal with hiding the habit from his mother while living at home, had limited his consumption initially to cigarettes he scrounged when drinking or joints he smoked with his friends. The occasion for his return to the habit had come only a couple of months earlier, when stopping at a small snack shop to buy a Milo during one of his walks, he'd observed the man in front of him asking for three single Gold Leafs, paying for them and collecting them from the counter with a self-satisfaction that made him wonder what was stopping him from doing the same. He'd asked for a Gold Leaf and a box of matches when it was his turn, had walked for a while with the cigarette tucked carefully in his shirt pocket, bringing it up to his face every so often to savor the smell of the tobacco. Crouching at the corner of a small, deserted lane, he'd struck a match and put the flame delicately to the tip, taking pleasure in each of the various motions, in ashing the cigarette with a sharp tap of his index finger, in bringing it leisurely back to his lips, listening to the burning of paper as he sucked in slowly and watching the smoke waft up in the air as he exhaled. He smoked a cigarette at the halfway point of each of his next few walks, soon began buying not one but two, one for smoking immediately and the other for before he went to sleep, transporting the extra cigarette with care in his shirt pocket, taking pains to ensure it remained crisp and unbent, going out to the balcony later in the night when no one else was awake to smoke in silence under the stars. The number of cigarettes he smoked proliferated in the weeks that followed, so that soon he started buying packs instead of singles and replaced his matchbox with a lighter. Smoking became a way to help time pass, an activity he could look forward to in the intervening periods, something that made the present more bearable even when he wasn't smoking because it meant the present was leading to something good. Unlike the prospect of going out in the nights, which engendered hopes and expectations that were ultimately illusory, the pleasure of smoking a cigarette was a real one, a pleasure, however modest, that was itself and nothing else, that contained no false promises, and that he knew he could rely on as long as his supply of cigarettes remained steady. He didn't stop going out in the nights or trying to meet new people, but smoking allowed him to accept that there was nothing more than what was visible before him, opening the present up, making it more expansive but also more inhabitable, so that even when he returned home with none of his hopes for the night fulfilled he was consoled by the certainty of one last cigarette before bed.

Looking up Krishan saw that he was coming to one of his preferred spots for smoking, chosen because he could sit there by the water without being visible to pedestrians on the road. Veering right from the pavement he made his way up the grassy mound to the railway tracks, paused to make sure there was no train coming, since there was a news story almost every month about a pedestrian or cyclist being knocked down somewhere or other by a train, then crossed to the other side. He walked

down to the slender outcropping of rocks that formed the
boundary between land and sea, where making his way to a
section that was relatively free of rubbish, he took out his pack
of cigarettes and lighter and lowered himself down. There was
a young couple sitting a good distance to his right, their bodies
not touching but their heads leaning together as though sharing a secret, while far off to the left a few men in tattered clothes
were fishing on the rocks closest to the water, appearing and
disappearing among the thick clouds of spray. Krishan turned
and looked out at the silver-gray sea that stretched out calmly
in front of him, at the golden-gray sky, backlit by the sun, suspended like a canopy over the horizon. Drawing a cigarette
from the pack he rotated it slowly between his fingers, as if
surprised by its insubstantiality, then turning away from the
water and hunching to guard against the breeze, he lit the cigarette and took in a long first drag. He tried to direct his thoughts
toward Rani, toward the unexpected and slightly absurd nature
of the way she'd died, the strikingly mechanical tone of her
daughter as she'd relayed the events over the phone, but found
himself dwelling, for some reason, not so much on Rani or her
daughter as on the scene he'd glimpsed through the keyhole of
his grandmother's door, the sight of his grandmother so un-
knowingly, helplessly asleep. Why the sight of her sleeping
bothered him so much was hard to say, especially when there
was something far more urgent and important to think about,
but gazing out at the water that extended from the rocks at his
feet, his eyes drifting across its shifting gray surfaces, all he
could think about was the vulnerability that had emanated
from her sleeping body, a vulnerability that should have been
obvious but had caught him by surprise, as if the real condition

of his grandmother had been invisible to him all this time, as if he himself had been complicit in keeping it hidden.

His grandmother's withdrawal from the world had begun, of course, long before he was born, but the event that first made him conscious of its inevitable trajectory, Krishan could remember, the event that first made it clear to him that she would not remain in his life forever, had occurred when he was twelve or thirteen, when his grandmother must already have been seventy or seventy-one years old. She'd been working in the garden that afternoon, according to what she told them afterward, plucking out weeds from a spot in the corner where she planned to plant a few bitter-gourd seeds she'd obtained. It hadn't been strenuous work but she'd found herself, as she came up the stairs afterward, panting in a heavy, alarmingly hurried way, and despite going straight to her room and sitting down on her chair to rest the panting had become more pronounced, followed shortly afterward by a kind of shivering that radiated out from deep inside her chest. They'd taken her at once to the hospital, where a battery of tests run in quick succession indicated that one of the arteries near her heart was clogged. She hadn't exactly had a heart attack or a stroke, the doctors said, but she was in fact in danger of both, and it was advised that something called a bypass surgery be performed, an operation in which the length of a vein that ran from her right ankle to her right calf would be extracted and used to replace the problematic artery near her heart. Of the days that followed, Krishan could remember only his surprise at how easily his grandmother seemed to submit to everything that took place, how willingly she seemed to give her body up to the authority of the doctors and nurses around her. When she returned home after the two weeks of monitoring that followed the surgery, seemingly healthy and flattered, clearly, by all the attention being lavished upon her, she'd given no sign of seeing the events of the previous month as anything but a brief, almost refreshing interruption of her daily existence. With a satisfaction she hardly concealed she furnished all the relatives who visited her in the following days with a detailed account of everything that had happened, from the initial panting and shivering, which she always clarified was not a heart attack or a stroke, to her final discharge from the hospital three weeks later, dwelling at length on the quality of the various meals she'd been served before ending her account by lifting her sari to display the operation scar on her right leg, as if to provide evidence that all she'd described really had occurred, that nothing had been fabricated merely for the sake of her audience's entertainment.

It had been his habit, at the time, to go to her room in the nights to talk to her before she went to bed, and he could remember how, in the weeks and months after the operation, as the nervousness and excitement of the event were finally absorbed back into the mundane exigencies of daily life, Appamma's conversation during these nighttime visits came more and more to center on the subject of her health. Her health was something his grandmother had always talked about to some degree, but it became now the topic toward which every conversation with her invariably converged. He would go to her room just as she was turning off the lights, around nine o'clock when the last TV show she followed for the day had finished, and lying on the bed next to her in the darkness he would listen as she discussed how many times she'd walked up and down the hall that day for exercise, how she still cooked and cleaned and was therefore fitter than other people her age, how any medical professional who met her for the first time was always astonished when she revealed how old she was, since she looked much younger, they never failed to tell her, than any other person in their late sixties they knew. He would speak from time to time during these conversations, either to show his grandmother he was listening or when it was obvious she wanted him to confirm or verify something she said, but mostly he remained silent, detecting in the way she spoke something that made him hesitant to change the subject or interrupt her, a kind of confessional quality in her voice and the room, as though what she was sharing with him were not something she would share with anybody else, a kind of fear or anxiety that she was reluctant to communicate directly but which, as they lay next to each other in the darkness, their faces invisible to each other, he could sense in her body beside him. Only rarely did this fear or anxiety enter the actual words she spoke, usually only after she'd been talking for some time, when she'd established to her satisfaction that she was still as healthy as before despite having needed the surgery, which, in her view, was nothing but a precautionary measure. She would mention at these times, lowering her voice as though making a parenthetical remark or an unimportant aside, that so long as she could take care of herself she would be fine, that the only thing she didn't want was to become incapacitated, to be unable to walk or dress or bathe herself, to be confined to her bed, a nuisance and a disturbance to others. Not knowing what to say at first Krishan responded to these admissions with silence, but as he grew accustomed to them he learned to tell his grandmother that she was wrong, that she wouldn't be a nuisance or a disturbance to look after, that he at least would take care of her happily, without any sense of obligation. It was a response she appreciated but usually chose to ignore, preferring to focus instead on the possibility that she would never be immobile or confined to bed, that she would always be able to take care of herself and would never have to worry, therefore, about being a burden.

The years that followed had brought with them various signs of deterioration, the first appearance of the swelling that eventually beset both her legs, the discoloration of the small patch of skin just above her collarbone, the jarring whiteness of which none of the ointments she applied could efface. Most of these developments Appamma dismissed as either temporary or irrelevant, and it was not till five or six years later, when relatives were visiting from Toronto and they'd decided, on the last day of the visit, to go to a nearby Indian restaurant for dinner, that she was once more forced to confront the fears and anxieties that had surfaced in the months following the operation. There'd always been a kind of buried tension in Appamma's face when she was compelled to leave the house and traverse the unfamiliar terrain of public spaces, an anxious strain in her features as she navigated the slender line between shame and danger, shame, on the one hand, of the ungainliness of her body and uncertainty of her feet, of the fact she was slowing down everyone else in the party and becoming an object of pity, danger, on the other hand, of trying too hard to keep up, of making a misstep and falling, which would of course have only made her even more an object of pity. Krishan always tried to slow down in such situations, letting the rest of the party go on ahead while he walked in step with his grandmother, pretending they had the same natural pace so she would feel less pressure to keep up with everyone else, sometimes also offering her his own arm for support, though this was a gesture she usually rejected, thrusting his hand aside as if it were an insult. These offers to help were, in fact, mostly unnecessary, but it was at just such a moment, approaching a part of the restaurant where the floor was very slightly raised, wanting to show their relatives she was capable of walking without help, that rejecting his hand with a flourish Appamma had tripped and fallen facedown, striking the floor in a strangely soundless fashion, as if the impact had been absorbed wholly into the soft mass of her large body. In the sudden rush to help often witnessed at such times—the immediate scrambling of the rest of the party, the quick, purposeful strides of waiters moving toward the scene of the accident, the scraping of chairs as diners stood up and tried to express concern on their faces—in the sudden rush Appamma struggled to assert herself, to smile dismissively despite being visibly shaken, to get up on unsteady legs and continue moving toward their table. Someone immediately brought over a chair and she was made to sit down right there in the middle of the restaurant, given a thorough examination while all the waiters and diners looked on uncomfortably, unsure whether or not to retain their postures of concern. She'd managed somehow to avoid the hard edges of the tables and chairs on her way down, but despite her protests and to her great embarrassment—it had been just a little fall, she argued almost indignantly, the kind that happened to everyone from time to time—it was decided that they should ask for takeaway and have their dinner at home.

It was partly at the instigation of the relatives who'd witnessed the fall that Krishan's mother had bought the walking
stick, a somewhat costly purchase that Appamma reacted to
with an irritation bordering on hostility. She refused to use the
walking stick despite all her daughter-in-law's attempts to persuade her, and because she'd become noticeably more cautious
after the accident, moving more circumspectly around the
house, clutching the furniture and walls for support, her
daughter-in-law's insistence eventually fell away. The walking
stick assumed a more or less permanent position in the corner
of her room next to the TV, like a souvenir from a trip or a me-
mento of a special event, and the question of her mobility was
forgotten until a weekend three years later, when standing in
front of the gas cooker in the kitchen, frying the sardines Krishan ate for lunch—the only real cooking she was allowed to do
by that point, and which she insisted on doing so he would feel
indebted to her in some way—Appamma had once more collapsed to the ground. Once more she somehow managed to
avoid striking her head on the way down, and when she was
rushed to the hospital immediately afterward it was discovered
that her heart had stopped beating for a few seconds while she
was cooking, as a result of which she'd lost consciousness and
fallen. The natural signaling system that was responsible for the
regular beating of the heart sometimes weakened with age, the
doctors explained, more to Krishan and his mother than to Appamma, who looked on powerlessly from her wheelchair as
they discussed her condition among themselves. If, for whatever reason, a signal didn't go through properly, the heart could
skip a beat, which could sometimes lead to dizziness or faint-
ing. The only way to prevent a more serious accident happen-

ing in the future was to install a small battery-operated device called a pacemaker inside her chest, which, by producing its own electrical signaling, would keep the heart beating steadily even if its natural signaling system failed momentarily or broke down.

Appamma had feared she'd be forced to use the walking stick upon returning home, and buoyed by this unexpected diagnosis, which indicated that she wasn't to blame for the fall and that it wouldn't happen again if a pacemaker were installed, she energetically assented to being operated upon a second time. Sensing that her daughter-in-law would probably try to make her use the walking stick regardless, she began rehearsing arguments she could use to defend herself, that the unusual curvature of the walking stick's handle made it difficult to hold, that the walking stick actually increased the likelihood she would fall, that it was in fact safer for her to walk holding the walls and furniture for support. She returned from the hospital ready to negate her daughter-in-law's efforts, feeling as strong and vital as ever, as if with the aid of the battery-operated device installed in her heart she was now invincible. Entering her room she found, waiting for her next to the bed, not the walking stick that had been bought three years before but a new apparatus, a walker consisting of four hollow, rubber-tipped aluminum legs, joined at the top by a U-shaped frame with foam grips on each of the three sides. Caught off guard by this new device, Appamma's feeble attempts to object were easily countered by Krishan's mother, who was prepared this time to put up a fight. She'd already been lucky twice, his mother argued, and if she fell again, for whatever reason, she could be bedridden for the rest of her life—if that happened it was she,

her daughter-in-law, no one else, who would have to bear the
burden of looking after her. Appamma immediately fell silent,
pierced by the thought of being reduced to an obligation. When
her daughter-in-law left the room she simply sat there staring at
the walker, as if at an unwanted guest she could not send away,
and for the next three days she hardly spoke or left her room.
Krishan's mother wondered whether she'd been too harsh,
whether she should relax her demand or find some other way
to appease her mother-in-law, but then after lunch on the fourth
day Appamma emerged from her room clutching the walker
tightly with both hands, her eyebrows pinched in concentration
as she inched her way matter-of-factly into the hall. She didn't
say a word as she sat down in her usual place on the armchair
in front of the TV, as if there were no significance in the fact
she'd come out of her room with the walker, as if there'd been
no adjustment or concession to reality in her decision to use the
new apparatus. Sensing her reluctance to acknowledge the
change Krishan and his mother exchanged sidelong glances but
pretended not to notice, and from then on, as if she'd gone
through a kind of metamorphosis over the three days cocooned
in her room, Appamma used the walker whenever she needed
to go anywhere. She would push the walker forward a short
distance, lean her weight on it, then take a step forward before
repeating this sequence of movements, which soon became so
second nature that it was hard to imagine her moving differently. When relatives came to visit she would demonstrate its
different features, how the height could be adjusted by means
of the metal knobs on the legs, how the frame that connected
the front legs to the back legs could, by swiveling, allow for a
greater range of movement when she turned, as though she'd

come to see the walker not as a mark of weakness or vulnerability but of strength and capability, as something that postponed and even halted her withdrawal and therefore something
she could accept as part of herself.

The walker didn't help her negotiate the staircase, of course,
and over the course of the subsequent years Appamma was
forced to limit the frequency of her visits downstairs. She
would decide to make the journey a full day in advance, and
approaching the stairs with intense focus when the moment
arrived she would clutch the banister face-on and move not forward but sideways, parallel to the banister, first bringing her
lead foot down to the stair below and then, looking down to
check that the foot was firmly planted, bringing her back foot
down beside it. Krishan or his mother would stand on the step
directly below watching every movement, ready to catch her in
case she stumbled, and when after several tense, painstaking
minutes Appamma made it all the way down she would take a
moment to catch her breath, exalting in a combination of tri-
umph and relief. Clutching the walker, which was always
brought down beforehand, she would head immediately in the
direction of the kitchen, where moving along the counters
with renewed vigor she would throw open all the drawers and
cabinets, peer inside the various compartments of the fridge,
try to take stock of all the kitchen's contents so she could form
some notion of what had changed and what had stayed the
same, like an emigrant who returns from exile to visit her native land and is consumed with understanding how things
stand. The loss of this knowledge would have been too great to
bear, and when the trips downstairs finally came to an end Appamma compensated for her loss of physical access to the

kitchen by means of more oblique strategies, the most important of which was to ask, pointedly and unceasingly, as many
questions as possible about what was happening downstairs.
Appamma had always asked about matters she couldn't verify
directly—why had Krishan been late from work, who'd rung
the doorbell, how come her younger brother in London hadn't
called in so long—but she began making these inquiries with
much greater frequency and insistence than before, piecing together theories about the external world on the basis of the information she gathered like an injured general who cannot
participate in the battle and is forced, as a result, to rely on secondhand reports and satellite images of the fighting. Having
little else to do on weekday afternoons and weekends, when
there was nothing to watch on TV, she devoted herself to the
formulation and development of these theories, coming up
with more and more questions to ask as they grew in complex-
ity, since there came, with the increase in theoretical complex-
ity, a need for further, more specific information by which they
could be confirmed, disproved, or elaborated. Krishan and his
mother found themselves, soon, in thrall to endless questions
about a world that neither of them had any interest discussing. They would tiptoe past Appamma's room, hoping she
wouldn't hear them and call out to them, would cut short their
conversations with her as if they had somewhere else to be,
Krishan's mother especially, who was burdened enough having
to do all the shopping, cooking, and housework without being
forced to justify every banal detail to her mother-in-law. Even as
she became aware of their attempts to avoid her Appamma
pursued her quest for information relentlessly, asking them
both the same questions so as to cross-check their answers for

consistency, furrowing her eyebrows and pursing her lips till she had every detail down correctly, as though the continued movement of the world upon its axis hung upon whether the small chili plant in the garden was bearing fruit or whether leftovers remained from the previous day's fish curry, as though something catastrophic could happen to the transition of day to night and night to day if she failed to properly oversee these matters from afar.

Krishan had always thought of death as something that happened suddenly or violently, an event that took place at a specific time and then was over, but thinking now of his grandmother as he sat there on the rocks, it struck him that death could also be a long, drawn-out process, a process that took up a significant portion of the life of the dying person. It was an obvious fact, in retrospect, but perhaps because of how his father had died, in the Central Bank bombing of 1996, perhaps because of the frequency of sudden and violent death in the country in which he was born, he'd never really stopped to consider the fact that people could also die slowly, that dying could be a process one had to negotiate over the course of many years. Ever since he was old enough to follow the news he'd been hearing of people dying in abrupt and unpredictable ways—in road accidents and race riots, by snakebite, tidal wave, and shards of shrapnel—and it had never really occurred to him that for most people in most places, even Sri Lanka, death was a process that began decades before the heart stopped beating, one with its own logic and trajectory. It was a process that began almost imperceptibly, with the minor changes in appearance that one was inclined at first to regard as merely superficial, the loosening of the skin, the thinning of the hair, and the deepening of the lines of the face, which only afterward began expressing itself in deeper, more unsettling ways, in the stiffening of joints and flattening of reflexes, in the subtle but suggestive deteriorations of motor activity that led sooner or later to constant second-guessing, making it impossible to see what was happening as merely skin deep. Changes occurring deep inside the body began making themselves felt, changes in energy, menstruation, metabolism, and libido that appeared with the force of inevitability, and tests taken, if one had the privilege of taking tests, showed that cholesterol or sugar or blood pressure had increased and that the body's internal indicators would need to be more carefully monitored, unless they didn't, in which case the relief that accompanied this news forced one to prepare for the occurrence of such developments anyway. In either case one began to treat oneself differently, in either case one became wary of overexerting oneself, of not eating in the right ways, not sleeping enough, or not doing enough exercise, in either case one began acting with increasing restraint and participating in life more selectively, a decrease in participation that was not so much a personal decision as the defining feature of aging: of the slow, meticulous process by which the same body that once moved so freely and easily between environments begins, gradually, to withdraw from what is called the world. The bones became brittle, the muscles slackened, and soon one could no longer walk at the pace of others; one's aptitude and reliability decreased, one was less able to do one's work, whether one's work was inside the house or outside. Vision worsened and so did hearing, things had to be repeated because they went unheard or were forgotten, and soon one ceased working altogether, venturing out into the so-called real world even less. Soon one became even less aware of what was happening to other people in other places, frequenting only a few specific locations, the hospital for checkups and the houses of a few relatives, so that soon, scarcely able to move, one was confined not just to one's house or flat but one's room. Interaction with the outside world slowed to a stop, leaving one with no idea what to do or how to pass the time, with nothing to think about but oneself and one's drastically reduced future, so that when at last it was time for one's natural death, which was in fact far less natural than a sudden or violent death, being mediated at every juncture by doctors, nurses, tests, and medications, when at last it was time to leave behind what remained of the body, one's first, most intimate environment, the small section of world over which one earlier possessed full mastery, it was something that one was if not exactly prepared for then not at least surprised by, since it was only, after all, the last stage in a withdrawal that was already long under way.

Krishan's notion of the elderly had always been of people who accepted this condition—some of them only begrudgingly, doing what they could to make the process easier, irritable about their situation but on the whole resigned to its inevitability, others almost gracefully, capable even of laughing at their age-related limitations. Appamma, on the other hand, was simply incapable of accepting her withdrawal from the world, and though there was something childish in this, as if she alone were unable to handle this process that so much of humanity had to experience, it struck Krishan now that maybe there was also something admirable about his grandmother's response to her situation, something deserving of more than just pity or condescension. In a way it was hard not to admire the resoluteness with which she'd fought against what was happening to her, her unwillingness to compromise on what she took herself to be entitled to, even if this unwillingness lacked the grace or the practicality of her peers, even if part of her resistance involved lying to herself and others, even if it was doomed, in the end, to failure. Her participation in the world had never been great—she'd never finished her schooling, had been married at a young age, had never had control or influence over anything but domestic matters—but she'd fought to preserve this participation as single-mindedly as she could, ceding the territory she saw as hers only after defending each inch of it to the utmost of her ability. He remembered how, on one of her final trips to the garden, exhausted from the journey downstairs and her visit to the kitchen, Appamma had walked haltingly over the grass to a pot she'd planted some seeds in a few days earlier, wanting to see whether there was any sign of life emerging from the soil. Two tender little shoots were visible, each of them a bright fragile green, but most of the surface was covered with weeds that seemed well entrenched in the soil, for despite tugging at them several times they didn't budge. He had been on the verge of going and offering to help when he saw Appamma's jaw suddenly clenching, her eyes flashing with anger, when he saw her bending down to almost a right angle, taking hold of the weeds one by one, tugging at them with such force and such vigor, her whole body somehow electrified, that they came out together with several clumps of soil. She flung the weeds into the corner of the garden, patted down the disturbed top layer of the soil, and inspected the two delicate green shoots that, miraculously, had remained unharmed in the center of the pot. She regarded them for a while, caressing the shoots with a delicacy totally at odds with her previous action, had then turned toward him and smiled, a luster in her eyes that remained for some time and returned, or so he imagined, whenever he came back to her with a positive account of how her plants were faring. What his grandmother found so captivating in such matters Krishan couldn't say, but it was mostly to tend to such things that she fought to remain in the small, self-contained spaces that had become for her the world, and he couldn't help feeling there was something worthy of admiration in this fierce and humble loyalty to life, in the way she preserved and nourished this life however she could, with all the resources at her disposal, even as her body was being inexorably broken down, even as the people around her ceased needing or depending on her, even as Rani, her last link to the wider world, was now gone.

3

FLICKING HIS CIGARETTE into the water at the base of the rocks, Krishan stood up slowly and stretched out his arms and legs. He'd planned to be gone just a short amount of time, since he didn't have his phone and knew that his mother might return his call, but wanting to remain outside a little longer he crossed the tracks, made his way down to the pavement, and resumed his earlier path, watching as the vehicles to his left accelerated and decelerated in spurts, as the walkers and joggers on the pavement pursued their destinations intently in both directions. The section of Marine Drive along which he was walking had changed little since the end of the war, still comprised of the same modest houses and flats, the only additions a few small cafés and restaurants that had sprung up here and there, mostly to cater to the influx of Tamils who'd begun visiting from abroad and wanted to stay near relatives. Among the various signboards Krishan saw the red cross of the small pharmacy he'd frequented in the past to buy medications for Rani, an establishment he hadn't entered in several months now and which, he realized, he'd hardly even noticed on his recent walks. He remembered the slight awkwardness with which he would slip Rani's prescription across the counter, the quiet, composed manner with which the thin, dignified pharmacist would read the long list and begin retrieving the items from the shelves. The pharmacy always had all the items on the prescription— the antidepressants, the antianxiety medication, the sleeping pills, blood pressure tablets, and liver medication—and usually they stocked multiple brands of both the antidepressants and the antianxiety medication, suggesting a much wider demand for these medicines than he would otherwise have suspected. He'd often wondered after his visits how many other people in the area took medications for psychological issues or mental illness, whether there was anyone else nearby who came to the pharmacy in need of a similarly diverse assortment of drugs, and he wondered now whether there was anyone else who'd moved to the area from the northeast after experiencing a catastrophe like Rani's. He continued making his way down Marine Drive, his movement stiff and somewhat forced, and it was only when looking up after a while, seeing that he was nearing the mouth of the Kirulapone Canal, that he felt his body beginning to loosen. The canal was the union of several smaller canals that moved silently through the inland parts of the city, the culmination of a centuries-old drainage system that collected the city's rainwater, channeled it toward the coast, and cast it out to sea. Its dark green water was calm and leisurely, its motion invisible except around the tips of the ferns that dropped down from the stone walls, pricking its otherwise smooth surface, and making his way along the walkway Krishan felt his quick steps giving way to a longer, more composed stride. Listening to its gentle gurgle during the lulls in traffic, he imagined the quietly profound meeting of waters that was taking place beneath the pavement, the slow, placid water of the city giving itself up to the deep, heavy, undulating water of the sea, and it occurred to him that it was perhaps this sense of an invisible but constant renewal taking place below that was the source of the reassurance he so often felt while crossing the canal, the intimation that subterranean processes might be occurring deep inside him too, even when, on the surface of his life, everything remained exactly the same.

Resuming his way along the unpaved path on the other side, Krishan's thoughts returned not to Rani, exactly, but to the trip to London his grandmother had made two years before, the ill-advised journey from which she'd returned in a state of almost total collapse, the ill-fated journey that had been responsible, eventually, for Rani's entry into their lives. The trip had not actually been his grandmother's first time abroad, for unlike his mother and him, who'd only been to the UK once in their lives, on an extended trip several years before that took them first to London and then to Toronto, Appamma had actually visited London four or five times over the previous twenty years, each time as the guest of her youngest brother. Her brother, who was actually her half brother and eighteen years her junior, had been raised by Appamma for several years in Jaffna, and despite their different personalities and trajectories the two siblings had remained close, speaking on the phone at least once a month ever since they'd moved to different places. Her brother had joined one of the smaller separatist organizations operating in

Jaffna in his twenties and had been forced to leave the country in 1986, traveling first to India and then to Europe before ending up finally with asylum in the UK. He'd already been well into his thirties when he arrived in London, had never finished his schooling and spoke hardly any English, but was handsome and charismatic and had ended up managing a supermarket not far from where he lived. Unable to return to Sri Lanka on account of his former activities, having no wife or children that he needed to provide for, he would buy return tickets for his eldest sister every few years, so she could come and stay with him in London for five or six weeks. Appamma had always looked forward to these visits, in part because of the prestige of flying, the sense of power they gave her, in part because of the reassurance they provided that she wasn't completely dependent on her daughter-in-law, that there was someone else in the world who wanted to see her and spend time with her. Her brother had none of the scruples her daughter-in-law had, was more than happy to let her wander into the small back garden of his house or spend afternoons in the kitchen preparing lunch, dinner, and various greasy desserts, and the prospect of being in a foreign environment—even if she seldom left the house—was a perennial source of invigoration for her. The idea of traveling abroad broke the monotony of life confined to her room by giving her something to look forward to, an event in the future around which to organize the otherwise shapeless passage of the months, a longer-term correlate of what her TV programs did for each day and what her Sunday baths did for each week, coming, over the years, to be indispensable to her manipulation of time.

Her brother would buy her tickets six months ahead of her

departure in order to get the best price possible, and from the
moment Appamma was informed of their purchase, the abstract notion of going abroad becoming tied to a concrete date,
she would begin anticipating the journey ahead with a kind of
slow, sweeping pleasure. Her preparations began a full two
months in advance of her departure, with the chili powder she
always took for her brother and other relatives, a process she
would spread out over a couple of weeks, first leaving the curry
leaves and chili out to dry in the sun, then having them ground
together with coriander, turmeric, fennel, and cumin, sealing
the resulting powder in airtight plastic bags so it was ready to
be packed for international travel. The chili powder done, she
would begin taking out the various items of clothing she'd kept
stored in her armoire since her previous trip, mostly some nice
saris and a few sweaters and socks she had no use for in Colombo, washing and folding them then laying them neatly
aside. She would start pressing her daughter-in-law to begin the
visa process, to buy the supply of heart and pressure medications she would need during her time abroad, would begin
looking through her drawers for the various miscellaneous
items, safety pins, rubber bands, pens, and batteries, that would
come in handy during her stay. Finally, three weeks before the
trip, she would order Krishan or his brother to bring out the
two battered suitcases that were stored under their beds, leaving them open in a corner of her room, partitioning them into
different compartments, and carefully filling them with the
things she'd gotten ready. She would finish all her packing at
least a week in advance of her departure, would spend the remaining days visualizing her daily routine in London to make
sure there was nothing she was forgetting, making small addi-

tions and modifications to her bags, taking pleasure in their order and fullness, in the fact that she was prepared for any outcome or eventuality, so that when the day of her flight finally came all that was left was for her body and her suitcases to be flown to London, her mind having settled serenely in the spare room of her brother's house long in advance.

When her brother had called three years before to suggest she make her next visit the following June, proposing they use the occasion to celebrate her eighty-fifth birthday in style, inviting not just their relatives in London but those who could come from Europe as well, Appamma had, needless to say, been flattered by the suggestion. Despite her attempts at nonchalance she was visibly gratified by the notion of going to London to celebrate her health and longevity, by the thought of having all eyes on her, the old but still vigorous matriarch of the family, the fulcrum around which the members of their dispersed family were brought together. Krishan and his mother had been a little more hesitant, for though Appamma's trip four years before had been without any issue, her health had been declining steadily in the time since. Her body had become frailer, especially her legs, as a result of which she'd abandoned her trips downstairs, and her bladder had become less reliable, so that sometimes she went to the bathroom once every two or three hours, which in turn affected her ability to sleep. Her hearing too had gotten weaker, though she refused to use the hearing aids she'd been prescribed, making conversations more difficult to sustain and even her regular TV shows harder to follow. Increasingly forlorn as a result of her deepening isolation, the idea of a birthday party in London struck Appamma as precisely the intervention needed, energizing her so dramatically that neither Krishan nor his mother had the heart to air their reservations. In the weeks that followed she began exercising more, practiced moving without her walker over short distances; she became vigilant about what she ate and obsessed about her appearance, applying a cream with clinical regularity to the rash that had begun spreading across the back of her neck. Her initial excitement about going abroad, it soon became evident, was turning into anxiety about how she would perform on the trip and above all at the party, about whether she would be able to impress their relatives with her mental and physical vitality, and it was this anxiety perhaps that was responsible, as her departure drew nearer, for the unforeseen further decline in her condition, her loss of weight, her forgetfulness and repetitiveness in conversation, the increasing time she spent in bed.

By the time the trip was two months away both Krishan and his mother had begun to doubt it was safe for her to go at all, and his mother decided at last to broach the subject with her, suggesting that maybe the flight should be postponed or that maybe it was better for her not to go. Appamma shrugged the suggestion off lightly at first, but when it became apparent that her daughter-in-law was serious she responded with uncharacteristic rage. She would be able to handle the long flight perfectly well, she stammered in fury, there would be attendants to wheel her through the airport, and during the journey all she had to do was stay seated. It would be a complete waste of her brother's money to change plans now that tickets had already been bought, and if her daughter-in-law was tempted it could only have been out of jealousy that she herself didn't have the chance to travel abroad. Krishan's mother replied that she didn't care about going abroad, that it was only concern for her mother-in-law that was prompting her to intervene—how could Appamma hope to fly halfway across the world, she asked, when she couldn't even make it down the stairs? Appamma had turned away angrily, and after the exchange they were both cautiously taciturn, each acting as though it were obvious the other would soon concede. The issue came to a head six weeks before the flight, when Appamma asked Krishan's mother why she hadn't begun the visa application, whose outcome couldn't be taken for granted and which in the past she would have initiated much earlier. His mother ignored the question, and Appamma responded not with argument or accusation but a profound silence, refusing to eat or to speak a word, rising from the chair in her room only to go to the bathroom or when it was time to sleep. Krishan's mother pretended to ignore what she saw, hoping her mother-in-law would soon give in, but Appamma held firm in her fast and vow of silence till two days later, fearful she would collapse, his mother was forced to concede, informing Appamma through Krishan that she would apply for the visa, that she didn't want to cause anyone such misery and that if going to London was so important then she might as well go. Appamma's condition improved in response to the victory, and by the time the visa arrived Krishan and his mother both felt less nervous about the trip. Watching through the glass divider a few weeks later as an attendant whisked her through check-in they felt confident that nothing disastrous would happen, that the flight would go smoothly and that she would be handed over without issue to her brother on the other side, so that waving goodbye as she was wheeled off toward immigration neither of them could suppress their anticipation for the six weeks they would be able to spend by themselves.

They received a call from Appamma's brother in London the next day, informing them she'd arrived safely. She was tired from the flight and hadn't wanted to eat, her brother had said cheerfully, but she was jet-lagged and would be better after she slept. He called again the next day, some alarm in his voice, to say that Appamma still wasn't eating. She had trouble moving, wasn't really talking, and didn't seem herself somehow, though what was different he couldn't really say. He called each of the following days, repeating each time that he wasn't sure what to do and that he was worried she would get worse, and then on the eighth day called to say he thought it best to send her back as soon as she was well. Appamma was eating now and had gotten a little better, he told them, she still wasn't quite herself mentally, but would very likely keep improving in the coming days. She would soon be fit enough to travel, he felt, and though it would be expensive to change her ticket it was probably a good idea for her to return sooner rather than later, just in case her condition deteriorated again. They'd have a small gathering for her the following Saturday instead of a birthday party, would take her the day after to the airport so she could board a direct flight to Colombo. It wouldn't quite be the party they'd planned, since their relatives from Europe wouldn't have arrived, but there was, in his opinion, no other sensible option given the circumstances. Krishan's mother hadn't objected, knowing it would be hard for Appamma's brother to look after her in London if she did become unwell. A week later she and Krishan left once more for the airport, sitting beside each other in nervous silence the whole journey and arriving an hour in advance of the flight. They sat down in the cavernous hall for arrivals, their gazes shifting between the notifications board that hung from the ceiling and the automatic doors through which newly arrived passengers emerged, most of them tourists from Europe, Russia, and North America, large, oblivious-looking people who'd begun flocking to the country ever since the end of the war. Appamma's brother had already called twice to ask whether Appamma had arrived, his impatience betraying real concern about how she would fare on the flight back, and they sat there in a state of tension till finally the arrival of the flight was announced. They kept their eyes pinned to the automatic doors, scanning each new wave of passengers several times over, trying to determine whether they matched the demographics they expected of a direct flight from London, or whether they were likely to have come from elsewhere. Half an hour passed without any sign of Appamma, and unable to remain sitting Krishan's mother got up and elbowed her way to the crowd standing up front. Leaning on the railing between tour operators holding up their signs she rotated her phone anxiously in her hands, her eyes darting to the sides of the hall as though there might be an entrance she was unaware of. Another half an hour passed and then another, they began to feel sure something had happened, that they needed to find an official to speak to, and just as they were about to abandon their positions they saw the door slide open and a wheelchair being pushed slowly into the hall.

It took a moment to register that the person being wheeled out was the same person they'd said goodbye to eleven days earlier, for Appamma had lost so much weight that her sari gathered in folds around her body. Her blouse was falling loosely over her right shoulder, her bra strap visible over her skin; her cheeks were slightly hollowed and there was a glazed, uncomprehending quality in her eyes as she looked in disorientation at the wide, high-walled hall. Krishan and his mother signaled to the man pushing the wheelchair and quickly ran toward her, but seeing them Appamma only clutched her handbag and gave them a look devoid of recognition, the black of her pupils completely dissolved in the indistinct brown-gray of her irises. They repeated her name several times, heedless of the obstruction they were creating and all the people watching, and though something seemed to resolve in Appamma's eyes each time her name was pronounced they dissolved back quickly into indistinctness, glistening like drops of oil behind the soft, drooping folds of skin that enclosed them. It was only when Krishan's mother took her hands and introduced herself, slowly and loudly, as if to a child, that a partial clarity emerged in Appamma's face, her features drawing together in recognition, and watching her during this brief moment of awareness, which couldn't have lasted more than a couple of seconds, Krishan felt sure he could see a glimmer of embarrassment or shame in his grandmother's eyes, as if she'd understood, in that brief moment, everything that had happened, the fact that all her hopes and plans for the trip had gone astray, that she'd come away having won not admiration from their relatives but pity. She mumbled something about her brother, her birthday party, and how time either had or hadn't come around, repeated the latter several times before lapsing, once more, into a state of confusion. It was a condition she remained submerged in during the long days and weeks that followed, days and weeks in which she was unable to string words into coherent sentences, unable to feed or wash herself, urinating and sometimes even defecating on her bed, and thinking of that moment at the airport now as he continued making his way down Marine Drive, Krishan couldn't help feeling that his grandmother had chosen to abandon her lucidity on purpose upon recognizing them that day, that she'd sensed in that moment that remaining conscious would mean accepting the powerlessness of her situation and decided, in some interior part of herself, that it was preferable from then on to be absent.

The number of pedestrians on the pavement had begun to diminish, the vehicles on the road moving faster now on the emptier roads, and looking up at the deepening blue of the sky Krishan realized that it was getting late, that he'd come a significant way from the house. In the distance ahead, on the other side of the road, was the little Pillayar temple that was the last of the landmarks he used to measure his progress on Marine Drive, and deciding that he would continue walking just a little longer, smoke one last cigarette before turning back, he glanced quickly in both directions and crossed to the other side of the road. The temple was more of a shrine than a temple, consisting of no more than a single, tiny room, but like the canal closer to their house Krishan was always reassured by its presence on his walks. Approaching it now he paused and looked in through the iron grille, at the Pillayar's childlike smile flickering behind his trunk in the light of the small lamp, nodding at him in a kind of acknowledgment before he turned and continued walking. The temple had no official name, but growing up Krishan had always heard it referred to as the Visa Pillayar temple, since it was to petition for the granting of a visa that most people went to pray there, a petition that, in many cases, the Pillayar was said to have answered favorably. Flicking through Google Maps shortly after his return to Colombo he'd noticed the temple had been labeled Visa Pillayar by Google too, that thanks, no doubt, to the efforts of a grateful Tamil abroad whose visa had been granted, its colloquial name was now legitimized with a semiofficial status. No one he asked seemed to know much about how the temple had become associated with visas and emigration, and his main source of information about the place came from a long, nostalgic account of its history that he'd discovered in an anonymous comment on some diaspora blog. It was a comment that had clearly been authored by someone who'd lived many years in the area and then moved abroad, perhaps the very same person who'd campaigned to have the temple named on Google Maps, there were so many diasporic Tamils who haunted the internet in such ways, he knew, people who'd left or fled the country and now lived in bitter cold on the other side of the world, people who spent their free time trying to convince themselves that their pasts on this island really had taken place, their memories more than fantasies or hallucinations, representing people and places that really had taken up space on the earth.

According to the comment what was now the site of the temple had originally been an ordinary middle-class residence, a small, single-story house that had been vacated by its owners in the early nineties, when the government was reclaiming land close to the sea in order to construct the road that would become Marine Drive. Among the rubble of the half-demolished house that was visible to passersby afterward was an abandoned stone sculpture of Pillayar, sitting there with his usual placid expression despite being plastered in dirt and exposed to the elements, too heavy, the anonymous poster hypothesized, for his owners to have taken to their new residence. Flowers would occasionally be seen strewn in front of the Pillayar, sometimes even an offering of fruit, and at some point someone had washed off the dirt encrusting his face and trunk, cleared a path through the rubble so he could be accessed easily from the street. This had been in the mid-nineties, when thousands of Tamils displaced from the northeast had come to Colombo hoping to find a way to leave the country from there, to make it somehow to Canada or the UK or Europe or any other place that could be identified with the possibility of future prosperity. Most of these people stayed in Wellawatta, where they had the relative security of being in a Tamil area even in the country's far south, and it was some individual or group of individuals from among these displaced people, according to the anonymous commenter, who'd first built a small shed for the Pillayar, so he didn't have to sit under the open sky. A small brass lamp had been placed in front of him soon afterward, not long after a till box for donations as well, thus setting up the makeshift shrine that, over the course of a few years, thanks to donations received from local residents, soon became housed by a permanent concrete structure, a structure that deserved to be called a temple, the commenter stressed, despite being maintained not by male Brahmin priests but by older women of presumably different castes.

The darkness around him was becoming heavier as Krishan left the temple behind and entered the final, deserted stretch of Marine Drive, where there were hardly any shops or streetlights, silence except for the occasional passing car and the gentle breaking of water against the rocks. There was a bus parked with its lights off by the side of the road, and making his way around it he saw that he'd come to the unmarked stop for overnight buses that made direct journeys between Colombo and Jaffna, the same spot he'd been picked up and deposited on so many of his visits home while working in the northeast. There was nobody there now, it was still a little too early for departures, but he continued walking till he'd gone a good distance past the bus stop just in case, stopping finally at a narrow, unlit lane that went up to Galle Road, one of the last such lanes before Marine Drive came to an end. Standing with his back to the wall of an empty lot he looked past the road and tracks at the water stretching out darkly from the shore, the shimmering lights of cargo ships visible now in the distance, charting their heavy, patient paths between port and sea. He remained there unmoving for a while before he drew out a cigarette, turning away to light it then looking back at the water as he took a first drag, remembering for some reason the time when Rani, who didn't of course smoke cigarettes, had told him she chewed betel leaf. It was a confession he'd found hard to believe at the time, partly because it was a habit he associated with laboring men, partly because he'd never seen Rani chewing betel at home. He'd never seen Rani getting up and going to the toilet or garden to spit out the viscous, blood-red cud, and she'd hardly ever left the house by herself either, certainly not enough to maintain an addiction or even a mild habit. She only chewed betel when she was back home in the village, she'd told him with a smile, obviously proud of her self-control, it wasn't something she'd let herself do in another person's house. It wasn't something she'd always done either, she told him, she'd started only recently, about a year or so after the end of the war.

She liked chewing betel, found that it soothed her, though she was careful not to do it too much, since she didn't want to become too dependent on it. He hadn't asked her more at the time, perhaps because it would have felt too intrusive, perhaps because he simply hadn't thought to, but thinking of her confession now Krishan wished he had, for there was always something more to how people began such habits, not just with betel or cigarettes but with other, more addictive substances too. Whether an addiction came about quickly, before one knew what was happening, or whether it happened more gradually, with the tacit consent of the individual involved, there was always a story that divulged something about the specific or general sense of absence that allowed the dependency to develop. Addictions were, so often, at the beginning at least, a way of tolerating or managing yearnings that were too intense or too painful, a way of catching hold of desire that floated too freely, without an object to which it could be fastened, functioning for so many people as a means by which desire could be taken hold of and brought back down to the earth, relocated in easily acquired and reassuringly concrete objects like cigarettes, betel leaves, and bottles of liquor. Rani's habit of chewing betel had been a response no doubt to everything she'd seen and lost during the war, but what specific role it had played in her last years, what specific consolations it had given her, he had no idea, and having failed to ask or find out when she was still alive it would remain unknown to him, he realized, like so many other things about her life.

Rani was so different from them, her history and experiences so far from anything they were familiar with, that thinking of her now Krishan found it hard to believe they'd shared a living space, that their lives had intersected in any substantial way at all. The first time he encountered her, he remembered, had been more than two and a half years before, on an afternoon when he'd been taking a tour around the psychiatry ward of the General Hospital in Vavuniya, where he'd gone to speak with the doctor in charge about a program for trauma victims being run by his organization in Jaffna. He'd been walking with the doctor just outside the ward, no longer talking about the program specifically but about how things worked at the ward more generally, when glancing through the tall iron gratings that looked into the ward he had noticed, sitting up on one of the beds, quietly reading a book of some kind, a woman in a neat purple frock. The woman was heavyset, her skin blackened around the eyes, and lowering her book as they passed she'd looked up and smiled gently. Struck by the disjunction between her calm, reflective demeanor and the slightly unhinged appearance of the other occupants of the ward, most of whom seemed to be in varying states of psychosis, he'd asked the doctor once they were past earshot who she was and what she was doing there. The woman, the doctor told him, had had three children, two boys and a girl, and had lost both sons during the war. The elder one had been killed while fighting for the Tigers in 2007, and the younger one, only twelve at the time, had been hit by shrapnel on the penultimate day of fighting in 2009. The woman was suffering from post-traumatic stress disorder with severe depression, and came to stay at the ward for a few days every month, officially to get medication and to receive electroshock therapy, but also just to be able to leave home for a while, where she was plagued by endless thoughts of her sons. She was better now than when she'd first begun receiving treatment, the doctor told him, but it had been three years since then, and there was no hope of her condition improving while she remained at home. At home she was forced to spend too many long stretches of time by herself, trapped in her own mind, and there were too many associations with her two sons for her to be able to move on, not that moving on would ever be fully possible for cases such as hers.

It wasn't long after this encounter that Appamma had made the trip to London, and though Krishan's mother was able to take care of her by herself for a while, it soon became clear that someone else would be needed to look after Appamma when school started and his mother's teaching duties resumed. A professional nurse or caretaker turned out to be too expensive, and his mother spent several weeks asking almost everyone she met whether they knew someone who might be willing to stay and look after Appamma for a salary of some sort. Failing to find anyone as the start of the term drew closer, exhausted and having no idea what to do, she'd remembered the story Krishan had told her about the depressed woman who needed to leave home in order to get better, had asked him to get in touch with the doctor to see if the woman might be interested in taking the job. The suggestion had seemed out of the question to Krishan, not only because Rani hardly seemed capable of looking after herself, let alone another human. She'd lived through the last two years of the war, losing both her sons and seeing unimaginable violence all around her, and even if she said yes he would feel uncomfortable about her living with them in their two-story house in Colombo, would feel guilty living opposite someone who'd suffered so much and now had nothing, not even her mental health. Her status in the house and the work she did would be ambiguous too, since she wasn't a professional nurse, and there was no guarantee she would be treated respectfully by Appamma either, who was sometimes extremely irritable in her state of infirmity. His increasingly exhausted mother refused to let go of the idea, pointing out that if what the doctor said was true then maybe it would be good for Rani, that in any case the choice was hers to make, that it wasn't for him to decide whether or not she should take the opportunity. Krishan finally gave in, confident the idea would be rejected as absurd, and apologizing on behalf of his mother he put forward the suggestion to the doctor, who, to his surprise, immediately agreed. It would be good for Rani to leave the north for a time, the doctor said, and perhaps looking after someone else would help get her mind away from her own troubles—he would ask her if she was interested and would let them know. Two days later he called to say that Rani was indeed interested, that she would come the following week.

When he went to pick her up at the Pettah bus station late at night the following Sunday, Krishan had found Rani standing near the station entrance, hair disheveled, sari full of wrinkles, the duffel bag containing all her things thrown over one of her hefty shoulders. She was looking at the city around her uncertainly, at the density of bright lights, private vehicles, and tall, multistoried buildings, at the paved streets and the people around her speaking a language she couldn't understand. It must have been unsettling, Krishan realized as he descended from his three-wheeler, to be seeing Colombo for the first time, to come here after having lived all her life in a small village on the far side of the country, under Tiger control for more than fifteen years. It must have been unsettling to have looked out the window of her bus at the miles of continually built-up area that led, through the densely populated outskirts and suburbs, into the central parts of the city, to see up close the money and power of the state against which so many people she knew had given up their lives trying to fight. When she saw him coming toward her Rani had smiled as though he were an old acquaintance and begun walking in his direction. She didn't say much on the ride home, despite his attempts at making conversation, not so much out of shyness, it seemed, as from simply having nothing to say. There was something confident about her manner, even in the uncertainty of the new environment, and unpacking her things as soon as they arrived at the house she made herself at home with relative ease. She did everything that was needed of her, with more attention to detail than Krishan or his mother had been able to give, not hesitating even when she needed to help Appamma in the toilet or the shower. The first week passed without any of the discomfort Krishan had feared, and soon he felt he'd been wrong to be skeptical about Rani coming to stay with them, that maybe it had been a good idea after all. There were occasional tensions with Appamma, of course, who especially early on, when the childishness brought on by her condition was still strong, disliked not being the main subject of attention, but Rani didn't seem to take issue with any of her occasional rude or insensitive remarks, either because she knew Appamma was not in her right mind or because she simply didn't care. She smiled in his presence and engaged in conversation with all three of them, though she rarely initiated a conversation herself, and except for her appearance, her darkened eyes and often uncombed, unruly hair, the only sign she gave of being less than well was the way her gaze sometimes seemed to slip away from what was in front of her, as if there were other things on her mind than the work that occupied her hands. Krishan wondered what she was thinking at such times, whether she was remembering her sons or what had happened during the last months of the war, but he'd never dared broaching the subject explicitly, and in the first few weeks the closest they got to acknowledging her life in the northeast were moments in which she discussed the family she still had left, when she had reason to mention her alcoholic son-in-law, or the stepdaughter she'd helped raise, or her two young granddaughters, who, it was clear, she cherished more than anyone else alive.

It was strange to reflect on the fact that Rani was dead, this person who'd lived in their home for over a year and a half, this person to whom each of them had, in their own particular ways, become so attached. It was strange too to think that after having survived so many shells and so much shrapnel during the end of the war she'd died the previous day in such an arbitrary, almost careless way, her neck broken at the bottom of a well. Her nephew too had died in an accident after the war, he had learned from Rani during conversation one day—he'd been nineteen or twenty, his motorcycle had collided with a lorry, and he'd died on the spot, his body thrown up in the air by the force of the impact. That incident too had felt strangely arbitrary when he heard about it, strangely careless given all that the boy had seen and survived during the last two years of the war. Krishan had dismissed it simply as coincidence at the time, as yet one more of the cruel flukes of the world they lived in, but the thought occurred to him now that perhaps the boy's death hadn't been purely accidental, that perhaps Rani's death hadn't been accidental either. There'd been so many stories of accidents in the northeast in the years since the end of the war, drownings, fires, mine explosions, and road accidents above all, so many brief second- or third-page news items that noted how some or another unknown person from the former war zone had died in some or another bizarre or unexpected way. Accidents happened everywhere, of course, but these accidents had to have been more than just bad luck, for how could such hardy people, people who'd gone through so much and still come out alive, allow themselves to die so easily now and with such docility? It was as though there was some other, more obscure logic at work than mere chance, as though death was in some way following these people who'd managed to survive, as though they were in some way marked, the various statistically high probabilities on which ordinary life was based beginning, for them, to alter, to change more and more in favor of their unforeseen demise—as though they themselves walked with open arms in the direction of these seemingly accidental deaths, as though they themselves welcomed them or even willed them to take place.

Standing there with his back to the wall, his gaze following the lights of a ship lost in the black water, Krishan thought again of Rani's daughter's voice on the phone, her affectless tone and her eagerness to be done with the call. It made sense, of course, since she'd probably had to repeat the same story countless times, since she probably had a lot of work to take care of before the funeral, but all the same he had the feeling she was trying to hide something. He would have to leave early on Sunday morning for the funeral, he realized, and he would have to go alone, the journey there and back was too demand-

ing for his mother, who would anyway need to stay home to
look after Appamma. It would be his first time returning to the
northeast since he'd moved to Colombo, his first time in almost
a year, and he'd be going not just anywhere he knew but to Kilinochchi, ground zero of the war. He would have to go to the
town, which the army made a show of keeping oppressively
clean and well organized, would have to travel through miles of
impoverished countryside to find Rani's village, which he
would be seeing for the first time. It was the place she'd grown
up and spent all her life in, which she'd been displaced from
with her family during the fighting and returned to afterward
without her sons, and the thought of being there made him
suddenly uncomfortable now. He wanted to go, wanted to pay
his respects to Rani, to acknowledge her in some way and to
have that acknowledgment be seen by her family, but he would
feel guilty in front of her family members, none of whom he'd
ever met before. He would feel guilty seeing the well in which
she'd died and guilty for the fact he'd done nothing to prevent
her death, which even if accidental he felt certain now had been
foreseeable and even predictable somehow. Krishan remembered the way Rani would hug him when he visited Colombo
on his breaks from work, the way she would press his face
tightly against her ample cheeks, as if welcoming back a son
she hadn't seen in years, and standing there looking at the darkness of the sea he felt his eyes beginning to water, the significance of the phone call at last beginning to sink in. He heard,
approaching from outside his field of vision, the faint clanging
of heavy iron, and looking to the right saw the hazy yellow
headlights of the commuter train in the distance, their circles
becoming sharper and brighter as the train advanced along the

faint arc of the coast. Its movement became louder and more convulsive as it drew nearer, the pounding of its wheels on the tracks almost deafening by the time the front carriage hurtled by and cut off his view, each subsequent carriage superimposing itself so rapidly over the preceding one that the train appeared stationary while it moved. He watched as the open-door carriages passed motionlessly one by one, their fluorescent light falling on the multitude of bodies sitting and standing and leaning out, fixing their postures briefly against the night, the scene unchanging for what felt like an impossible amount of time till finally the train vanished and the jolting faded and only he remained, gazing at the water from the deserted road.

JOURNEY

4

HIS BODY HEAVY from having woken up so early, Krishan was sitting on his haunches, leaning back against one of the tall iron posts that rose from the platform, watching the people around him with the dense, trancelike clarity that often takes hold when one is up before the day, when everything outside is still shrouded in the pitch-black darkness that directly precedes dawn. The train, which was scheduled for a quarter past five, had not yet arrived, and the platform had filled up with people, with middle-aged men, older couples, and families sitting or standing in the cool darkness of the morning, gazing out in silence at the trains arriving and departing on the other tracks. He was watching a family of five who had stopped not far from where he was sitting, standing in a circle near the edge of the platform around three large pieces of luggage. The mother and father were looking around the station with quiet but focused curiosity, as if they might be called upon to draw the scene

from memory later on, the three teenage children, two girls
and a boy, leaning on the bags with seeming indifference, lost in
the dim blue glow of their phones. The parents looked like they
might still live in the country, but it was obvious from the appearance of the children that the family was visiting from
abroad, their foreignness, like that of many diasporic children,
immediately recognizable by the clothes they wore, their tight,
branded shirts and tank tops, their loose tracksuits and formfit-
ting jeans. On another day Krishan might have tried to specu-
late about the family's origins and the circumstances under
which they'd left, studying how the parents were dressed,
whether the children spoke Tamil or the language of their
adopted home, how nervous or at ease they seemed to be returning to their place of origin. Today, though, he simply gazed
at them without curiosity, not in the mood to analyze or con-
jecture, content to give sensation precedence over thought as
he sat there waiting for the train.

He'd been in a strange mood over the last day and a half,
distracted and somewhat removed from himself, unable to
shed any tears since his walk on Friday evening, unable for any
sustained period of time to think about Rani, who'd once more
begun to seem distant and elusive in his mind. He had told his
mother the news on returning home from his walk and they'd
decided it was best not to inform Appamma till the next morning, so she wouldn't have to spend the night reflecting on the
death by herself, and retreating to his room he'd spent the rest
of the evening trying to read, his thoughts drifting now and
then to the email he'd received from Anjum, the question of
how to respond. When they told Appamma after breakfast the
next morning she hadn't been as shocked or upset as they'd

feared, responding with surprise as she asked for all the details and then falling silent as the information sank in. She was sad but her sadness was muted, calmer and more thoughtful than they'd expected the night before. Shrugging her shoulders, her eyes watering slightly and a kind of wistful smile on her face, she told them that Rani had suffered a lot, poor woman, that maybe it was for the best she was gone. She'd been silent for a while and then asked his mother to take out twenty thousand rupees from her bank account, to be given to Rani's daughter to help with expenses for the funeral. It was money Krishan didn't know his grandmother had, money she'd apparently saved up over the years from her monthly pension payments, modest sums she received because her husband had been a teacher in their village in Jaffna. He'd been surprised to learn Appamma had a bank account, that she was actively keeping track of the money she received, had been even more surprised at the generosity of the gesture given the childish self-absorption he'd come to associate with her old age. He'd known his grandmother was close to Rani, that the two of them had spent nearly every day together for almost two years, but the majority of their relationship had taken place while he was elsewhere, it made him realize, while he was busy with other things, and listening to his grandmother reminisce about Rani at various points over the previous day he could tell, despite her measured response, that the two of them had been intimate in ways he had no inkling of.

The platform began to resound beneath his feet, lightly at first and then more heavily, and looking to the right Krishan saw that their train was approaching the platform slowly from the distance. The exterior was a dull red that had been stained over the years by rust, smoke, and grease, not one of the sleek new models bought recently with loans from China but one of the older, heavier, boxier trains purchased decades before from India. Everyone who'd been sitting and standing as if half-asleep immediately clutched their bags and began hurrying in search of their carriages, roused by the thick smell of diesel, but Krishan remained where he was, watching as the family from abroad began making its way through the crowd, the three children listlessly following their parents toward the front of the train. He waited till they disappeared into the crowd, then standing up heavily and throwing his backpack over his shoulder, proceeded to the second-class carriage where his own seat had been booked. He climbed the vertical steps up to the carriage, and squinting in the harsh fluorescent light of the compartment made his way to his seat, which, he discovered to his satisfaction, was by the window. The boy in his early twenties sitting next to him smiled and stood up to let him into his seat, probably Sinhalese from the look of him, which meant, Krishan noted happily, that he would probably be getting off somewhere in the south, that there was a chance the seat beside his would be empty for the remaining portion of the journey. Resting his bag on his lap he sat down and looked out at the now much emptier platform, listened to the calls of the men who went up and down the platform selling tea, coffee, and peanuts to passengers through the windows. He wondered whether he should try to sleep, since he'd only gotten three or four hours that night, but decided he would try to stay up despite his fatigue, to preserve for as long as possible the calm focus that had held his mind since waking. He took out of his bag the book he'd brought, a book about Indian militarism and the occupation of Kashmir that he'd wanted to read for some time but had been struggling to make progress with in the previous few weeks. He flicked through the pages thoughtlessly, more to hear the sound of the flicking than to find the place he had stopped, till a heavy clanging sounded from deep inside the train and caused the carriage to shake—the familiar yet always surprising sound that signified the train's imminent departure and came, he liked to assume, from the massive pressure of the brakes being released. The train jerked forward a little bit, hesitated for a few seconds, then began to stagger forward. The fluorescent lights in the carriage went off, shrouding everything in the blue darkness of dawn, and grateful that reading was no longer a possibility Krishan put the book down and leaned back as the train made its way out of the station. The thin floor reverberated beneath his feet and the glass windows trembled against their frames, the clanging of the wheels against the tracks growing heavier and more rhythmic as the train picked up speed. It was his first time traveling all the way north by train, and looking out at the abandoned carriages and cluttered workshops just outside the station, at the shanty settlements strung out along both sides of the tracks, strangely desolate in the small, bright circles of light cast by occasional lamps, he began to feel, despite his fatigue and the somber purpose of his journey, a mood of anticipation rising gently inside him, the same sense of possibility he'd always felt when embarking on long train journeys, the sense that he was leaving behind everything that limited and constrained him, moving toward some vast and unspecifiable future.

It had been some years since he'd felt this mood of optimism while traveling, for though Krishan had traveled fre-

quently between north and south during his time in the
northeast, he'd always traveled by bus on these journeys. The
train hadn't been functional till the previous year, the northern
section of the line having been completely destroyed during the
war, and bus in any case was the more utilitarian option, faster,
cheaper, and more easily arranged at the last minute than train.
There was something much more stressful about traveling by
bus, Krishan felt, for traveling out of Colombo by road you
were constantly blocked or impeded by traffic, especially in
buses because of their unwieldy size and the narrowness of the
roads. Bus drivers were so often in a state of physical tension,
their hands tightly clutching the steering wheel and the gear-
stick, their feet constantly pushing down on the pedals, suddenly accelerating and breaking in the pointless attempt to
overtake slower vehicles, attempts borne out of a deep anxiety
to finish their routes as soon as possible despite the fact that it
was impossible, no matter how quickly they went, to speed up
even the longest journey by a meaningful amount of time. The
constant frustration of the drivers, which invariably communicated itself to the passengers too, seemed only to make them
tenser, to spur them on more recklessly, pushing them to overtake on bends and when vehicles were approaching on the opposite lane, a frustration that was no doubt one of the major
causes of the road accidents that took place around the country
each day. They spent the majority of their lives in such a state,
Krishan knew, and imagining these drivers as they lay awake in
their beds at night, their bodies still caught up in the tension
and strain of the day's driving, he wondered sometimes what
their dreams were like when they were finally able to fall asleep,
whether they saw visions of broad, empty, smoothly tarred

roads unlike the ones they came across in real life, roads that stretched out into the horizon and down which they could accelerate into infinity, endlessly and without obstacle, as long as they pleased.

Traveling by train was different, for even if there were occasional delays and breakdowns there was never any traffic on train rides, no effort or strain required as you were borne smoothly and inexorably toward your goal. Looking out at the silhouettes of the city passing by in the darkness, Krishan thought of all the hours he'd spent on trains during his time in India, when he was on holiday from university and had the chance to leave Delhi, to see other parts of that vast, seemingly endless country. He'd spent most of those journeys sitting or lying on his seat or berth, reading, listening to music, or simply looking out at the small, unpeopled rural stations, the hot wind rushing into the carriage through the open doors and windows, allowing him to breathe in the air of the places they passed and absorb their smells, as if he were in some kind of communion with these small towns and villages as they flitted by. The constant movement of wind through the carriage would feel like a calling to him from outside, and leaving his seat he would go down every so often to the linking section between carriages, where standing in a corner he would look to make sure nobody was watching, light himself a cigarette, and pull open one of the heavy train doors, one hand tightly clasping the grip on the door frame so he didn't fall into the passing landscape, the other holding the cigarette in front of his body so that no one passing behind would see that he was smoking. The warm, fragrant air of the countryside buffeting his face, he would look out at the wide expanses of farmland, brush, and forest, at the plains that went by for sometimes hours at a stretch without stopping, and he felt, at such moments, something close to a sense of liberation, if not quite liberation then the sense at least of being on the verge of liberation. It was as if, at such times, he was permanently suspended in the blissful but always vanishing space between desire and satisfaction, in that region of the self where one is no longer anguished by the absence of something one feels to be necessary for one's salvation, but not yet saddened by the disappointment that attainment of desire always seemed to bring, for strong desire, desire that radiates outward through all the regions of the body, always seemed to involve the hope or belief that attainment of the object of desire, whether a person, place, or situation, will change everything completely, will end all absence and yearning, all effort and struggle, that it will stem, somehow, the slow, sad passage of time. We experience, while still young, our most thoroughly felt desires as a kind of horizon, see life as divided into what lies on this side of that horizon and what lies on the other, as if we only had to reach that horizon and fall into it in order for everything to change, in order to once and for all transcend the world as we have known it, though in the end this transcendence never actually comes, of course, a fact one began to appreciate only as one got older, when one realized there was always more life on the other side of desire's completion, that there was always waking up, working, eating, and sleeping, the slow passing of time that never ends, when one realized that one can never truly touch the horizon because life always goes on, because each moment bleeds into the next and whatever one considered the horizon of one's life turns out always to be yet another piece of earth.

His thoughts had often returned to *The Cloud Messenger* during those long journeys, the famous Sanskrit poem of yearning that he'd read in translation early on during his time in India, before he'd begun to understand how intimately the Sanskrit language was tied to the mythology of Hindu nationalism, before he'd begun to understand the everyday racism of North Indians toward people of darker skin like himself, a racism that hadn't affected him greatly but had, nevertheless, played its own small part in his desire to leave. The language and imagery of the poem had moved him so much all those years ago, and looking out now as the darkness of early morning gently let up, he found himself thinking, once more, about the painful longing so elegantly expressed in its verses. The unnamed main character of the poem was a yaksha, a kind of divine or semidivine spirit who served the god of wealth, and the poem began with an account of how, as punishment for neglecting his duties, the yaksha had been exiled by the god of wealth from Alaka, his beautiful native city in the foothills of the Himalayas. He'd been compelled to wander far south to the plains of central India, thousands of miles away from the cool climes of his birthplace, a parched, arid wilderness that to the author and his audience of elites must have signified the outer limits of civilization, an area of total darkness. The yaksha had already been wandering alone in this wasteland for many months at the start of the poem, unable to stop thinking about the city he'd been exiled from and above all the wife he loved so much, losing so much weight from the sadness of separation, according to the poem's narrator, that even the bracelets on his thinning arms had slipped off. It was late July or August, the time of year when the annual monsoon rains finally began to reach the plains of

central India on their northward journey from the southern
coast, and climbing up to the top of a mountain in his dazed,
hopeless state the yaksha had noticed a single dense, dark cloud
heading in his direction from the south, descending so low it
almost touched the peak of the mountain before pausing there
as if for rest. Gazing at this cloud the yaksha was lost for a long
time in thought, hardly able to hold back his tears, until realizing at length that the cloud was a forerunner of the imminent
monsoon, that it would, in all likelihood, continue traveling
north till it reached the Himalayas, it occurred to him that he
could ask the cloud to carry a message for him to his wife. Although most rational beings know, the narrator remarks in the
fifth stanza, that a cloud was nothing but a conglomeration of
vapor, light, water, and wind, an object incapable of being ra-
tionally addressed, individuals consumed by love were unable
to distinguish between the sentient and the insentient, as
though to the individual overcome by passion the whole world
was populated by beings whose sole purpose was either to support or thwart their love. So taken up was the desperate yaksha
by the possibility of communication with his wife, the narrator
goes on, that looking up he began to address the cloud out
loud, praising its beauty and auspiciousness before asking it
whether it would be willing to bear a message from him to his
wife on its way north.

All this took place within the first six stanzas, and the large
substance of the poem that followed, one hundred and fifteen
stanzas in all, consisted of the detailed set of directions that the
yaksha gives to the cloud in order to find his city and wife, directions, the yaksha assures the cloud, that will lead it through
all the grandest, most opulent cities of the subcontinent, allow-

ing it to stop, on the way, at wide-flowing rivers and dense jungles so it could gather itself and rest, absorbing water into its body and rejuvenating itself so it could maintain its bodily integrity as it continued the long journey north. It should begin, the yaksha tells the cloud, by heading north from their present location and then a little west toward the Vindhya mountain range, whose flanks are covered with wild mango trees and kutaja flowers, where welcomed by the cries of watery-eyed peacocks it would be able to drink to its heart's content at the source of the Narmada River. Though it might want to dwell there in the mountains for some time, the yaksha goes on, it should try not to tarry too much and should continue quickly on its journey, which would as it knew take several weeks to complete. Heading north from the Vindhyas the cloud would reach the country of Dasharna, its garden hedges white with the buds of ketaki flowers and its trees busy with the nest-building of crows, flocks of flamingos dwelling on the forests of rose apple at its outskirts. At its capital, Vidisha, the cloud would be able to drink from the waters of Vetravati, the yaksha says, after which it should continue north, going a little out of its way in order to see the famous city of Ujjain with its terraced mansions, where the morning breezes carried the drunken warble of cranes and were fragrant with the scent of blooming lotuses, a city so beautiful it looked like a fragment of heaven on earth. The cloud should visit the famous shrine to Siva in Ujjain and then spend the night there, asking its wife, lightning, to descend in silence every now and then to give light to the women who were making their way secretly to their lovers. From Ujjain the cloud should head farther north, past the Gambhir River in Rajasthan toward Devagiri, where it could

worship at the temple to Siva's son Skanda. It should then proceed toward the Chambal River, where again it could rest and
take up water, and from there it should travel northeast past
Kurukshetra, the battleground of the famous ancient war depicted in the *Mahābhārata*. The cloud should afterward make its
way east toward the city of Kanakhala, the yaksha says, where
it could drink from the great Ganges, continuing its journey
north till it reached the source of the Yamuna River, a mountain white with snow where the rocks were fragrant with the
musk of deer and bamboo swayed softly in the wind. On the
last leg of its journey it would have to travel north around
the flanks of the Himalayas till it reached Mount Kailasa, home
of Siva, the snow on its slopes white as freshly cut ivory, and
once there it should head toward the waters of Lake Manasa,
full of golden lotuses, where the gossamer on the wish-fulfilling
trees by its banks was fanned continually by the misty breeze.

It was from the banks of Lake Manasa, the yaksha says, that
the cloud would finally be able to see his much-longed-for city
Alaka, which it would recognize at once by the enormous mansions with bejeweled floors and the soaring palaces with turrets
that kissed the sky. The city itself was located in the lap of the
mountain and contained enormous parks and gardens where
the flowers of winter, spring, summer, and autumn were all in
simultaneous bloom, a detail that had struck Krishan when he
first came across the poem, as though the narrator was suggesting that all seasons were collapsed there into a single season,
that time itself stood still or that all times were contained in a
single time—as though, the narrator was suggesting, in ordinary life we are pulled in different directions by our contradictory desires, so that what we imagine as heaven is a place where

these conflicting longings are somehow reconciled, in which the separate and seemingly incompatible times of their fulfillment are brought together, uniting our otherwise divided souls. The citizens of Alaka, according to the description the yaksha gives to the cloud, consist of male and female yakshas obsessed with love and sex, the male yakshas constantly drinking aphrodisiacs, carrying flowers in their hair that looked like the reflections of stars, while up in their private chambers the female yakshas, torn between embarrassment and desire in the company of their lovers, threw fistfuls of powder at the tall-flamed lamps while their lovers untied their robes. His own home, the yaksha tells the cloud, was to the north of the god of wealth's own house, recognizable by its arched gate and the young mandara tree beside it. There was a tank with emerald-paved steps, its waters crisscrossed by golden lotuses, and to the side of the tank was a rockery with a girdle of golden plantains where his wife often spent time, in the center of which was a golden perch where a peacock came to roost at day's end. By these signs the cloud would recognize his home, and if it went down discreetly to the house and cast a glance inside, it would finally be able to see his wife. The intense longing of separation would be weighing her down, her once beautiful appearance having changed like a lotus laid waste by frost. Her face will have become swollen from crying, her lower lip discolored from the heat of many sighs, and when the cloud saw her she would probably be painting pictures of him, the yaksha went on, or speaking to the caged mynah about him, or perhaps trying to play a song on her lute to remind herself of him, wetting its strings with her tears. She might be marking out the days and weeks left for his exile to end, or perhaps lying there on her bed fantasizing about the two of them in the throes of passion, for these, he explains, were the many ways that lovers whiled away their time when separated. The cloud should wait until night-time before alerting his wife to his presence, since it was at night that loneliness would most affect her, when she would be most in need of his words. It should go down to the window of his wife's chambers, and if she was sleeping the cloud should let her sleep on for the first watch of night, just in case she was dreaming of him. When the first watch was over, he goes on, it should wake her up by sending in a cool breeze through the window, and it is only at this point in the poem, after addressing the cloud for an entire eighty-nine stanzas, that the yaksha finally shares the message he wants to send.

The cloud should begin by announcing to his wife that it has been sent by her husband, he says, which will guarantee that she listens attentively, since to a person separated from their lover, news of the lover was almost the same as being physically united again. The cloud should inform her that her husband is alive and well, that he is wondering how she is doing, and that he cannot stop thinking of her. He sees her image everywhere around him—her arms in the slender vines, her flirtatious eyebrows in the ripples of a stream—and he wonders constantly how to make the rest of his allotted term of exile pass more quickly. He asks her not to become disheartened or grow suspicious of him, promises that he will be back as soon as possible, and with this the yaksha ends his brief message, a message that, after his richly described account of the path the cloud should take on its journey, after his meticulous instructions for how to find Alaka and how, having arrived there, to recognize his home and his wife, strikes the reader as remarkably superficial. It is as

though, after giving what amounts to an extended literary map
of half the subcontinent, a vast poetic travelogue of all its great
cities and natural wonders, the yaksha realizes he doesn't actually have much to say to his wife, that words will never bridge
the distance between him and her, the geographical but also
the temporal and psychic distance, the distance between all that
has happened and all that has changed in the time since their
separation. Having delivered his message the yaksha looks up
at the cloud, which has not, of course, said a single thing during
his entire monologue, then expresses his hope that the cloud
will carry his message without delay, adding that in no way
does he consider its silence a refusal. His request is unusual, he
acknowledges, but the cloud should take pity on him, and he
will pray, in the meantime, that the cloud never be parted in a
similar manner from its wife lightning. It is with this last statement that the yaksha ends his speech and the poem too comes
to an end, though Krishan could never think about the poem's
last lines without dwelling also on the image suggested so
obliquely by its ending, the image of the yaksha looking up
from that lonely mountaintop as the monsoon wind blows in
from the south, the image of that desperate, homesick, divine
or semidivine being watching helplessly as the cloud is ushered
north, its edges slowly dissolving as it is pushed farther and farther into the distance, its bodily integrity imperceptibly dwindling and with it the message entrusted with so much longing,
till finally, like the dissipation of desire into yearning, it evapo-
rates soundlessly into the nothingness of the horizon.

Recalling this image of the separated lover as day opened
out over the scenes passing by outside, the small, cheaply constructed houses and huts rushing by, the vegetation between

them becoming increasingly unruly, Krishan thought once
more of the trip to Bombay he'd made by train with Anjum
almost four years before, during his last year in Delhi, that short
but somehow timeless trip that had been the prolonged climax
of the overwhelming months they'd spent together but also, in
retrospect, despite having stayed together for some time afterward, the point he first began to sense that their relationship
might not last forever. He could still see Anjum sitting opposite him on their berth that day, cross-legged in her beige shal-
war kameez, her head propped up on her hands, the mahogany
of her eyes brighter and more vivid than usual in the light that
seeped in through the window, could still see the way she would
glance at him and then look away as she talked about her time
in Jharkhand, about the small village where she and the few
activists she worked with had been running a workshop on
labor rights for women working in the mines. They hadn't seen
each other in three weeks when they'd met that morning outside the station, had hardly spoken or texted either, Anjum not
being the kind of person who liked calling or texting unless it
was necessary. After just a quick, lighthearted embrace they'd
made their way to the platform without further physical demonstration of their feelings, each of them conscious of the other's physical presence but neither making any attempt to touch
or hold the other after that brief contact, as if in tacit agreement that they had to maintain strict distance from each other
in that intensely public place. They'd booked an upper and
lower side berth, so they wouldn't have to share the uncomfortable intimacy of a four-person compartment with strangers
who'd spend the entire trip trying to figure out whether they
were married, but the positioning of the side berths, which ran

along the side of the train, still subject them to the gaze of others, put them directly on view to the people in the compartments opposite and to anyone walking through the carriage. He'd tried to listen as Anjum described the village, which was strikingly verdant despite the aridity he generally associated with Jharkhand, as she described the struggles of the women living there and how the right-wing Hindu politicians in the area, suspicious of what was going on, had ordered their people to keep tabs on the workshop. He'd wondered almost every day, while she was away, how she was spending her time there, what she was thinking and feeling and saying and doing in that small village in that state he'd never been to, but sitting opposite Anjum on the berth, finally in her presence after three weeks of separation, he found himself paying more attention to the small movements she made with her body than to what she actually said, to the way she kept running her hands through her short hair, or rotating the ring she wore on the middle finger of her left hand, or pulling up her sleeves, which, for some reason, kept falling back down onto her forearms. It was unsettling to sit so stiffly and so far apart from this person with whom he'd spent so much time in various states of union, this person he was unable or reluctant to disentangle himself from in private, even to go to the bathroom or pick up his phone, and it was because perhaps of this physical distance that they also avoided sustained eye contact with each other as they talked, because their inability to touch seemed to give the small space between their bodies a palpable erotic charge, so that despite and also because of this distance it felt like they were touching each other when they were in fact only looking at each other, as if with their eyes they were reaching out and caressing each

other in front of everyone else there, so that even their eye contact became overly intimate and uncomfortable, not just because it alerted their neighbors to the nature of their relationship
but also because it exposed the superficiality of all their attempts at verbal communication, made obvious all the ways it
fell short of what they really wanted from each other as they
sat there opposite each other on that train hurtling heavily
through the plains.

Conversation did become a little easier as the journey went
on, as the gazes of the other people on the train fell away and
they adjusted to their new situation, reconciled themselves to
being next to each other without losing themselves in each
other, they had done it before, after all, whenever they chose to
meet in some public place rather than in one of their flats, a
postponement that often brought its own particular kind of
pleasure. They talked about various things as the train made its
way south and west, what exactly he could no longer say, but
after a while conversation seemed to dwindle, as if they were
running out of things to relate to each other, which worried
him a little, though it also made sense, Krishan told himself, for
they would be on the train for almost twenty-one hours, it
would be impossible to talk the whole time, a realization that in
a way signaled the true beginning of their three-week-long trip
together, the moment when silence as a way of being together
took precedence over speech. They ate the greasy samosas
they'd gotten at the station for lunch, passed most of the warm,
lazy afternoon reading or gazing out at the passing landscapes,
listening to the rhythmic clanging of the wheels against the
tracks, occasionally breaking their silence to share something
from what they were reading or to mention a thought or story

that found its way to their minds. Krishan did his best to read the book he'd bought but found it more and more difficult to concentrate as the afternoon wore on, reading and rereading the same few lines as his thoughts drifted again and again to Anjum, to whether she still felt the same way about him as he did about her, the same way she had seemed to feel before their three-week separation. He couldn't help feeling there was some subtle but noticeable change in her attitude toward him, even if it was true she'd been glad to see him at the station, even if it was true she'd wanted to talk to him about her time in Jharkhand, to share with him at least a significant part of everything that had happened. Looking up at her without trying to hide it—she was so absorbed in what she was reading that she didn't even notice him looking—he couldn't help suspecting that her feelings had changed, that she no longer felt the same overwhelming urge to put aside everything else so they could give themselves up to each other, for why, if she did, were they still sitting so far from each other, why were they making no attempt, at least covertly, to touch each other, to let their toes at least graze?

It couldn't have been fear of disapproving looks from the other people on the train, Krishan knew, for Anjum wasn't the kind of person to care about such things, was always ready to confront people who voiced their disapproval about how she dressed or spoke or conducted herself. It could only have been that her feelings had changed somehow, maybe she had met someone during her time in Jharkhand, another activist like her perhaps, a woman or a man whose life was more similar to hers than his and who she could identify with more than she could with him. Maybe she'd never even felt the same way about him as he did about her, maybe he'd been mistaken thinking his feelings reciprocated to begin with, in the four months they'd known each other she'd been reluctant to give their relationship any kind of name, after all, would dismiss any attempt he made to share his feelings with her explicitly, closing her eyes, shaking her head, and smiling in a slightly ironic, playful manner, as if to say he should know better, that there was no need to make such statements, that such statements were always false or cheapening or manipulative. It was a view he agreed with on principle, knowing enough by then to be suspicious of the ready-made expressions and conventional sentiments with which new lovers usually tried to allay their fears, expressions and sentiments which, he knew, if they weren't deployed with utmost caution, always had the consequence of domesticating love, of containing and constraining its vastness. Anjum's insistence on avoiding such statements had bothered him though from the very beginning, perhaps because of the single-mindedness with which he could sense that she pursued her convictions, and thinking about their namelessness he began to feel even more anxious as he watched her sitting in front of him, totally absorbed in her reading. In the absence of concrete words and gestures, which had a solidity you could cling to in a way you could not cling to unexpressed feelings, he found himself doubting all his convictions about the time they'd spent together, as if his memory of that time might be wrong or inaccurate, as if that time might not even have taken place at all, as if it might have been nothing more than a dream, the person sitting opposite him a total stranger. Sitting there pretending to be as engrossed in his book as she was in hers he began poring over the past several months, trying to find in that slow cascade

of images and sounds some moment that would give irrefut-
able proof against his doubts, that would allow him to dismiss
the distance he felt from Anjum as merely an illusion, no more
than the ordinary, temporary impasse that lovers often felt on
reuniting after a separation.

The first time he'd encountered Anjum had been at a panel
he'd gone to in Delhi with his roommate Rajiv five or six
months before, the subject of which was the relationship between the modern Indian state and queerness, the ways in
which Indian nationalists, mimicking the white rulers of India
before them, had sought to eliminate or to conceal queerness
in the subcontinent. The event had been delayed slightly due to
technical issues, and the two of them had been standing in the
small garden outside, smoking in silence, when they noticed
Anjum walking in through the gate, tall and long-limbed, her
skin darkly lustrous, hair cut short, wearing jeans with a large
shirt that hung loosely from her shoulders. She'd come with
two other people, a girl and a boy, the girl good looking but in
a more conventional way, the boy quite average. The three of
them had gone inside, then learning the panel hadn't started
had come out to the garden to smoke. Krishan tried to find
something to say to Rajiv, to give the impression of being absorbed in conversation, but neither he nor even Rajiv, who was
only attracted to men, had been able to stop themselves from
looking at Anjum through the corner of their eyes, at the elegance with which she brought her cigarette to her mouth and
then drew it away, at her sharp, judgmental features and boyish
grace, the strange quality of not belonging to the world that
seemed to emanate from the way she held herself and the way
she moved. When the panel began she sat down with her

friends on the floor in front of the stage, hidden from where he and Rajiv sat toward the back of the hall. Despite being unable to see her Krishan couldn't help wondering what her response was whenever one of the participants said something of interest, whether she was smiling or nodding or impassive, whether she was furrowing her eyebrows in agreement or indignation, as if his own responses to the discussion onstage would be ill-judged or in poor taste if they didn't cohere with hers.

When the panel finished everyone began making their way haphazardly outside, and spotting Anjum in the crowd Krishan tried discreetly to lead Rajiv closer to where she and her friends were standing. Leaning back against the wall in a performance of casualness he did his best once more to seem engaged in conversation, privately devoting his mental resources to discerning the nature of the relationship between Anjum and her attractive female friend, who, he felt sure, must also have been her lover. He lit one cigarette after another, trying not to seem distracted as he spoke to Rajiv's various friends, glancing back whenever he had the chance at Anjum and the people she was talking to, all of whom seemed far more intriguing and far more attractive than the people he was with. He wasn't close enough to hear anything she said but could tell that she was aware of the attention she commanded as she stood there, a cigarette in her right hand, her left hand sometimes on her hip and sometimes gesticulating as she talked, her upper body leaning forward as she spoke and moving back slightly when she laughed, her manner full of ease, as though she was at a friend's home and not in a public or semipublic place. When, midway through his third or fourth cigarette, she and her two friends left with two other boys, it was as if something had been extracted painfully but soundlessly from deep inside him. Everything remained exactly the same as before and yet her silent departure left the scene in the garden feeling empty and arbitrary, the crowd around him suddenly devoid of interest. It wasn't so much that he'd failed to introduce himself to Anjum or to insinuate himself into one of her conversations, such strategies didn't suit him, he knew from experience, he was still too shy and too awkward at the time to go up to people he didn't know in such contexts. What he'd wanted was simply to continue being in her presence, to continue occupying the same space that she was occupying, as if simply by being in her proximity something might happen that might somehow be of significance, in the same way perhaps that in the East Asian tradition of Pure Land Buddhism, which he'd been reading about at the time, devotees who felt Buddhahood to be too great a challenge for them as individuals could attempt, instead of striving to achieve nirvana, simply to be physically near the Buddha, to obtain a place in the strange force field like sphere that surrounded him no matter where he went, a space that assumed the aspect of heaven and that was, according to the tradition, the next best thing to enlightenment that a human being could strive for.

He'd been unable, in the weeks that followed, to forget Anjum, the stern beauty of her face and her distinctly southern darkness, the way she'd walked in so silently and unexpectedly through the gates of the building and into his mind. Images of her would rise to the surface of his consciousness unannounced at various moments of the day and he would think of the way she'd seemed to move through space that evening, her strange ease and ethereality, as though she subsisted not in the ordinary atmosphere but in some other medium, as though the path she carved through each day was light and effortless, free of resistance, her movement through the world like the long, fluid, unbroken descent that a diver makes through the air before cutting soundlessly into the water, disappearing beneath its surface. He'd come across such people before, of course, not frequently but from time to time, girls but also boys, people who were sometimes strikingly attractive in appearance but who always aroused in him much more than merely an urge to thrust forward or upward with his hips. He'd had glimpses of such people on the metro, in supermarkets, or simply walking down the street, people who seemed to materialize into the midst of everyday life, their faces sharp and angular, their bodies slender, their penetrating gazes directed high above the throng of other humans, as if nobody they saw could possibly interest them, as if everything they needed was already contained in the place they were headed, people who possessed that same quality of seeming to belong to a different, more timeless world that Anjum had, a quality he thought of, for lack of a better word, as beauty. Such people had always drawn his attention, made him stop what he was doing and turn around, made him wish he could follow them to wherever they were going, but watching them disappear into the crowd, a painful twinge in his chest, they would sooner or later leave his thoughts. Why he was unable to stop thinking about Anjum on this occasion, by contrast, it was difficult to say. Rajiv had mentioned that he'd seen her before at other queer events, that he'd been introduced to her briefly once before but had been too intimidated to talk to her, and perhaps she'd stayed in his mind because he sensed they were vaguely part of the same larger circles, that there was a chance he might come across her again in the future. He felt, upon learning her name from Rajiv, that he'd obtained a real, concrete connection to her, a thread that would lead him to her eventually, and the first thing he did was try to find her on Facebook, going through all the listed Anjums as well as the friend lists of dozens of Rajiv's friends, not knowing at the time that Anjum didn't use social media at all. He daydreamed of running into her at random places, on his way to or from campus or while out with his friends, imagining these encounters would lead to a life completely different from the life he lived, to a life that lay, in some way, outside time. He believed in the possibility of these encounters so intensely that he actually felt cheated when he failed to encounter her at a bar or party or a political event or panel, deciding with a little bitterness, once he was sure of her absence, that the place had nothing to offer him. It was funny how similar desire was to loss in this way, how desire too, like bereavement, could cut through the fabric of ordinary life, causing the routines and rhythms that had governed your existence so totally as to seem unquestionable to quietly lose the hard glint of necessity, leaving you almost in a state of disbelief, unable to participate in the world. You could follow the thread of habit day in and day out, lost in studies and in work, among friends and colleagues and family, clasping this thread tightly with both hands so as not to lose your way, and then all of a sudden one morning or afternoon or evening, sipping on a cup of tea at work or going to a friend's house on the weekend, you could come across a person or place or even an image of a person or place that suggested other possibilities, that brought to mind a completely different life, a life you might have lived or might still live, so that suddenly the life you'd been living for the last so many months or years, a life that till that very moment seemed fulfilling, satisfactory, or tolerable at least, became, with the soundless flicking of a switch, empty and hollow, lacking any connection to the person you felt you were or wanted to be.

It was hard to understand now how he'd been so drawn to Anjum when he'd known nothing about her at all at the time, not that she was from Bangalore, not her financial situation or her political views, not that she didn't like having her picture taken, that she slept without a pillow, or that she showered with cold water in the mornings, not even whether she was attracted to men. He'd become obsessed after that initial encounter with not so much a person as the image of a person, an image lacking a caption containing even the most basic details, had begun to long and pine for someone he knew nothing about but who, nevertheless, he imagined could somehow save him. In a sense his response to Anjum was no different from that of so many people, men especially but women too, who seeing someone whose external appearance could sustain all their fantasies, proceeded to project everything they desired onto this person, acting surprised when they realized, weeks or months or years later, that the actual person was different from the image they'd formed, that the actual person had a history and an identity of their own that would not remain silent, responding to this discovery with indignation, as if they'd been lied to or misled, sometimes using persuasion, manipulation or force to compel the unsuspecting person to conform to that initial mental image. And yet his obsession with Anjum could not have been simply an idealization, Krishan knew, for how else could it have turned out, if the image in his mind had been nothing but the blind projection of his own desires, that the more he got to know Anjum the more his desire for her seemed to intensify, how could it have turned out that everything he learned about her subsequently served to expand and elaborate the image in his mind rather than contradict it, filling it out, giving it dimensions and solidity, adding to his desire rather than undercutting it? There must have been more to it than mere projection or mere idealization, even if he'd known nothing concrete about Anjum after that first encounter, for a lot could be said after all on the basis of a single image, a lot could be learned about a person even on first glance, from the composition of the face, which was shaped not just by bone structure but also by the muscles around the cheeks, eyes, and jaw, each of them sculpted in different ways and to different degrees by the ways they were used, each mood and expression requiring a different combination of flexion and relaxation in the different parts of the face, so that one could learn, if one was perceptive enough, to tell whether a person spent most of their time in a state of attentiveness or indifference, melancholy or exuberance, skepticism or hopelessness or earnestness. One could tell by observing the movement of their eyes whether a person spent most of their time feeling shame or self-assuredness or desire or yearning or self-containment, one could tell from the readiness of the smile how vulnerable a person was and from the furrows above the brows how much they were plagued by anger or anxiety, could tell by the posture and the gait and the movement of the hands how lively they were, how open to the influence of others and how ready to influence others, so that perhaps his longing for this person he did not know was due not so much to projection or idealization as to the sometimes almost prophetic nature of a glance, which under the right light and the right circumstances could reveal so many of the possibilities and tendencies of a person's character, which was also why, perhaps, when everything finally ended between them, this too, in retrospect, had seemed like something he'd known about right from the very start, something he'd already glimpsed in that first, silent, one-sided encounter but chosen, subsequently, to ignore.

5

TWO MONTHS AFTER that first encounter, when he learned about a screening organized by a group that Rajiv knew, Krishan had waited all week with anticipation, knowing there was a chance he might encounter Anjum there. Queer events occurred in Delhi with greater frequency than they did in other big Indian cities, but they were still relatively rare, lacking places to host them and money to fund them, as a result of which when they did occur they functioned as a kind of meeting point, a gathering place where people could show their faces and reassure each other that they continued to exist. The event was at a small office space in South Delhi used by a wedding photography business during working hours, and entering the space Krishan had looked around for Anjum almost immediately, despite having told himself he wouldn't. He loitered near the entrance chatting with people he knew, his eyes returning to the door whenever someone walked in, and when the event began with still no sign of her he went reluctantly to find a place to sit with Rajiv, chastising himself for his foolishness as he tried to prepare himself for the screening. The film was an independent documentary about the long marginalized community of transwomen in Hyderabad, hijras, as they were usually referred to in India. It depicted the community's preparations for one of their year's most important festivals, touching also on the relationship between the hijra community and the small but relatively new and more mobile community of queer activists in the city. Krishan found himself being drawn slowly into the film, into the perhaps misleading intimacy with which it showed lives he would otherwise have no access to, and it was only toward the end of the film, after the thought of her had long disappeared from his mind, that he noticed Anjum sitting on the floor close to the front of the room, not far from the door, the light from the screen playing on the slant of her attentive face. Despite doing his best to continue paying attention he found himself unable to concentrate on the film, his heart beginning to beat faster, a tension beginning to spread through his arms and legs. Something inside his chest or stomach seemed to lunge each time he noticed her shift her weight from left to right or cross and uncross her legs, each time she smiled or shook her head in response to something in the film, and feeling that he wouldn't be able to wait another two months to see her again he began to wonder whether he should find a way to talk to her afterward or whether, rather, it was better to wait, there was something inappropriate, he knew, in him showing overt interest in a woman in such a situation, one of the few spaces in Delhi explicitly intended to support less normalized modes of desire.

It turned out, to Krishan's scarcely containable joy, that Rajiv knew some of the people that Anjum had come with, and chatting outside in a group of nine or ten afterward it was suggested, to his even greater joy, that they go to someone's flat nearby to hang out and smoke weed. Trying not to show too much excitement, though in the privacy of his mind he was unable to believe how effortlessly their paths were converging, Krishan nodded his assent to the plan, too hopeful and nervous to really talk to anyone as they walked toward the flat, which was only fifteen or twenty minutes away by foot. He did his best, over the course of the evening, to avoid looking at Anjum more than was appropriate, not wanting to impose himself on her, on the one hand, but also not wanting to alert anybody in the room to his interest in her. He was unable to shake the sense, whenever he was looking elsewhere, that she was looking at him, but each time he glanced up her gaze was in fact directed elsewhere, usually toward whoever was speaking, her long, thick eyebrows furrowed in a kind of skeptical curiosity, her eyes darting tirelessly from one person to another as the conversation shifted from political matters to personal updates to lighthearted teasing to gossip, breaking up from time to time into smaller conversations before coalescing back into a larger one. There was something about Anjum's gaze that elevated its object above everything else in the environment, he felt, so that whatever her eyes were resting on seemed more important than anything else in the room, whichever person she was listening or speaking to more interesting or attractive than anyone else, as if her gaze bestowed not merely significance upon what it was directed toward but existence itself, as if while she was present nothing existed except what she was looking at.

She would smile generously and sometimes laugh in response to what the others were saying, occasionally making her own comments or jokes or qualifications or rejoinders, all of which she expressed with a kind of irony, a skepticism not so much about the particular subject matter of her speech, he felt, as about whether speech in general was worth the effort of speaking. He used every occasion she spoke to study her, grateful to have an excuse to look at her without seeming conspicuous, and he tried too to participate in the conversation, not just so she might pay attention to him but also so he didn't seem out of place in that room full of mostly unknown people. As the evening wore on, as the group slowly grew smaller and those remaining grew progressively more stoned, their eyes did begin to meet more frequently, he sensed, perhaps because he was glancing at her a little more boldly as he grew more intoxicated, perhaps because sooner or later a person always came to know when they were the object of another person's gaze, the eyes had a strange power of attracting the attention of whoever they were looking at, after all, whether the person looking was immediately in front of you or on the other side of a large room, as if simply to look at another human, to recognize them, was also to ask or demand silently to be acknowledged back. On the first occasions they both looked away somewhat quickly—not too quickly, since looking away too quickly gives the impression of having something to hide or some ulterior motive—but after a while Anjum began holding her gaze for longer periods of time, in what felt like an intentional way, as though challenging him to make clear the intent of his own. There was something excruciating about the way her dark brown eyes bore into his at these points, something impenetrable about her own face that made these moments of recognition doubly difficult to withstand, even though they could have lasted at most a second or two, and looking away from her each time he would scold himself immediately for his cowardice, increasingly hopeful, at the same time, that these extended moments of contact were not just accidental, that some kind of silent communication was unfolding between them, that it wasn't just his desire leading their eyes to meet but hers too.

The two boys who Anjum seemed to know best in the group left after a couple of hours, and not long afterward Rajiv made an excuse and took his leave too, leaving only him, Anjum, and the two girls who shared the flat, one of whom immediately began rolling another joint. Anjum didn't seem to know either of them particularly well, which gave Krishan the hope that maybe she was staying behind because of him, and when the joint was finished and Anjum indicated that she needed to leave, that it was getting late, he took the initiative and asked whether she too was planning to take the metro. She was, it turned out, she was heading in the same direction that he was, both of them living in the north of the city, and it was decided that they would make their way to the station together. Taking leave of their hosts, they went downstairs, she first and he following, opened the gate and headed in the direction of the main road. It was only a week after Diwali, as most North Indians referred to the festival, and the air was thick and smoggy, still heavy with fumes from the firecrackers and fireworks of the week before. The only light came from the mute sodium glow of occasional streetlamps, which served more to underscore the lack of visibility than to improve it, and there was a postapocalyptic quality in everything they passed, in the empty roads, devoid of life, the closed shops and lightless buildings, everything around them coated in dust, even the leaves of the plants and trees, as if the city had been abandoned for years. Making their way through this desolation they found themselves talking about the differences between north and south, a subject Krishan had wanted to bring up since learning earlier in the night that Anjum was from Bangalore, sensing it would be a way of bringing them closer together, of giving the two of them some kind of shared racial or mythical origin that would put them in league against the city around them. She'd left Bangalore when she was nineteen to come to university in Delhi, Anjum told him, hadn't lived there or anywhere else in the south since then. For several years she'd hardly visited either, though she'd gone back twice in the year before last, a situation that had to do, as Krishan learned later, with the end of the three-year relationship with her ex-girlfriend, a relationship she'd told her parents about and that had compelled her to break ties with them for some time. The physical distance between them seemed to lessen as they walked, their arms brushing lightly against each other as they negotiated their way through the unlit, uneven roads and pavements, physical contact that momentarily obliterated Krishan's consciousness and which he had to try hard not to be overwhelmed by. Reaching the station they descended the long, steep staircase into the gleaming interior, where slowing down for a moment in uncertainty, stunned by the fluorescent brightness after walking so long in near darkness, they made their way through the long corridor that led to the main lobby, their movements suddenly stiff, almost embarrassed, keeping more distance between their bodies as they walked, their footsteps resounding behind them in the silence. They kept their gazes fixed ahead or on the floor in front of them, as though they couldn't look at each other, as though the brightness of the station exposed a vulnerability that they'd managed till then to keep hidden from their faces, for it was only in the darkness, after all, that you could look at a person you desired without fear of exposing yourself, which was why parties and liaisons and intimacies and sexual transactions were almost always reserved for the night, the lights kept to a minimum or even turned off completely, so you could see well enough for eye contact to be made but not for your need to be revealed. It was only in the darkness that you could approach another person and let your desire be known without allowing the sense of insufficiency or abjection that is so often part of desire to become visible, those desperate, vulnerable parts of the self you always had to skirt or sidestep during flirtation and which, when flirtation failed, when the veneer of coolness or nonchalance suddenly fell away, were painfully betrayed on your face. Krishan tried to find something to say to ward off this possibility, making a silly comment about how clean and well-lit all the metro stations in Delhi were compared to the deserted city above, a comment Anjum responded to almost immediately, to his gratefulness, saying that in a way she found them both similar, especially at night when the metro stations were largely empty, the large echoing halls and long underground corridors a strange futuristic mirror of the city above.

Entering the lobby the two of them went through security, he through the men's queue and she through the women's, putting their bags through the machines, walking through the purely ornamental metal detectors, letting themselves be frisked carelessly by the listless soldiers on duty. They went down the staircase to the mostly empty platform, the flow of their conversation back to normal, the moment of danger successfully averted, and no sooner had they stopped near the middle of the platform than they saw the lights of a train within the tunnel to the left, its twin circles becoming larger and more distinct as it entered the station almost silently, slowing to a soundlessly smooth stop in perfect alignment with the markings on the floor. They entered the carriage, surprisingly crowded given the emptiness of the station, and carving a space to stand just in front of the doors, fell silent as the train began to move. Several of the men in their section of the carriage were looking at them, Krishan could tell, a few of them studying him out of a kind of secondary interest, but most of them looking at Anjum, who was, he noted with discomfort, the only woman in the carriage. They looked at her not with that gaze with which men so often looked at women in Delhi, eyes reaching out like hands about to take hold of inert everyday objects, a glass of water or a remote control, but with a slightly more subdued, slightly more respectful gaze, a respect they gave only begrudgingly, Krishan knew, because of his presence beside her. Anjum had told him at length much later about what it was like for women to move through public spaces in Delhi, about how the gaze of men in Delhi seemed to lack a kind of shame, there was no other explanation, she felt, for the persistence with which men of all classes would try, simply by staring, to pull the inner life out from inside the woman who was their object of interest. You could feel the gaze of men in cities like Chennai and Trivandrum and Bangalore too, she had told him, but men's gazes in most other parts of the country, in most parts of the south, for example, felt somehow less relentless,

less direct, and less violent, more likely to falter when they were responded to or challenged, as if the gazer, upon being gazed back at, could feel he was doing something wrong and withdrew. In Delhi and many of the Hindi-speaking states more generally male stares were different, were intensely unselfconscious and intensely unrelenting, so that even when you weren't being harassed in more explicit verbal or physical ways you still had to use all of your psychological resources to resist these gazes over the course of each day, to prevent these men from trying to enter your soul through your eyes, like strangers who enter the privacy of your house without permission and without even bothering to take off their shoes. You had to employ these psychological resources so constantly over the course of the day, losing even the freedom to think autonomously in your own mind, that by the time you returned home you were always utterly exhausted. The cumulative effect of years of being subject to these gazes was that women who lived in the capital had learned to curb the movement of their own eyes to remarkable degrees, restricting their gazes in public spaces to areas where their eyes couldn't be intercepted, toward their feet or their laps or into the screen of their phones, though she herself made a conscious effort not to constrain her vision, Anjum added, to let her eyes move as freely as she wanted, which was also why she made a point of never using the women-only carriages at the front of the train, no matter how crowded the other carriages were.

He'd thought many times since that conversation about what Anjum had said and the words and images she'd used, not just because it was one of the first examples he'd had of her striking eloquence, the sharpness and intelligence of which he hadn't encountered anywhere in his university, despite having just begun coursework for his PhD. What she'd said had helped him understand not just the entitlement with which men in Delhi used their eyes on women but also the amorphous tension that lay over interactions between men in Delhi too, the vague and omnipresent air of threat that sometimes seemed to hover like an electric charge over the entire city, a charge you felt that at any given time and in any given place might coalesce and then explode without warning into a sudden eruption of physical violence. He remembered sitting opposite a man on the metro one night, relatively light-skinned, strong jawed, a roughness about his face emphasized by the small scar above his right eye that cut into his brow. He was in his mid- to late twenties probably, wore the uniform of mutely colored shirt, sleeveless sweater, trousers, and sandals so common among men in the city, and was sitting beside two friends who seemed a little more well off than him, one of whom had his arm slung around his shoulder, though the man who'd caught Krishan's eye wasn't really paying attention to either of them, was simply staring at the floor in front of him, listening to music with earphones on. Sensing perhaps that he was being watched the man had looked up at Krishan, his face devoid of expression, causing Krishan to look away immediately with embarrassment, as if he'd been caught doing something wrong. After a while, when he felt sure the man had forgotten about him, Krishan looked at him again, why exactly he wasn't sure, there was something intriguing about his presence, about his rough handsomeness and the way he seemed totally absorbed in his thoughts. Again the man looked up, holding his gaze this time, causing Krishan, after one or two seconds in which neither of them gave any indication what they were thinking, to look away. Staring down at the floor he could feel the man continuing to look at him, his gaze like a physical weight forcing his eyes down, and he felt suddenly not curiosity or embarrassment but fear mixed with shame, fear for what the man might to do to him, shame for having looked away and for continuing to avert his gaze from this stranger who was, he felt, now intentionally staring him down. There was always something so unbearable when two strangers looked at each other for an extended amount of time without obvious reason or purpose, a kind of tension that built up from each person's sense that the other person could see inside them, into everything you wanted to keep hidden and out of sight, a tension that soon became so uncomfortable you felt compelled to smile or frown or speak, to do anything, whatever it was, to distract the other person from what they might see through your eyes. Looking at a person in such a way was an act of great intimacy, which was also why it could give rise so easily to violence between men who didn't know each other, each man interpreting the other as attempting to penetrate him, to make him vulnerable and to possess whatever these vulnerabilities offered. It was for this reason too that there was, so often before these sudden eruptions of violence, a kind of staring contest that took place between the men involved, as if each was trying to challenge the other to enter him with his eyes while also trying to enter the other with his own, a contest that had become standard fare during televised boxing matches, when the two boxers stared at each other during weigh-ins or right before the fight began, a staring contest that starts out as a performance but soon becomes very real, a contest that was actually less about peering into another than showing one's willingness to be peered into, about showing that there was nothing one was ashamed of or afraid of exposing, nothing one would not put on the line.

Krishan chastised himself for looking away, which was beginning to feel like an unacceptable act of cowardice, for though he was looking down he could feel the man continuing to stare at him, almost gloating. He kept his eyes averted for the next couple of stops, trying to work up the courage to look up at the man, not out of curiosity now but out of self-respect, despite his fear, as if to prove to himself that he had nothing to be ashamed of, that he too could own himself in the way that was required to withstand another person's gaze. He looked up finally, and the man, who had returned to looking at the floor, looked back up almost immediately with the same expressionless gaze as before, though now there was something menacing about his look, which had become almost a leer. Krishan forced himself to keep looking but the longer the two of them stared at each other the more nervous he grew, the man seemed tough, he was with his friends, they could beat him up easily if they wanted, nor would he be able to defend himself in an argument, his Hindi was too poor to come to his aid in such situations and would give him away as an outsider, which would of course only embolden them. Unable to bear the weight of the man's eyes but not wanting to concede and look away, he had tried finally simply to smile, to give, at the last minute, a nonviolent direction or interpretation to their staring, a smile that the man responded to by leaning forward and continuing to stare at him for a few seconds longer before suddenly, to Krishan's surprise, himself breaking out into a smile, a wide, friendly smile devoid of aggression, after which he called the

attention of his friends, stood up, and pushed his way through
the crowd—they had just arrived at a station—out through the
doors of the train. It was a response that had left him confused
at the time but also greatly relieved, acutely aware, as he
breathed out heavily and rested back against his seat, of the
power that human eyes had, their power not just to beckon
other people silently from the distance but their power also to
inquire, assert presence, and threaten, to enter another person
with or without their will, the way they were used, by so many
men, almost as a sexual organ, a tool of penetration and recep-
tion. There was an intense vulnerability that the gaze of another could make you feel, for the eyes were, as was so often
said, a window into the soul, though what a gaze meant, he had
realized that day, whether it meant intimacy or violence, was
also dependent on the features of the face that surrounded the
eyes, on the meaning given to the gaze by the lips and cheeks
and eyebrows, so that when two people looked at each other it
was a moment both of total knowledge and of total indetermi-
nacy, a way of acknowledging another person that was open to
the most radical of interpretations, so that when the meeting
of eyes was unaccompanied by a determinate expression on the
face or a determinate purpose or context it was one of the few
moments in ordinary life when it seemed, somehow, that the
rules that governed normal interaction between humans were
suspended, as though for a moment at least, within the slender
line that existed between their gazes, anything at all was possible between strangers.

Krishan was pretending to look at the little electronic sign-
board above the door that indicated the stops on the train's
route, and realizing after a moment that Anjum was looking

straight at him he lowered his head and tried to return her gaze. She was standing with her back to the doors, one hand holding the grip that hung from the ceiling and the other folded behind her back, her body loose and relaxed as she swayed gently with the movement of the train. Her expression was difficult to read, the dark brown of her irises thinned to a rim around her dilated pupils, and she was gazing at him as though totally oblivious to the fact that the two of them, especially she, were the center of attention in the carriage. He waited for her to speak but she remained silent—anything they said would be immediately audible to the people around them, even if they kept their voices low—and realizing that she'd been looking at him for some time, that this looking was, moreover, intentional, Krishan felt even more uncomfortable in the crowded, brightly lit carriage, not just because he once more felt exposed but also because Anjum's gaze was intended now, he couldn't help feeling, as a provocation to the men staring at her, as a kind of demonstration that she refused to curb the movement of her eyes and the desire it contained, a demonstration not just for the sake of the men staring at her but also, he felt, for him, as if she could tell he felt threatened by these gazes and wanted him to know that she, unlike him, was not. Not wanting to show his discomfort he forced himself to respond to her gaze, doing his best to avoid her eyes and look instead at the other parts of her face, at her dark, curved forehead, fully visible because of her short hair, the light furrows between her eyebrows, which contributed to the sternness of her gaze, the stud on her left nostril, and her lips, though each of her features always led him back to her eyes, large and dark and insistent, or perhaps it was her eyes themselves, staring earnestly at his, which constantly drew his gaze back to hers. They were almost the same height, he only an inch or two taller, and standing opposite her he noticed how perfectly aligned their bodies were, that if he moved just a short distance forward his chest would be pressed against her chest, his waist against her waist, his groin against hers. He'd been aware since the beginning of Anjum's physical presence, both her stature and also the way she had of moving, but standing in front of her now—he was careful to keep his eyes on her face, not to look down at the rest of her—he felt newly alert to her body, as if realizing for the first time that it existed in the same space and time as his body, a body that could come into contact with his, that could rock and press and shift and push with and against his own. He still didn't know whether she was attracted to men, everything he'd interpreted till then as possible interest could just as well be disinterested friendliness, and even if she was attracted to men in general it didn't, of course, imply that she was attracted to him. Her gaze, though, was gradually becoming gentler, more open and more suggestive, no longer seeming to challenge or interrogate him so much as to be making a kind of invitation, and the longer he looked at her the more everything else seemed to fade away, the gazes of the men around them diminishing in force, becoming almost mute, the sounds around them too becoming fainter, the announcer's voice as they approached various stations, the whoosh of the doors sliding apart, the shuffling of feet as people entered and left the train, as if only the two of them existed on the train as it wound its way through the subterranean city, everything else reduced to a faint echo from a distant world. He felt their bodies moving closer together, their foreheads almost but not quite touching, as if they were about to share a secret with each other though neither of them said a thing, no longer because they feared being heard by the people around them, none of whom existed anymore, but because it seemed there was no more need now to speak, because conversation was no longer required to distract from or conceal what each was feeling, because it was somehow becoming clear, standing opposite each other in the heavy, rhythmic clarity of their intoxication, that they were interested in one and the same thing.

Krishan didn't know how long they stood there looking at each other, stoned but with total lucidity, their bodies rocking gently with the movement of the train but never touching, but at some point Anjum leaned toward him so that her mouth was near his ear and asked whether he had to sleep early that night, whether he wanted to smoke a little more before he went his own way, a question that even if Krishan wasn't exactly expecting didn't exactly surprise him, and to which he'd responded with a silent nod of his head. Getting off at her station, which was only two stops past his, they took a three-wheeler in silence to her flat, their knees pressing against each other over the course of the bumpy ten-minute journey, she looking out on her side at the pavement cascading under the wheels of the three-wheeler, he looking out on his side at the passing streets, desolate as a moonscape, their hands covertly making their way toward each other so that they could clasp each other while continuing to look out their respective sides. When they arrived Anjum whispered that they needed to be quiet, and leading him up several flights of stairs, unlocking her door, she took his hand and guided him through the darkness of the flat. He waited by the door as she went in and turned on a light, a small bedside lamp on the floor that lit up the room with a soft yellow

glow. The room was small and bare, empty of furniture except
for a wooden desk in the corner and a thin mattress on the floor
along the wall. The walls were lined with folded clothes piled
on sheets of old newspaper and several stacks of books in English and Kannada, the English ones mainly political or histori-
cal, as he came to learn later, the Kannada ones mainly poetry.
Anjum put her things in a corner and sat down cross-legged on
the mattress, her back against the wall. Krishan sat down next
to her, not against the wall but facing her at an angle, watched
as she took from beside the mattress an engraved metal box, a
small clay lamp containing the butts of several old cigarettes,
and a slender volume of Kannada poetry. She took out from
the box a small, marble-sized ball of hash, which, she told him
as if by way of explanation, she'd been gifted by a friend, hash
being too expensive for her to buy herself, then heating the
hash up gently under the flame of a lighter, she began to break
the softened ball up with her fingernails into tiny crumbs that
she deposited onto the cover of the book. Not quite able to
believe that he was alone with this person he'd spent the previous two months fantasizing about constantly, Krishan watched
as she mixed the little shreds of hash with tobacco from a cigarette and then rolled the joint with elegant, practiced fingers.
She put the book away, dusted off the mattress, and lit up the
joint, and he asked as she took her first drag whether she read a
lot in Kannada, to which she responded that it was mainly poetry she read in Kannada, most of it from a slightly older generation of female poets in Karnataka. She didn't really enjoy
poetry in English or Hindi, the other two languages she spoke,
the emotional valences of the words and images not resonating
as much with her as they did in her mother tongue. She wrote

in Kannada too, in her journal or notebook—she preferred not calling it a diary—but that had been a relatively recent development, something she'd begun doing only in the last two or three years. When she lived in Bangalore she'd preferred writing in English, probably because in Bangalore, where she spoke mainly Kannada, English had been a way for her to remove herself from her environment, to feel, when she was alone with herself, that she was far from everything around her. It was for this same reason probably that she'd started writing in Kannada again now, because in Delhi of course she communicated primarily in Hindi and English, so that now writing in Kannada rather than English had become her primary mode of being elsewhere, not necessarily a way for her to be back in Bangalore or back in Karnataka, places she felt quite ambivalent about, but a way for her to feel elsewhere at least than Delhi.

Their fingertips came into quiet contact each time the joint passed between them, each of them taking long, indulgent drags before passing it on. It shortened quickly, faster than Krishan would have liked, and taking the last drag, stubbing the joint out firmly in the clay lamp, Anjum looked up at him silently, a shy but assured smile on her lips. There was nothing in their hands to distract them now, nothing to help them pretend they weren't sitting next to each other, alone and unhindered, free to do what they wanted. Both of them shifted slightly where they sat, and Anjum put her hand lightly on the inside of his knee, tracing it upward across his thigh. Krishan brought his face forward to kiss her but leaning to the side she skirted his mouth and kissed him not on the lips but on the side of his jaw, near his ear, then down toward his neck, only gradually making her way up toward his lips. In the soft, effortless sequence of movements that followed almost instinctively, as if the ground beneath them was giving way and holding each other they'd begun falling downward through space, their clothes came off and she sat astride him, her movement slow at first, then more voracious. He lay beneath her, contributing to this movement and supporting it with his hips, his hands moving from her thighs to her waist to her sternum just as hers moved from his chest to his shoulders to his neck, occasionally becoming conscious of what was happening, regarding the woman on top of him with quiet amazement before becoming submerged again in their deep motion, clutching her body more tightly in their increasing momentum as though to prove to himself that she really existed, that the image he'd carried of her in his mind was in fact more than an image, something solid, not fleeting, made of flesh and skin that he could hold and clasp, which gave off smells he could breathe in and sweat he could feel his hands slide over. Her breathing was becoming faster, her groin pressing harder and more intently against his, and sensing what was happening he did his best to hold himself in check, to focus his mind as he tried to accommodate her increasing urgency, though soon he felt himself being overwhelmed and joined her in reaching, unexpectedly, a breathless, briefly overlapping peak. When it was over Anjum leaned forward, still astride him, and buried her face between his neck and head, her chest pressing against his as she breathed heavily in and out. She stretched out her legs so she was lying flat on top of him, her feet upon his, each of them listening as the quick beating of their hearts against their chests became slower and more measured. They lay there in silence, each of them buried in the quiet exhaustion of their bodies, watching as their intoxication surfaced slowly from the ruins of their urgency, neither of them feeling any desire to speak, as though swathed in the warm afterglow of exertion and pleasure they were fully suspended in the present moment, without thought of past or future, a present that like a womb seemed sufficient to contain everything they needed so long as their bodies remained in contact.

They remained this way for fifteen minutes, half an hour, or maybe even an hour, it was difficult to say, it was as if time wasn't passing, or as if all time was contained in this one time, though at some point, shifting onto her side, Anjum placed her hand on his thigh and traced lightly up toward his groin in inquiry. Her hand dwelled there till she sensed a shifting, which soon turned into another series of movements, which led them again to a slow, vigorous immersion into each other, this time longer and more explicit, each of them plundering the other more boldly now, taking as much pleasure in taking as in being taken from. They shifted from one position to another, consuming each other in turns with their eyes and hands, each of them torn between the urge to physically possess the other body and the urge to be able to admire the other body at a remove, caught between the conflicting needs for proximity and distance so central to desire. When they slowed down once more they lay side by side on their backs in exhaustion, his right leg sprawled over her left leg, her left arm stretched out over his stomach, each of them staring at the ceiling in the warm glow of the lamp. They were silent for some time and then began to speak, Krishan could no longer remember about what, to speak with the strangely confessional intimacy that so often arises between new lovers as they lay beside each other after sex, an intimacy that sometimes feels artificial or performed but which, when two individuals have been longing for each other so much that their desire isn't exhausted in the act of union, can feel strangely profound, an intimacy in which each person feels that what they are sharing is something they've kept deep inside themselves all their lives and have only now, in the safe vulnerability of the moment, become capable of expressing. It was an intimacy Krishan had felt once or twice in the past with other people, but which was magnified now to a degree he'd never experienced, as though the words he spoke at that moment to Anjum and which she spoke to him would not, as most words did, fade gently into the world's endless stream of sounds and silences, as though their words were somehow really being heard or really being received, being given some kind of objective validation outside the boundaries of their individual selves, as though in speaking at that moment within the warm cocoon of their bodies they were writing their souls out into the sky or inscribing it into the earth, making themselves, by means of their words, permanent somehow or eternal.

They did not sleep that night, moving continuously in and out of these states of vigorous exertion, peaceful exhaustion, and quiet, confessional revelation, as though none of these states were distinct from each other, as though none of them had any beginning or end but were all simply different aspects of the same larger condition. At six or six-thirty in the morning, knowing he would have to go home before going to campus, Krishan got up to search for his clothes in the mess of things beside the mattress. He put them on with some awkwardness, knowing that Anjum, naked under the sheets, was watching him, then kneeling down on the mattress he kissed her on the cheek with a chasteness she did not seem to expect and took his leave. Outside the day was colder than he'd expected, perhaps because he hadn't been outside so early in the morning in a while. The morning light was pleasantly dusky through the thick fog and dust, and he felt as he walked a gentle invigoration from having not slept all night and not eaten. Despite the poor visibility the scenes around him possessed an unusual clarity, the edges of things sharp and their surfaces distinctly colored, the tea shops already open, fruit and vegetable sellers already pushing their carts, laborers going here and there, the roads packed with cars, vans, buses, and three-wheelers throwing up large quantities of noise and smoke into the air. Looking at all the people around him already beginning the day, already fully engrossed in obligations, in the routine of their daily lives, he felt as though he'd stepped from one realm of existence into another, each of which seemed to deny the possibility of the other. As though the appearance of the world of everyday life, which had seemed so far away just a few hours ago, called into question now the existence of the world he'd just left behind, a world so different in nature that he might actually have begun to doubt its existence had he not been carrying the smell of it still in his body, the scent of sweat and bodily fluids and the faint pungency of condoms, all of which enveloped him against the morning cold like a warm, invisible layer, a constant proof and reminder of the night before. The scent remained with him on the ride home and even after he had showered, changed his clothes, and gone to campus, leaving him only after he'd slept in his own bed that night and then bathed again the next morning, and perhaps it was its dissipation that was responsible for the quiet anxiety he felt in the following days, as if reimmersed into his ordinary life without any physical token of the ever

more distant world he'd shared with Anjum, he could no longer be sure whether the profundity of the experience had been
real or just imagined, whether Anjum had felt the same way or
whether, blinded by his heavy intoxication, he had misread the
situation, in which case, it occurred to him, it was possible she
might not even want to see him again. They did in fact meet a
few days later, this time at his flat rather than hers, and this second night too had gone the way of the first, the two of them
again hardly sleeping, again moving in and out of those different modes of bliss, and again followed, not long afterward, by a
kind of anxiety, less this time about whether he'd actually felt
what he remembered feeling or even about whether Anjum
had felt the same way, but about whether, rather, what they'd
experienced together could possibly continue, whether it
wouldn't somehow just vanish into thin air. Even if their two
meetings had been as revelatory for her as they'd been for him,
how could he be sure she would continue to find in their encounters that same quality and pitch, how could he be sure it
would continue, not just for her but for him too, for how after
all could such intense desire and attraction really last, how
could a way of being so manifestly at odds with the so-called
real world possibly be sustained?

In the three or four months that followed, time that felt, in
his memory, strangely outside time, Krishan had oscillated continuously between these two conditions, between the thought-
less, rapturous, and seemingly endless present that he
experienced in physical proximity to Anjum, and the restless,
agitated uncertainty that he felt when they were apart. They
met each other usually no more than once a week and sometimes even less frequently, depending on Anjum's schedule, for

most of her free time was devoted to her political work, to organizing, going to protests, and running workshops, for which she often traveled out of Delhi on weekends too. When they did meet they would spend extended periods of time together, sometimes, if they met on the weekend, up to two days without break holed up in one of their rooms, smoking cigarettes and hash, having sex, talking and reading to each other, the sleepless nights followed by mornings and afternoons in which they drifted continuously between dreams and coitus. Even in the excursions they made out into the world to eat or to obtain fresh air they were unable to break away from the cocoon they formed together in bed, so that even sitting in tea stalls and smoking cigarettes, walking together directionlessly in parks, standing opposite each other on trains, they were as though wholly ensconced in each other, unable to break away from each other, as if the world consisted of only the two of them, as if everything outside them was some kind of trick or illusion or lesser reality, a feeling no doubt related to the strange quality that time seemed to acquire while they were together, for though this time could be measured objectively, could be counted, once it was over, in terms of hours and minutes, it seemed at the same time recalcitrant to the metrics of standard time, as though it had a duration that was fuller or vaster than the time that constituted the other parts of their lives, as though while they were with each other they were held together in a single, depthless moment that could be stretched out forever and that, while they were in it, went on endlessly, though eventually of course it always came to an end. The longer they spent together in this way, hardly eating and hardly sleeping, as if their time together were some kind of ascetic practice, the more dangerous being together somehow seemed, their personalities beginning to disintegrate, their private moods beginning to dissipate, as if in the time they spent together they were pushing farther and farther into some realm of existence or being that was connected to the so-called real world by only the slenderest of threads, so that the farther they went into this other realm the more possible it seemed that the thread might be cut, that they might find themselves suspended, suddenly, in some other place, unable to return to their familiar selves. It would seem more and more urgent for each of them to obtain brief moments alone so they could verify that they continued to exist as individuals, so they could attempt, in whatever small ways, to preserve at least scraps of their individuality, one of them going outside in order to buy cigarettes, taking what was obviously a longer amount of time than necessary, the other spending several minutes in the bathroom, answering the various messages that had accumulated on their phones under the pretext of having to use the toilet. Having reassured themselves of their separate existences they would lose themselves once more in the world they formed together, this dissipation or disintegration of the self holding such an ineluctable pull over them, despite the need they felt for self-preservation, that they couldn't stop themselves from spending more time together, though eventually of course it would be necessary to separate, eventually the pull of the outside world and their separate lives grew so strong that they could no longer continue ignoring it even as they tried, postponing their social or personal commitments and sometimes even canceling them, extending or prolonging the moment of departure in small ways, one last cigarette, one last cup of tea, or one last quick, urgent ripping apart of clothes, so that five minutes more became half an hour and half an hour more became three full hours.

When they did finally manage to part ways Krishan always felt a quiet relief, mingled with the sadness of having to confront the strange nonexistence of his person, a nonexistence he felt as a blissful, exhilarating condition in the presence of Anjum but that, as soon as he was on his own, he experienced only as an unsettling loss of self. Too exhausted to think or feel or do anything productive he would go home and lie down for a while, and when he finally recovered the strength he would go to the bathroom and shower, attempting, by washing his body, to recover something of his former self. He would try then to do something quiet, to sweep his room, the rhythmic, repetitive motion of which always comforted him, to read, which allowed him to feel he had an inner life of his own, to try in whatever way he could, in other words, to rebuild his depleted resources and reconstruct a self that was independent of Anjum. Sooner or later though he would feel the need to contact Anjum, to hear from her and to obtain from her some kind of external corroboration of the thoughts and feelings still lingering in him from their encounter, some kind of proof that these thoughts and feelings were justified, a consolation for the loneliness he began to feel as their separation became more concrete. Anjum rarely responded quickly to his texts once they'd separated, often taking hours to text back, sometimes more than a day. Her responses were sometimes sweet, sometimes more matter of fact, but they were never long and seldom conducive to further conversation, as though she wanted to maintain some distance from him once they were no longer in the same physical space. Maintaining such distance was healthy, Krishan knew, it was necessary for regeneration, which was necessary in turn not only for the endless task of daily living but also, more importantly, in order to be able to see each other again. He did his best not to seem desperate or needy, not to create the impression that he wanted her more than she wanted him, never sending more than one text message at a time, never sending a second message till he received a response to the first, always waiting at least an hour before replying to the messages he finally received, even if he wanted to respond immediately. He did his best to appear unbothered by Anjum's silences, but obtaining little reassurance from her that she was thinking about him as much as he was thinking about her, that she wanted to see him as soon as he wanted to see her, he would begin in the days following their meetings to feel anxious, to wonder whether he might have said or done the wrong thing, whether she was beginning to get bored of him, whether the profundity of their time together was being lost to repetition and routine. Such anxiety was, of course, experienced to some degree by every person newly in love, by every person who finds in another a bliss or rapture that they were unaware till then was possible and that they became terrified, having experienced, of losing. It was an anxiety that usually diminished as time passed, as interaction became a little more habitual and as each person became to the other someone whose continued presence could be taken for granted, and Krishan's anxiety too began to diminish a little with the passing of time, as he became more confident that the quality of transcendence in their encounters was not going to subside just because they were becoming more familiar with each other. He could tell how much Anjum liked him, not just his body but his sensibility and the things he said, could tell how interested she was in him from all the questions she asked about his youth in Sri Lanka, which seemed to her like a distant, mythical place. He could tell from how she sometimes held him while they slept that she was opening herself up to him, allowing herself to become more attached to him, but even as she seemed to become more vulnerable, even as he sensed, in the way she sometimes looked at him or sometimes touched him, that she too was perhaps developing the tenderness that marked the transition between falling in love and actually loving someone, Krishan couldn't suppress the sense that in some private way she was resistant to becoming too close to him, that despite being willing to abandon herself fully when they were actually beside each other, she was wary of spending too much time with him or of incorporating him into the rest of her life—as though she felt that what they experienced together could not go on forever, that it would inevitably cease to be gratifying or fulfilling if it did, as though the yearning for other worlds he sensed so vividly in her could be permanently satisfied only by something else.

He'd wondered initially whether this resistance might have to do with wanting to be with other people, for Anjum would often express her attraction toward people they knew or saw in passing, both boys and girls, making these remarks almost conversationally, as if she couldn't possibly imagine him being affected by what she said. She sometimes mentioned lovers she'd had in the past and during her previous relationship, which had been open for two years, and it occurred to him that maybe she wanted to sleep with other people—maybe women in particular, who could give her something he could not—that possibly in fact she already had other lovers, which was maybe why they

saw each other no more than once a week. Or perhaps she was
in some way embarrassed by him, embarrassed to be seen in a
conventional relationship with a male, and maybe this was why
she seemed so reluctant to meet him at social events and in the
company of friends. He didn't raise the issue with her explicitly,
partly out of shyness and partly out of fear of what he would
learn, and it was only two or three months into their relationship that he began to sense that Anjum's distance came not so
much from desire for others or embarrassment at their relationship as from the fact, simply, that she didn't seek transcendence in sexual or romantic relationships at all. She liked
intimacy, of course, had a strong, sometimes overwhelming
need for sex, and was clearly capable of losing herself in the
rapturous world they experienced when they were alone, but
for some reason it was as though she didn't fully trust this world
of theirs, as if she didn't believe it could do justice to what she
ultimately yearned for. This yearning, Krishan began to understand as they spent more time together, as he learned more
about her life outside their meetings, was a yearning she saw
only her political work as capable of fulfilling, not exactly the
utopian vision that animated this work, since she was too cyni-
cal to imagine that a perfect world could ever be brought about,
but the life she hoped to create with the community of people
with whom she did this work, with her comrades, as she liked
to call them. Listening to the way she talked about the various
cases of gender and caste violence she saw at her job, the way
she talked about the protests she went to and the police violence she'd witnessed, the fervor with which she discussed
plans and visions for future work, always collaborative, always
with comrades, it dawned on him that Anjum was willing to

give up everything for these plans and visions, that if the circumstances were right she would drop everything for their sake
and disappear, and though he sometimes hoped, in moments
when he felt close to her, that he too might be able to share in
this life she sought, that she might at some point be willing to
invite him into it, he couldn't help suspecting, at other, weaker
moments, that she viewed the time they spent together as only
a distraction, that no matter how much she liked or even loved
him their relationship was something she allowed herself only
as a break from what really mattered to her, that she was, like
the female Tiger cadres he'd read about and listened to in so
many articles and interviews, one of those people for whom
love, no matter how otherworldly it seemed, was always bound
to the so-called real world, a world whose basic structure she
could never accept, that she was, in other words, one of those
people whose being was so taken up with yearning for another
world that no single person, no love or no romantic relationship, could ever fill the absence in her soul.

6

IT WAS THIS thought Krishan kept returning to as he sat opposite Anjum that evening on the train to Bombay, he pretending to read while all the time stealing glances at her, hoping she would glance up from her book and give him a sign, that she would reach out with her hand to touch him or raise her head up to look at him at least. He was able, usually, to suppress such anxieties when next to Anjum, not wanting to let them affect their time together, but having not seen her in three weeks and having hardly heard from her at all, unable now, even in her presence, to obtain the instant reassurance that her touch always gave, Krishan couldn't help worrying that something had changed during her time in Jharkhand, that the urgency for union he'd always sensed when they met in person was no longer present, as if the distance she so often tried to maintain when they were physically apart had crystallized now into something more definite. Dinner was beginning to be served in their carriage, the staff moving quickly from berth to berth with trays marked vegetarian and nonvegetarian, and becoming aware of the commotion around them Anjum had closed her book finally and looked up. She asked him how his novel was going, and looking down at the book still open in his hands he replied that it was going okay, that he'd read a little too much for the day and wasn't really in the mood to keep reading. She too was a little distracted, she told him, a little too upset to read. He looked at her inquiringly, surprised at this admission, and after hesitating for a moment she told him she'd been fighting with her mother, that no matter how much she tried to put the matter aside it had kept returning to her thoughts. Krishan waited for her to continue, but she seemed unsure about whether to share more, and it was only when he prodded her a little, asking what had happened, what was the reason for the fight, that Anjum sighed and began to explain. It had started with an accusatory comment her mother had made on the phone three weeks ago, chastising her for having not returned to Bangalore in so long. She'd gone twice the year before but hadn't been back in the previous year, and her mother had been pestering her continuously about her next visit. She'd told her mother it wasn't her fault, that her work had been overwhelming and that she simply hadn't had time to visit, but her mother, who'd been irritable from the start of their conversation, had insinuated that there must have been some other reason. What did she mean, she'd asked, what other reason, and her mother, without skipping a beat, had told her that her ex-girlfriend must have been the reason, that either she'd gotten back with her ex or that she was wasting her life away in some other infantile way. Anjum had been silent at first, not having expected this accusation, then remembering all the things her mother had said in the past concerning Divya she'd suddenly become furious, had shouted and hung up the phone. On both occasions her mother had tried calling since then, ostensibly to patch things up, the subject had come up again, neither of them backing down, and on both occasions the line had been cut amid shouting and recriminations.

Krishan had heard a little about how Anjum had fallen out with her parents over Divya, but it was something she'd never seemed to want to dwell on at length, despite his attempts at inquiry whenever the subject came up, and he was a little taken aback now by how patiently she began to relate the story behind the recent fight, a story that was, she made a point of telling him, nothing particularly surprising or remarkable. She'd been together with Divya for almost two years at the time, she told him, had been living together in the same flat with her for several months, and because she'd felt certain the relationship was going to last she'd decided that she should finally let her parents know. It was a matter she'd known they wouldn't respond to well, especially not her mother, but her parents were relatively permissive and understanding so far as parents went, had always supported or at least sympathized with whatever she and her sister wanted. She'd assumed that eventually they would come to accept the relationship, even if they had to go through a long period of adjustment before that could happen, even if they never made any effort to meet Divya or bring her into their lives, which wasn't, in any case, something she particularly cared for. She'd fully expected the fury of her mother's initial response, had fully expected the long campaign of manipulation that came afterward, the tears her mother frequently

shed in an attempt to make her feel guilty, her claims that Anjum's father was becoming ill in response to what she'd told
them. She'd expected the vicious remarks, calculated to induce
shame, had expected the quietly poisonous words that sank in
and took root long after they'd been spoken and heard, but
what she hadn't quite expected, what she hadn't quite prepared
herself for, was that she herself would be so affected by everything her mother said. She'd been close to her mother during
childhood, almost inseparable, but their relationship had become troubled when she was a teenager, and she'd made a con-
certed effort when she left to Delhi for university to distance
herself from her parents and her home. Her mother would still
make disparaging comments every so often about the way she
dressed or the way she looked, would chastise her if she didn't
want to spend time with relatives when she returned home, but
by the time she'd graduated and begun to work her mother had
become less controlling, sensing perhaps that she had less
power over her daughter now that she was making her own
way in the world.

She'd assumed, when she told her parents about Divya, that
no matter what her mother said she would be able to stay patient and composed, remain unaffected by the attempts her
mother made to bring the relationship to an end, but the truth,
she'd realized, stunningly obvious in retrospect, was that her
mother was still after all those years capable of piercing her, of
making her doubt not only her convictions but her sense of
self. She'd borne her violent words as long as she could, hoping
they would eventually come to an end, but the fighting had
continued for months, leading to deeper and deeper resentment, till finally, no longer able to hear her mother's voice with-

out feeling her chest constrict in anger, she'd been forced to break off ties. They didn't talk for a year and a half, not till several months after the relationship with Divya ended, and even then she didn't tell them about the breakup immediately, not wanting to give her mother the satisfaction of knowing it was over. When she finally learned what happened her mother took care not to seem overjoyed, persuading her to come home for a week, making her special curries and desserts almost every meal, never once making reference to the relationship. She'd known that nothing had really been resolved, that her mother would continue pretending she was straight, but she'd accepted the conciliatory gestures nevertheless, the reassurance and security of being in touch with her parents convincing her to let the matter go. As time passed and things became more normal she gradually forgot what happened, which felt increasingly in the past and increasingly insignificant, especially since things with Divya had ended for other reasons. It was only now that she was realizing how resentful she must have remained, for how else, when her mother brought Divya up on the phone, could all that rage have resurfaced, so suddenly and forcefully that it surprised even her? In a way her mother's intuition had been right—the fact she hadn't returned home in so long testified, no matter how she tried to rationalize it, to a smoldering anger about all the things her mother had said, an anger she'd suppressed for a long time and which, when her mother provoked her that day on the phone, had finally exploded into the open.

Anjum fell silent as their trays were brought to them, each of them moving to the edge of the berth and resting the trays on their laps. They opened the little plastic containers to examine what was inside, nothing but a few small, slightly soggy chapattis and a yellow-colored fish curry, and leaning forward to avoid spilling they began to eat. When the two uniformed men had served the opposite berths and moved beyond earshot, Krishan turned again toward Anjum and spoke in a low voice. Was she sure that her mother's pressure hadn't been partly responsible for her decision to break up with Divya, that her mother's role in the breakup wasn't the source of her unexpected anger? Anjum thought for a moment, looking at him as she finished swallowing what was in her mouth, then shook her head. No, she said. If anything her mother's response had made her even more determined to be with Divya, if anything it had made her stay with Divya even longer than she would have otherwise. She wouldn't have let her mother or any of her family members affect her choices, she'd been with other women too since Divya, and wouldn't hesitate to be with a woman again in the future, if that was what she wanted. She paused for a second, then smiling at him as if making a joke added that if she was spending time with him now, it was because she liked him, not because he helped her satisfy some subconscious desire to please her mother. Krishan listened as she began to speak about her previous relationship openly and at length for the first time, as she described Divya's possessiveness and the various other problems that had led to the end of their time together. Her voice was less grave now, more earnest, as if in talking about her mother and Divya she was getting something off her chest, and Krishan felt the anxiety he'd felt all afternoon melting away. He understood now why Anjum had been so out of touch these last three weeks, why she'd seemed distant for most of the day, and he could sense, in the way she was talking about Divya, that she was trying in part to reassure him, to convey that she hadn't ignored him on purpose and that there was nothing he needed to worry about. She was focusing on him fully, her eyes fully on his, and he couldn't help feeling grateful that she was telling him all these private, intimate details, she who was usually so reserved about what she shared, as if this person who'd maintained till then such a smooth façade of invulnerability was willing at last to open herself up to him. Sure that nothing had changed between them, that they had, in fact, somehow grown closer over the past three weeks, Krishan felt silly for all the anxiety he'd been feeling, anxiety that now felt misplaced and childish. He should have guessed that something else was happening, they were after all going on this trip to Bombay together, were going to spend three weeks with each other in a kind of semi-domesticity, something they'd never done before and that Anjum wouldn't have suggested if she wasn't in some way serious about him. She could have told him of course that she was fighting with her mother, in which case he would have tried to comfort her instead of getting worked up on his own, but that was just how Anjum was, she was secretive with her thoughts and liked to deal with things on her own, a quality that made her confidences all the more precious when she shared them. They stayed up talking as the passengers in the carriage around them began going to bed, turning off their compartment lights and drawing the curtains over their berths, their conversation moving from Anjum's mother and Divya to parent-child relationships, to the question of financial independence and other more far afield topics, Krishan becoming more and more cheerful as they talked, as if only now were things between them becoming normal again, making jokes, reaching out and touching Anjum on the knee or forearm, causing her to laugh and touch him back. When, around nine or nine-thirty, the main lights in the carriage were turned off and Anjum yawned, told him she was sleepy, he couldn't help feeling slightly let down, not because he'd thought any other end to the night was possible but because he'd only just begun feeling connected to her, and wanted to remain in that feeling. He watched as she stood up and pulled down her bag from the upper berth, began to spread out the sheets and cover, then getting up with some reluctance he began clearing the lower berth, dusting off the crumbs from their meal and spreading out his own sheets. When Anjum was done setting up her bed she came up from behind and touched his left elbow, squeezing it lightly as she leaned in close and whispered good night. Climbing nimbly up the small iron ladder, she made some last adjustments to her berth, then drew her curtain and disappeared from view.

Krishan finished making his bed and sat down at the edge of his berth, looked to his left and right and wondered what to do. There were no signs of life or movement in the carriage, the curtains had been drawn across all the berths but his, the bright fluorescent ceiling lights turned off and replaced by two small bulbs in the corners of the carriage that gave the darkness a dull amber hue. There was a reading light that he could turn on in the upper corner of his berth, he knew, but he didn't really feel like reading, especially not after having read or tried to read for so many hours that afternoon. The sudden and intense fluctuations in his mood that day had left him exhausted, in a quiet, ruminative mood, and what he wanted above all was to be with himself for a while. Deciding to lie down and watch what could be made of the passing night, he took off his sandals, brought his legs up onto the bed, and drew the curtain so he was enclosed in the darkness of the berth's womb-like space. Through the scratched horizontal pane of the window the countryside outside was flitting by quickly, shrouded ghostlike in the blue-black dark. He brought his face to the glass and tried to discern what kind of landscape they were passing, but couldn't make out anything except for very occasional lights in the distance and trees here and there, as though everything passing by was anonymous, only the continuous pounding of the train's wheels below to mark their progress against the immensity of the night. Raising his hand, Krishan caressed the soft leather underside of Anjum's berth. He could sense her presence above him, in her own separate enclosure, and the thought of being so close to her and yet so sealed off magnified his feeling of being alone, not in a way that caused anxiety or distress but in a peaceful, almost pleasant way. It had been a while since he'd last felt this kind of solitude, this sense of calm self-containment or self-sufficiency so different from the loneliness that had been taking hold of him in the past few months. Unlike that loneliness, which was full of a desperate, almost helpless desire to be in Anjum's presence, a constant anxiety about whether Anjum really wanted to be with him, what he felt now oddly was a sense of needing nothing outside himself, not even Anjum, a sense of being able to relinquish the world and everything it offered, to accept instead the person he was, incomplete though he was and so full of voids.

He'd never thought of himself as being needy—even now, in his state of calm, he found the word difficult to use—but the truth was that he'd become, in the last few months, so dependent on the signs of interest and affection that Anjum gave him, his moods so responsive to everything she said or failed to say, did or failed to do, that sometimes he seemed pathetic even to himself. He'd found himself becoming envious and even possessive on occasion, resentful of the fact that the time he spent with Anjum was determined solely by reference to her availability, and even if Anjum's own nature was partly responsible for these feelings—it was no coincidence, he felt, that Divya too had been possessive while she was with Anjum—he still couldn't help detesting himself for the pettiness of the thoughts he sometimes had. When his desperation was at its peak he often felt his only recourse was to pull back completely, to attempt to psychologically extricate himself from Anjum altogether, partly out of frustration or indignation or even perhaps a desire to wound, but above all to save himself from the pain of feeling desire too strongly. He would listen, at such moments, to a recording of the *Sivapurānam* he'd bought a few years before, not long after having heard it for the first time at a funeral in Colombo for some distant relative. A singer had been hired for the funeral, and listening to the man as he stood singing beside the corpse for the small audience, he'd been moved, despite having hardly known the deceased, to the point of shedding tears, entranced by the singer's rich, unornamented voice, by the slowly building, incantatory rhythm of the song, written in a Tamil from several hundred years before that he could hardly understand but which, he knew, was about the pain of being embodied, of having to live many different lives, as a blade of grass, a worm, and a human, of having to endure countless existences dominated by earthly desires while all the time yearning to give up earthly life, to be shorn of attachment and the weight of the body and joined to the feet of Siva. Listening to the song or singing the lyrics to himself in those moments of desperation he was able to more easily bear the uncertainty of being with Anjum, would feel consoled by these visions of total removal from the world, by the possibility of cutting off all ties with Anjum and leaving her completely, a severance that was at that point only a fantasy but nevertheless one that comforted him. There was probably something unhealthy, he suspected, about this need to either identify completely with Anjum or completely withdraw from her, about his difficulty finding a reasonable middle ground, and he wondered in less impassioned moments whether it was possible to relate to her differently, to accommodate himself better to this person who clearly wanted to be with him but seemingly only in a temporary or provisional way. He wondered whether he could simply be grateful for her presence when it was available and content by himself when it was not, whether he could take pleasure in her company when he could but remain unworried and unconcerned at other times, to avoid in this way the debilitating anxiety he so often felt when she was out of touch or vague about plans or withdrawn. He would think, listening to the *Sivapurānam*, of the sea in Sri Lanka as it was during the calmer months, specifically of the sea in Trincomalee as he'd seen it once on a warm, late June evening, the water a calm, waveless sheet of glimmering, glistening blue that stretched out silently toward the sky. He would think of how the water unfurled itself so softly across the gentle slope of the beach, how it swept over the smooth, polished sand with such tenderness and how reaching its full extension, just as it was losing all its momentum, it would pause as if taking a breath in a last brief embrace of the

earth, clasping the land for as long as it could before being
drawn back with a sigh into the sea. He would think of the sea,
rolling and unrolling itself softly and placidly across the edges
of the earth in this way, coming into contact with the shore so
lovingly and gratefully and then, when it was time, withdrawing so gracefully, and he would wonder whether it was possible
for him too to be in Anjum's presence and then return to himself with such grace and equanimity, to attach himself to the
thing he loved and then detach himself without each time ripping apart his soul, though the truth, he knew, was that such a
stance was only possible at certain moments, at least for him,
moments in which he was, for whatever reason, briefly in possession of himself, for it was difficult to be philosophical in the
midst of desire, it was difficult to be as removed from the world
as religious devotees claimed to be when you were caught up in
the bliss of union or in the desperation of being parted.

How long he sat there looking out the window it was hard
to say, immersed in the darkness of the world passing by and
simultaneously lost inside himself, but at some point, maybe
half an hour, maybe an hour after she'd said good night and
withdrawn for the night, Krishan heard the creaking of Anjum's berth directly above him, the sound of Anjum moving on
her bed. He assumed at first that she was simply shifting or rolling around, since Anjum moved constantly from one side to
the other as she slept, but a few seconds later he noticed the
flapping of the curtain on the far side of his berth, the momen-
tary entry of the carriage's amber light into the enclosure. A
hand parted the curtain and he saw Anjum's face looking in,
her eyes squinting as she tried to locate him in the darkness of
the berth. She was trying to determine whether or not he was

awake, he realized, and quickly drew in his legs to let her know he was up. Parting the curtain more widely, letting more light in, Anjum glanced around to make sure no one was looking, then entered the berth and drew the curtain so the enclosure was once more shrouded in darkness. She moved toward him on her hands and knees, her movement confident despite the berth's narrowness, and he slid down so that he was lying on his back and she was able to move closer. Their bodies weren't touching but her head was directly over his, their eyes trying to distinguish each other in the shadows, neither of them moving, neither of them, he could feel, breathing. They didn't need to speak, he could sense why she'd come and now that she was there felt no surprise at all, as if he had in fact been waiting for her to come all the while. He could smell the light perspiration on her skin, which he had not been this close to in three weeks, and despite feeling an urge to wrap his arms around her and bring their bodies together he remained unmoving, arms by his side, partly to preserve the self-possession he had just been feeling, the sense of not being in need of her or anybody else, but partly also to prolong his anticipation of the contact he felt certain was going to come, the loss of self he knew he was going to give into and that he wanted more than anything else despite, just moments before, having felt so self-possessed. He traced Anjum's thigh lightly with his right hand, wanting to draw her body closer to him but still wary of more solid contact, and Anjum lowered her head down and brushed her lips against his. Her mouth hovered above his for a moment, the warmth of her breath on his skin, then moving to his neck she began not to kiss him exactly but to caress him with her closed lips, making her way up from his neck to the side of his face, across his forehead and then down to his mouth, where again she did not kiss him so much as touch her lips to his, the rest of their bodies taut as this brief contact was made. A shaft of silvery blue light entered the berth through the window and then disappeared, and raising her head up to look outside Anjum became still. They were passing a station probably or perhaps some small town, nothing to worry about it seemed, and as another shaft of light passed into the enclosure, filling the berth with a soft, electric glow, she turned back and their eyes found each other wordlessly, she looking down at him and he up at her. Their faces were illuminated only for a moment but it seemed much longer to Krishan, as if in that brief silver light he could see every detail of Anjum's face simultaneously and with great clarity, the stud on her nose, the lashes over her dark brown eyes, the soft fuzz of her earlobes, like a dark room lit up by lightning so that everything is taken in as an instantaneous whole, each detail of her face imprinting itself so vividly in his mind that when the light fell away and they were engulfed again in darkness he continued to see her just as she was in that brief moment, their eyes locked, their bodies tense, still keeping their distance in case the train came to a stop and people began to enter or leave. The carriage continued rocking from side to side, the berth and the windows vibrating from the hammering of the iron wheels below, and breathing out softly Anjum lowered herself down again so their bodies were in full contact, each of them drawing deeper and more immersed in the other, each of them losing awareness of everything that existed outside the movement of their limbs and the smell of their skin and their hushed groans and murmurs as they were borne aloft together through the anonymous night.

They remained there for some time, each of them breathing slowly in and out, saying nothing for a while, receding back into their own separate worlds as they emerged slowly from their cocoon. Krishan asked whether she wanted to smoke a cigarette, a habit of theirs after having sex, and Anjum whispered back that yes, a cigarette would be nice. She went out first, and waiting a couple of minutes he began making his way down the darkened carriage himself, taking care to move quietly despite there being little chance that anyone was up. Opening the carriage door and going out into the small space between carriages he was met with a rush of cool air on his face, and squinting in the fluorescent light he found Anjum standing on the left, looking out through the open door at the passing scenes. He put his hand gently on her shoulder, and turning around immediately she unlatched the heavy iron door from the wall, closed it to stem the flow of wind. She reached into her pocket and took out her pack of cigarettes, offering him one and then taking one herself, lighting both cigarettes in the stillness of the enclosed space. Opening the door again and latching it to the wall, she resumed her earlier position as the wind rushed once more into the carriage, leaning against the doorframe in silence and looking out. He looked over her shoulder at the wide expanse of land they were passing, the silhouettes of occasional trees and scattered brush, everything engulfed in the seemingly endless night. It was cumbersome to smoke with Anjum immediately in front of him, and wanting to be by himself for a moment, to make sense of everything that had just happened, Krishan squeezed her lightly on the back of the neck and went to the closed door opposite. Pulling down on the handle, opening the door, and latching it to the wall so that he too could lean out into the landscape, he took a drag of his cigarette and watched as the foreground rushed past while the lightless horizon in the distance remained still, the wind buffeting his face, the thin steel floor trembling beneath his feet. They could have been anywhere in the immense stretch of land between Delhi and Bombay, could have been anywhere in that endless country that he'd always associated with both the beginning and end of human time, and staring out at the silvery outlines of trees and electricity pylons that punctuated the land's flatness he suddenly felt drawn again to Anjum, an urge to wrap his arms around her and tell her how much he loved her, how much he wanted her, to confess how sad he'd been while she was away. He finished his cigarette and flicked it out, watched as its fire glinted for a second before disintegrating into the receding darkness, then turned around toward Anjum, who sensing his gaze perhaps threw out her own cigarette and turned toward him. She stood there unmoving in the doorframe opposite his, her body leaning to the right, one hand still gripping the bar along the wall, the large shirt she'd changed into billowing in the wind. In the white light that fell from the ceiling her face was starkly visible, her eyes squinting slightly, her thick eyebrows furrowed, a tired, peaceful smile softening her sternly beautiful face. Behind her vast tracts of unlit land passed by each second, miles and miles of unknown places containing people living unknown lives appearing and vanishing every moment, but continuing to look at her, not taking his eyes off her as she gazed back at him, it felt like the two of them were lost in that distant night that the train was hurtling through, as if those vast distances were contained right there in the space between them, as if what was distant and what was proximate had collapsed somehow into a single space. He was unsure what was going to happen between the two of them, could tell in the clarity of the hour and the mild intoxication of the to-bacco that nothing was certain, that as long as he continued to be with Anjum he would continue experiencing those rapid, unsettling transitions between rapture and disquiet. Watching her as she watched him, the landscape rushing by behind her but aware only of the blinking of her eyes and the beating of his heart, Krishan was grateful that they were part of the same place and the same time, that for now at least they were to-gether in the same moment, a moment that contained not only what was proximate and what was distant but also what was past and what was future, a moment without length or breadth or height but which somehow contained everything of signifi-cance, as if everything else the world consisted of was a kind of cosmic scenery, an illusion that, now that it was being exposed, could quietly fall away. What for lack of a better word was sometimes called love, he had realized that night, was not so much a relation between two people in and of themselves as a relation between two people and the world they were witness to, a world whose surfaces and exteriors gradually began to dis-sipate as the two individuals sank deeper and deeper into what was called their love. Falling in love, or what deserved to be called falling love, he had realized that night, was not so much an emotional or psychological condition as an epistemological condition, a condition in which two people held hands and watched in silent amazement as the world around them was slowly unveiled, as the falsities of ordinary life began to thin and dissolve before their eyes, the furrowed eyebrows and clenched jaws, the bright colors and loud noises, the surface excitements and disturbances all dropping away so that what remained—time stripped bare—was the only way the world could truly be apprehended, so that even if this condition did not last, even if it was lost, as eventually it is always lost, to habit or circumstance or simply the slow, sad passage of the years, the knowledge that it has imparted remains, the knowledge that the world we ordinarily partake in is somehow not quite real, that time does not need to pass the way we usually experience it passing, that somehow it is possible to live and breathe and move in a single moment, that a single moment could be not a bead on an abacus of finite length but an ocean that can be entered into, whose distant shores can never be reached.

It had been almost four years since that trip, since that moment standing opposite each other on the overnight train to Bombay, and sitting now on this other train, traversing the length of his country of birth, Krishan thought once more about how much time had passed, about how much had happened and how much had changed. He'd thought several times, since reading Anjum's email on Friday afternoon, about what kind of message he might send in response, how much or how little he should share with her of the life he was now living, how earnest or aloof he should try to seem. He'd imagined telling her about what he'd been doing since his return to Sri Lanka, about his two years in the northeast, the initial fervor and subsequent disillusionment, about his recent time in Colombo, the books he'd been reading and his walks in the evenings. He'd wondered what her response would be as she read what he wrote, had imagined her impressed as she learned about everything he'd seen and done, as she saw how much more he understood now about himself and the world. She would respond not immediately but after an interval of perhaps a week or two, her response would lead to the growth of a slow, thoughtful, and somewhat confessional correspondence, and finally the two of them would meet at some halfway point, he fantasized, where she would be quietly taken aback to see him in person after four years, surprised by the way his body had grown into itself, his shoulders a little broader, his arms and legs stronger, his cheeks more hollowed out, by the confidence with which he now spoke and carried himself. The idea of writing such a letter had given him some hope on Friday afternoon, as if an unexpected possibility was opening itself up to him, the possibility of reconnecting with a past he'd left behind and perhaps even of reunion with Anjum, but thinking again about writing to her he began to second-guess these thoughts, to feel they were somewhat naïve. There was a tendency, he knew, when thinking about people from the past, to believe that they'd remained the same while you yourself had evolved, as if other people and places ceased moving once you'd left them behind, as if their time remained still while only yours continued to advance. The tendency in general was misleading, people and their situations were always changing, but with Anjum especially it was wishful thinking, Krishan knew, for Anjum especially was too quick and too active to remain the same, always inclined toward what was unknown, ready to absorb and assimilate it if she found it worth her while. She would probably not be too surprised or impressed by how he'd changed, for she too had no doubt experienced much over the last four years, she too had no doubt grown and developed, not just in opinions and outlook but probably in habits and mannerisms too. It occurred to him that he didn't even know whether she still tilted her head back in the same way when she laughed, whether she still had that habit of rotating the silver ring on her middle finger when she was thinking about something, whether she still even wore that ring at all. It was not where she was living and what she was doing that he wanted to know but these small details, these small, almost imperceptible changes in habit and manner that could signify, sometimes, a total alteration in a person's stance toward the world. He wanted to know whether she too had felt the weight of things increasing upon her in the last few years, whether she too had become just a little more fatigued with the passing of time, but it was precisely these answers that couldn't be communicated via email, precisely these answers that couldn't be given or asked for in words sent through the void. Even if he managed to compose an email he would, like the yaksha in Kalidasa's poem, be unable to share what he really wanted to share, for how would it be possible to convey all that had happened to him in the intervening years, to convey all the events and all the experiences, one change building upon another, accumulation upon accumulation, how would it ever be possible to really begin or end? What was the point of trying to account for all the time that had passed like a river between them, gone and impossible to retrieve, what was the point when all that writing could accomplish was to remind them how much they'd once shared, when the only way to respect what had existed between them was to remain apart, to acknowledge that no words could bridge the vast distance between them?

The train was slowing down, the boy on the seat beside him and others in the carriage beginning to stir, and looking outside Krishan saw that they'd arrived in Anuradhapura, the ancient

Buddhist center of learning and the last major Sinhala town before the north. Almost half the passengers in the carriage got off as the train came to a stop, almost all of them Sinhalese from what Krishan could tell, so that with the exception of a few neatly dressed, clean-shaven men with buzz cuts—soldiers who were returning to their various bases after having spent their leave in the south—it was mainly Muslim and Tamil passengers left now in the carriage. The station master sounded his whistle after a while, the train hesitated, then resumed moving with a jolt, and leaning his head against the window Krishan adjusted his gaze to the scene that opened up as the train left the station and town. The landscape had become flatter and drier, still a lot of vegetation and still occasional paddy fields but no longer the lush, overabundant growth of the south, no longer the same thick density of ferns and flowering plants, the dense clusters of bright green paddy shooting out of silvery water. The profuse foliage had been replaced by fields of tall grass interspersed with quiet stands of trees, and the villages they were passing too seemed emptier and sleepier, small single-story houses and huts deserted except for the occasional old man or woman sitting on a plastic chair, watching with boredom as trains passed by on the tracks. Krishan remembered that his mother had asked him to call when he reached Anuradhapura, and though he didn't really feel like talking, he pulled his phone out of his pocket and dialed her number. His mother picked up after a while, her voice lower and more somber than usual, and he told her they'd just passed Anuradhapura, that they'd probably get to Kilinochchi in the next two hours. He asked whether she'd heard anything from Rani's daughter, which she had not, then asked how Appamma was doing. She was not doing so well, his mother told him after a pause, she'd gone to her room in the morning and found her sitting with her face buried in her hands, the TV turned off even though one of her favorite programs was on. Her eyes were wet, she'd obviously been crying, and his mother had been at a loss for how to comfort her, since it was so rare to see Appamma cry. Krishan asked whether Appamma had been sobbing or just tearing up, to which his mother responded that she didn't know but that it seemed like she'd been crying a good deal. She hadn't wanted breakfast in the morning, she added, and had neglected to take her weekly head bath too. Krishan tried to inquire further but his mother became irritated with his questions, dismissing Appamma's state as a natural response to what had happened, a response that would eventually pass. They talked a little longer, his mother repeating the directions for how to get to Rani's village, asking whether the money he was taking with him was safe, then bringing the call to an end.

Putting his phone down on the empty seat beside him, Krishan turned listlessly and looked out again through the window, unsure what to think as he replayed in his mind what his mother had said. He was bothered by the image of Appamma crying in her room, since it was true as his mother said that his grandmother seldom cried, but even more unsettling was the fact that she'd neglected to take her Sunday head bath. Her head baths were one of the primary rituals by which his grandmother gave movement to her time, an activity that taxed her body but that she continued performing with meticulous regularity, so that if she hadn't wet her hair and shampooed it that morning it could only have been, he knew, because she'd been thoroughly shaken by Rani's death. He'd assumed from her initial response that the news would leave her saddened but mostly untouched, that it would leave her unaffected the way many of the seemingly important deaths in her life had, the death of her sister several years prior, for example, which she'd been upset by for a few days and then seemed to forget about completely, or even the death of her husband decades before, at whose funeral, according to his mother, she hadn't even cried. It was obvious now that Rani's death had the potential to affect his grandmother more gravely than these other deaths, that the psychological impact of the loss might be severe enough to have a physical effect on her too. It had been due largely to Rani that Appamma had been brought back from the brink, after all, due to Rani's nursing and attention during those first few weeks but also, even more significantly, to the constant human presence that Rani had provided in the subsequent months. She'd played a vital role in Appamma's overall recovery, putting an end to the isolation she experienced spending hours on end alone in her room, coming over time to represent the wider world from which she'd been sundered. Appamma had taken personal affront to her unannounced departure, to the fact that Rani had ended their relationship without even informing her, and it had required significant work on her part to forgive the betrayal, to come up with an acceptable narrative for why Rani had cut off ties so abruptly. Whatever the plausibility of Appamma's narrative, which appealed of course to Rani's instability and not to any dissatisfaction with her situation in Colombo, it was possible now, Krishan knew, that the connection to the outside world that Rani had symbolized could be severed by the news of her death. There was a real chance now that Appamma could return to her earlier state of isolation, to a life lacking in meaningful stimulus, her mood and energy once more beginning to deteriorate, her mental sharpness and along with it her physical vitality, her mind and body spiraling in tandem once more toward oblivion.

It was striking now to think about how close his grandmother had become to Rani during their time together, about how much his grandmother had come, in spite of all her initial suspicions and resentments, to trust Rani and depend on her, to become, even, a kind of friend. He'd been nervous at the beginning about how Appamma would receive her, about whether she would treat Rani as a nurse or whether she would treat her as a servant who was at her beck and call, whether she would give her the respect and understanding due to someone who'd lost so much. The first weeks of Rani's stay in Colombo had actually gone smoothly, Appamma still possessing only the most basic modes of awareness, scarcely even conscious of Rani's presence in her room, taking her for granted the same way a newborn child takes for granted the fact it will be fed and washed and cleaned. It was only in the weeks that followed that his initial fears had begun to materialize, Appamma becoming more cognizant of her surroundings, surfacing from her unconsciousness to find that her existence was now bound to that of a stranger. She saw Rani as an alien presence in the household, an imposter who symbolized her new helplessness and was constantly taking her family's attention away from her, attention, she felt, that belonged by rights only to her. With the gradual recovery of her speech and memory Appamma became, paradoxically, more infantile than before, incapable of recognizing anything but her own desires and far more irritable when those desires went unmet. Krishan remembered how, on

a weekend afternoon relatively early on, not more than two
months into Rani's arrival, he'd gone to his grandmother's
room and found Rani stretched out on the floor on her thatched
mat, her hands covering her face as if for protection from the
light. It always made him uncomfortable to see Rani sleeping
on the floor, as if this habit were a subtle critique of his way of
life, but she'd insisted on it despite him setting up his brother's
bed in Appamma's room, not being used to sleeping on a mattress, as she told him, preferring instead the cool hardness of
the floor. She had turned slowly toward him as he entered the
room, as though she hadn't been sleeping but lying there lost in
thought, her eyes red and her hair in greater disarray than
usual. He'd asked whether everything was okay, and she'd told
him she was fine, that she hadn't slept at all the night before,
that was all. She hardly slept on most nights, she said, she was
unwell, and her illness made it difficult to sleep. Krishan had
known what Rani meant by the word unwell, but it was the first
time the question of her mental state had come up explicitly,
she having brought it up herself, and wanting to let her say
more if she wanted he'd asked her what she meant. She'd show
him, she replied, and standing up a little unsteadily she went to
the corner of her room where her bag was kept, rummaged
through it till she found a cardboard folder. This is the reason
I'm unwell, she'd told him, taking out two medium-size photographs from the folder and holding them out for him to see,
the first of a boy about fifteen or sixteen, wearing a black suit
two sizes too big for him, taken in a studio with a sky blue back-
drop, the second of a boy about ten or eleven, wearing trousers
and a shirt, taken in the same studio with the same blue background. The first was her eldest son, she explained, the one

who'd died fighting, and the second was her youngest, the one who'd died in shelling on the seventeenth of May, the penultimate day of the war.

Taking the photos uncertainly in his hands Krishan looked at the two boys, both of whom held their arms awkwardly by their sides, neither of them, it seemed, having posed for a formal photograph before. He was wondering whether to ask Rani what their names were or whether to wait till she told him of her own volition when he noticed, through the corner of his eyes, that Appamma was beginning to shuffle around on the bed with irritation, as if to attract his attention. She didn't like him having long conversations with Rani, he knew, since in her mind she was the one who was ill and needed to be looked after, whereas Rani was perfectly well and was there only to look after her. Not wanting to encourage her indignation he kept his gaze fixed on Rani, who was beginning to describe the circumstances of her youngest son's death. It had been early morning when it happened, she was saying, and they'd been trying to cross the front lines from what remained of Tiger territory, which had been shelled every day and night for the previous several months. They had been unsure whether or not to cross for some time, afraid of being killed in the cross fire and about what the soldiers would do to them if they went over to the government side, but they'd decided finally that it was safer to try crossing over than to remain behind under constant shelling. Appamma, whose shuffling on the bed was becoming more conspicuous, interjected suddenly that the afternoon's film had been no good, that when there was no good film playing she preferred the TV to be off. This was irrelevant, of course, the TV in any case being off, and trying to show Rani that he was paying attention Krishan asked who she'd been with at the time. She'd been with her husband, her youngest son, her daughter, and her sister's family, Rani replied, all of whom she'd been together with throughout the various displacements. They'd been walking for about half an hour through the shelled debris of the camp, trying to find the best place to cross, when they heard a high-pitched whistling in the sky, a sound that indicated a standard-issue shell, she explained, for every kind of airborne weapon had its own sound, the cluster bombs, the rockets, and even the drones. They began to run, not knowing whether they were moving toward the shell or away, and after a few seconds it had fallen, not close but not far away either. Looking around in the rising dust and smoke she saw that her youngest son had fallen down and was unable to get up, and running toward the body she realized that he'd been struck by a piece of shrapnel in the stomach and died instantaneously, without so much as a sound.

Rani, whose eyes had been welling up, wiped away a tear, and as Krishan was wondering what he could say to console her he heard his grandmother calling his name from the bed. He tried to ignore her, but she repeated his name with irritation until he was forced to turn around. She was pointing to the dressing table beside the TV, at several tins of canned tuna that her brother had put in her bags before she returned from London. She'd forgotten about them till finding them that morning, she said loudly, that was how much her brother loved her, he was always thinking of her, even while she was sick he'd thought to buy canned tuna for her, knowing they were her favorite food. She wasn't planning on opening any yet, since there was plenty of fish available these days, she would save them for

later, she'd decided, when the price of fish was higher. Krishan
nodded quickly and turned back to Rani with a look of apol-
ogy, terrified she would be hurt or offended by the interruption, but Rani continued as though Appamma hadn't spoken at
all. They'd had no choice but to keep running, she went on,
they'd had no choice but to keep running since the shells were
continuing to fall. She wasn't able to bury her son's body, her
daughter had been with her, and she couldn't put her at risk by
staying there any longer—what happened subsequently to her
son's body she'd never managed to find out. Appamma, who'd
taken Krishan's curt response to her statement as a snub, raised
her voice and shouted across the room that some of the tins
were not ordinary tuna but were in fact flavored, some lemon,
some pepper, and some tomato, but Rani, too caught up in
what she was saying to take heed, simply raised her voice and
continued, describing how they'd escaped finally and made it to
the other side of the front lines, how they were frisked by the
Sri Lankan army, extensively interrogated, and then interned in
camps for more than a year and a half. Krishan kept his gaze
fixed on Rani as she told him how they'd lost almost all their
belongings in the last few months of fighting, how the only
tokens of her sons she'd managed to hold on to were the two
photographs he was holding in his hands. He didn't look away
till she finished her account, transfixed, despite his fear of another interruption, by the strange tension and immediacy in
her eyes, which were directed not into the distance as they often
were, not far away the way the people's eyes usually were when
describing an event from a different time and place, but vividly
alert and present, as if the world she was describing was some-

how in front of her as she spoke, as if she'd never left that other world behind.

Such incidents occurred a few times in the first two or three months of Rani's arrival, but Rani would always ignore them or respond to them quickly and sharply, rarely seeming to take them to heart. They became less common as time passed, partly because Krishan's mother made a point of scolding her mother-in-law whenever she overheard a rude remark or demand, but mainly because the childishness induced in Appamma as a result of her trip gradually began to subside on its own. As time passed and her condition improved, Appamma became more capable of seeing things from the perspective of others and more aware of how much she owed to Rani, in whom she had, she discovered, a person she could count on for all her personal and social needs, a companion who wouldn't desert her even when everyone else had said good night. It was to Rani that she directed her questions about what was happening downstairs, what they were going to have for dinner, how much the onions, coconuts, or brinjal cost, how the various plants in the garden were doing, questions that previously she would have had to ask Krishan or his mother and to which Rani, unlike the two of them, was compelled to give some response. Rani's eyes and ears and hands and feet became, over the course of her recovery, her proxy sensory and motor organs, and not only did Appamma's ability to understand and participate in the affairs of the household begin to improve but so too did her consciousness of the world beyond the house. Through Rani her conception of the world began to expand to include the north and east, parts of the country she'd grown up and spent her married life but hadn't seen in decades. She learned from Rani about the war and about Kilinochchi and Jaffna, about how things had worked in the areas under Tiger control and how they worked now under government control, and it was because of Rani too that Appamma began reading the newspapers, paying more attention to the evening news, forming political opinions and keeping abreast of political developments, things Krishan had never noticed her caring about till then. All this knowledge, this sense of being once more part of the world, together with the presence of a full-time interlocutor and companion, someone with whom she could watch TV, express her opinions, quarrel, and make jokes, had the effect of energizing Appamma, improving her moods, so that not only did she recover her condition prior to the trip to London but soon surpassed it too. She became healthier and more mobile, more youthful and more vital than she'd seemed in several years, making it obvious that her deterioration in the years leading up to the trip had its source not so much in the physical process of aging as in the withdrawal that came about as a result, the loneliness and isolation of having nothing to do and nobody to engage with, a withdrawal that led to the atrophy of the body far more quickly, it seemed, than any merely physical process.

Krishan remembered how another day later on, when all Appamma's faculties had been fully restored, he'd gone into their room in the morning and found the two of them talking, both of them in a seemingly good mood, Rani explaining to Appamma some development in the TV show they'd just finished watching. He'd said hello to Rani and asked his grandmother how she'd slept the previous night, to which she'd responded by slapping her hand dramatically against her forehead in a kind of mock frustration, a sly smile on her lips as she told him she'd spent the entire night looking after Rani, as if she were Rani's caretaker and not the other way around. He'd glanced nervously at Rani, unsure how she would respond to this statement, but she too was smiling, partly out of embarrassment and partly because of the liveliness of Appamma's account. She'd woken up the previous night, Appamma explained, to the sound of sudden screaming and shouting, had been worried there was a thief in the house or that some other terrible thing had happened. She'd sat up in a state of disorientation, not knowing what the source of the commotion was, then turning around had realized that Rani was the one yelling, that she was having one of her nightmares again. She'd gone over and begun shaking Rani by the shoulders, trying to wake her up, but even after she woke it had taken several minutes to calm her down. They'd tried going back to sleep but the entire night Rani had tossed and turned, mumbling loudly to herself, and two more times she'd woken up screaming and shouting. It was fine for Rani, Appamma went on, still pretending to be upset, the smile on her lips widening into a grin, for Rani always made up for her lost sleep in the afternoons. What about her though, she who could never sleep in the afternoons, what was she supposed to do? The three of them had laughed at Appamma's humorous narration but Krishan had been left somewhat unsettled, for the nightmares Rani had, he knew, were nightmares about the last months of the war, most often about the death of her younger son, sometimes about other things she'd seen or heard. For him these were subjects that had to be discussed with utmost gravity, subjects that had to be approached with

the solemnity reserved for funerals, and he found the lightness
with which Appamma treated them disturbing. He'd still been
living and working in the northeast at the time, but despite
coming across countless people who'd suffered just like Rani
during the war, he hadn't become close enough to anyone to
witness their traumas firsthand. It was only on moving back to
Colombo and living opposite his grandmother and Rani, observing the dynamic that had formed between the two women,
that he began to wonder whether it was his own stance that had
been misplaced. The trauma Rani had suffered during the war
was, for better or worse, part of her ordinary life, something
she couldn't help thinking about or reacting to, whether she
was waking up, eating, performing her duties, or sleeping, and
it had been foolish of him to think it belonged to some separate
sphere. Trauma for Rani was something that had to coexist
with all the various exigencies of daily existence, and precisely
for this reason she couldn't afford to treat it with the same
weight or seriousness that he did. In treating Rani as someone
she could tease, argue with, and exchange stories with, as someone with whom she had to compete for the attention of her
grandson and for power within the household, Appamma was
in a way treating Rani as an equal, as someone who was going
through something that was normal and not unusual, someone
who didn't have to be stopped and pitied or treated with exces-
sive caution. Even if she sometimes hurt Rani with her cavalier
stance, Appamma's way of dealing with her had probably made
Rani more comfortable on the whole, and perhaps it was this
nonchalance that had allowed a camaraderie and even a kind of
friendship to form between the two women, between that rap-

idly aging woman who was fighting to remain in the world and that invisibly wounded stranger who didn't seem to care about whether she stayed or left, a bond that despite all his guilt and despite all his efforts he himself, he felt now, had been unable to forge over the course of Rani's time with them.

7

IT WAS STRANGE to think of the two years Rani and Appamma had spent together in the latter's small room, the unlikely confluence of paths that had brought them together, one of them ostensibly the caretaker and the other ostensibly the charge, even though each was unwell in their own way, even though a remedy was being sought in the arrangement for both of them. Krishan had worried initially that Rani's trauma might actually be worsened by moving from her village to the south of the country, where she had neither friends nor relatives and could speak hardly a word of the majority language, but both he and his mother had sensed an improvement in her condition soon after her arrival, and even the doctor had said as much when she returned to Vavuniya for a checkup after two months in Colombo. Being in a different environment had helped her get some distance from her traumas, and having a job to do, however undemanding it was, gave her purpose and direction,

prevented her from spending her days lying about as she had
while living with her daughter. The fact she was earning more
than her daughter and son-in-law too had an important effect,
gave her new standing in her family, since far from being a burden she'd now become an essential source of financial support,
lending money sometimes to her daughter, sometimes to other
relatives who needed help too. She bought presents for her two
granddaughters whenever she went back to her village to visit,
dresses, hair clips, chocolates, whatever she could afford that
took her fancy, and whenever she spoke on the phone with her
daughter the two of them would grab the phone from their
mother, demand to know when their grandmother would next
be visiting. Talking about her granddaughters, Krishan noticed,
one of whom was five and the other seven, both apparently
very talkative, very intelligent, and very stubborn, was one of
the few things that caused Rani's face to visibly brighten. The
fact she took up so much space in their minds was obviously a
source of much joy to her, and it had occurred to him more
than once that Rani was trying in some way to substitute her
two lost sons with her two granddaughters, though perhaps
the pleasure she took in her granddaughters was just the ordinary joy that anyone who'd come in contact with so much
death took in the vitality of the young. The nightmares continued, of course, as did the bad days, days when Rani hardly
spoke a word, burdened by a weight none of them could see,
but for the most part this aspect of her condition seemed controlled, held within manageable bounds that allowed her to live
with relative normalcy. It was only well into her stay in Colombo, after a year had passed and she'd become fully inte-
grated into the household, inseparable from its routines and

rhythms, that Rani's trauma once more seemed to surpass these bounds, making its presence felt again in her mood and energy. The relapse had to do no doubt with the deaths of her husband and nephew within a span of a few weeks, her husband of cancer and her nephew in a motorcycle accident, but outwardly at least Rani didn't seem greatly shaken by either death, not even that of her husband, who she hardly ever talked about and who, as Krishan learned later, she'd married at the insistence of her parents despite being twenty years his junior. He couldn't help feeling that the deaths were only catalysts, that the resurgence of Rani's illness had more to do with the depth and the pull of her original trauma than anything else, a trauma she could never fully escape, which the novelty of her new life in Colombo had temporarily concealed and which, as she became more used to her new situation, had begun once more to exert its hold on her. Whatever its source, Rani began to talk less, to sleep less in the nights and more in the afternoons, to take less care of her physical appearance. She began complaining about feeling unwell, about dizziness and a constant, dull pain in the back of her head, physical symptoms, Krishan came to suspect, that signified psychological distress more than any specific bodily malady. She spoke to the doctor a few times on the phone, and began at his suggestion going up to Vavuniya more frequently for sessions of electroshock therapy, traveling north by bus every month and a half to spend a few nights in the ward.

Krishan had known for a long time that Rani received electroshock therapy, ever since that afternoon in the ward when he first encountered her and first learned who she was, but the idea of Rani sleeping next to psychotic patients during the nights and receiving current to the head during the days continued to bother him, as if her need to continue receiving the treatment was a mark of their own shortcomings, a sign that they'd somehow failed her. Electroshock therapy was a form of treatment that was no longer in use, he'd believed for most of his adult life, an obsolete mode of therapy from the long-gone era of asylums for the insane. His vague sense of it had been shaped by harrowing scenes in old American movies he'd watched about the mentally ill, scenes in which the patient was strapped into a chair or bed with a bit in their mouth and electrodes attached to their temples, in which a switch was casually flicked and heavy current passed through the patient's body like thunder and lightning, causing the eyes to widen, the jaws to clench, and the body to jerk, the veins on the neck and forehead to vividly distend. It was the most effective treatment for the severest, most recalcitrant forms of depression, the doctor had told him when Krishan first inquired about it, Rani was already taking several medications, medications for depression, anxiety, and sleeplessness, as well as for her liver, which was adversely affected by the other medications. None of them were having any significant effect except the electroshock therapy, the doctor explained, which wasn't painful, lasted only a few minutes, and was administered only after the patient had taken a general anesthetic, ensuring that no pain could be felt while the current was being passed. Krishan continued to be suspicious of the treatment despite this justification, and when the topic came up with Rani of its own accord one day he'd asked her what the treatment was really like, whether there really was no pain or discomfort. Rani had looked at him, almost surprised by the question, then shook her head. She never felt anything while it was actually happening, she told him, since she was never actually conscious during the treatment, and she didn't feel bad afterward either, mainly just a little groggy from the anesthetic. Krishan noticed that she did in fact seem better whenever she returned, more active, more talkative, and in a general way more present, though sooner or later she always seemed to return to her previous condition, taciturn, distracted, and lethargic, as if this condition possessed some magnetic hold over her that the electricity could only temporarily dispel. Each time she went back to the ward the doctor would deem it necessary to give her a slightly more intense course of treatment, so that whereas at first she received only one or two doses administered over two or three days, toward the end of her time in Colombo it had become three, four, or even five doses over six, eight, or ten days. In the months before she finally left Colombo she became increasingly forgetful as a result of the therapy, sometimes losing the thread of conversation, sometimes getting confused about whether or not she'd taken her medications, sometimes going down to the kitchen to get something and then forgetting why she'd gone. The treatment she received on her last visit to the ward was so severe that for several weeks afterward her hands and feet were shaking, leaving her unable to bring up Appamma's afternoon cup of tea without spilling. He'd called the doctor to ask what to do, concerned about the side effects but also wondering whether the treatment as a whole was making any difference, whether it was really worthwhile given all the side effects. It had been almost six years since the end of the war and the death of her sons, she'd been doing shock therapy for almost four, and she'd still shown no sign of permanent improvement—was it really sustainable, he'd asked, for Rani to continue receiving current to the head like this indefinitely? The doctor had told him that nothing could be done—he'd increased her medications but they were having no impact, and the side effects of the shock therapy would only be temporary, whereas if she didn't continue receiving treatment her condition would almost certainly deteriorate rapidly. It wasn't so much a question of helping Rani get better, which was increasingly unlikely as the years went by, as simply of helping her cope with ordinary life as best as possible. She herself had been asking for higher doses of therapy, was finding ordinary consciousness increasingly intolerable, and it was his opinion, given the situation, that nothing else could be done.

It was shortly after this conversation with the doctor that Rani had had the accident in the kitchen, Krishan remembered, an accident he'd forgotten about completely till then and which seemed now, in light of the news of Rani's death, to have carried with it a warning or omen that they hadn't perceived at the time. His mother had started asking Rani to come downstairs to cook with her in the evenings, partly because she needed help but also because she felt it would be good for Rani to move her body, to be involved in some physical activity and have a break from Appamma's endless chatter. Rani initially seemed to enjoy these hours in the kitchen with his mother, happy to have the opportunity to talk to an adult without Appamma's constant interjections, but her thoughts also often drifted while she was in the kitchen, leading her on two occasions to accidentally cut her hands while using the coconut grater. One evening Rani had been cutting vegetables while Krishan's mother was turned the other way, busy making batter for the thosa, the regular beat of Rani's knife against the cutting board audible behind her. At some point the sound of the slicing behind her came to a stop, and turning around his mother had found Rani standing totally still, her left hand held up in front of her face, bright red blood dripping profusely from her hand onto the bright orange carrots she'd been slicing. Rani was silent, looking at her hand as though at a curiosity, and Krishan's mother had screamed hysterically, asking what had happened, what had happened, rushing over to look and discovering that a chunk of flesh from the top of Rani's middle finger, about an inch long, was dangling from the rest of the finger. She'd cut it accidentally while slicing the carrots, Rani told her calmly, it was probably best to just cut the whole thing off now, and screaming again Krishan's mother had stopped Rani from picking up the knife, shouting that she was mad and calling for Krishan to come down. The two of them had taken her to the hospital immediately to get the severed piece of finger reattached, and all through the process Rani had been remarkably silent, as if she felt no pain or urgency, only an abstract embarrassment for having made herself the cause of so much concern. They had accepted Rani's explanation that it had just been an accident, like the two accidents with the coconut grater earlier, a result of her distracted state of mind, her inability to fully focus on what was in front of her. The event had soon been forgotten, but reflecting on it as he sat on the train now, it occurred to Krishan that perhaps it hadn't been accidental, that perhaps the incidents with the coconut grater earlier hadn't been accidental either, that perhaps on all of these occasions Rani had actively been trying to harm herself, that perhaps she'd been asking for higher doses of electric shock for the same reason too, out of a desire to extinguish her consciousness and all the heaviness it involved. He thought again about what he'd learned from Rani's daughter on Friday evening, about the way Rani had been found at the bottom of the well, and the thought came back to him that her fall had somehow been willed or intended. He'd tried to put the possibility out of his mind for the last two days, hoping it would fade away if he didn't think about it, but he was realizing now that suicide was a real possibility, that he wouldn't be able to rule it out till he went to the funeral and saw Rani's daughter face-to-face, till he actually spoke to her in person and searched her eyes for some indication of what had really transpired.

Krishan looked out to see if he could get a sense of how close they were to Vavuniya, whether they'd made it out of Anuradhapura district yet, but nothing in the monotonous vegetation that lined the tracks or the brief glimpses of landscape beyond gave any indication where they were. There was no sudden change in ecosystem between south and north, he knew, both sides of the border region looked more or less the same, mainly scrubland with occasional stands of trees but sometimes denser, more crowded sections of jungle too. He'd never actually traveled anywhere in the North Central Province, always having associated that part of the country with ancient Buddhist temples and ruins, places he not only had no interest in but generally went out of his way to avoid. Growing up he'd associated Buddhism mainly with the Sri Lankan government and army, with the statues they constructed all over the country to remind Muslims, Tamils, and other minorities of their place, and it was only during his time in India, ironi-

cally, as he finally began learning more about its history, that
he'd begun considering it a religion or philosophy in its own
right. It was during his time in Delhi that he'd learned that Buddhism was viewed as a religion of emancipation among the op-
pressed castes of India, that at one time there'd been Tamil
Buddhists in the south of India and even in northeast Sri Lanka,
that what most Sri Lankans called Buddhism was in fact just
one particular version of Buddhism. He himself had just as
much entitlement to the Buddha as most of the Sri Lankans
who called themselves Buddhists, he came to realize, and coming across a translation of *The Life of the Buddha* by chance in a
bookshop in Delhi one day, flicking through it and deciding it
was finally time to try to understand Buddhism with a more
open mind, he'd bought the book on a whim and begun to read
it on the way home. The poem, which was written by the north
Indian poet Ashvaghosha in the first century, under circumstances that couldn't have been more different from the Sri
Lanka in which he lived, had begun with a moving and detailed
account of the birth of the Buddha that was familiar but slightly
different from the versions he'd heard growing up. The young
prince Siddhartha, according to the poem, had appeared in his
mother's womb without any act of conception, and was delivered apparently without passing through her birth canal, his
skin gleaming like the sun, his large, dark, unblinking eyes capturing the gazes of those around him like the moon. Shortly
after his birth his father was visited by a highly revered seer
who'd examined the newly born child, declaring that he would
become either a conqueror of vast worlds or a conqueror of
the soul. Conquering the soul meant taking the path of renunciation, meant leaving behind family, society, and the world at

large, and the king was greatly disturbed by this news, not ever wanting to be parted from his son. Knowing that any exposure to pain or suffering could lead the young prince down the path of renunciation, he decided to raise Siddhartha in such a way that he experienced only the pleasures of the world, none of its bitterness, hoping in this way to ensure that he became a conqueror of worlds rather than a conqueror of the soul. As the young prince came of age, according to the text, he became a youth of startling beauty and intelligence, and the king assigned him chambers in the very top floors of the palace, where he spent the days and nights with male friends and female consorts. He was married at a relatively young age to a princess named Yashodhara, a woman of exceeding beauty and noble bearing, and not long afterward she bore him a son, which meant, his father thought happily, that the prince would be too bound to earthly life to ever renounce. Siddhartha continued to spend most of his time in his private chambers even after his son's birth, taking his pleasure with the women his father had sent to entertain him. Listening to the soft sounds of the women's golden tambourines, watching as their lithe bodies moved to the music, laughing and drinking with them in the evenings and sleeping with them in the nights, for many years he saw hardly any reason to descend from the cloud-topped chambers in which he lived.

It was only in his twenty-ninth year, according to the poem, hearing about the lush parks and groves in which his female consorts passed their time in the city, that Siddhartha began to wonder about what existed outside the confines of his chambers and the palace. Increasingly bored by his life of endless sensual and material pleasure, this curiosity slowly turned into yearning, and one day the prince asked his father for permission to venture beyond the palace grounds, something he'd never done before. The king was troubled by the request, but decided eventually to let his son be escorted around the city, though only on a predetermined route that would be shorn of anything that might upset the prince. He had the areas around the route beautified with flowers and banners, had all the poor, disabled, and sick removed from sight, and finally, at an appointed time, sent Siddhartha on his way with a trusted charioteer. Multitudes of people, women especially, who'd never seen a man so attractive, gathered around the road to try to catch sight of the young prince, and seeing the order and splendor of the city and the droves of respectful citizens, all dressed in clean, dignified clothes, the prince rejoiced, according to the text, as though he'd been born for a second time. Everything went according to plan till he caught sight, near the edge of the crowd, of a white-haired woman with a wrinkled face, her body slumped and her back unnaturally bent, holding a walking stick for support as she tried to catch a glimpse of him from the distance. Never having seen a person in such a condition before, he asked the charioteer what had happened to the woman and was told the woman had reached old age, a state in which beauty and strength were destroyed, in which memory dissipated and the sense organs deteriorated. Perturbed, the prince asked the charioteer whether such a thing could happen to anyone, or whether it was the fate of that particular woman alone. When the charioteer said it would happen to everyone who lived long enough, that it would without doubt happen to him one day too, the prince became dejected, and soon asked for the chariot to be turned around toward the palace, where he

retreated to his chambers to be alone. Unable to find peace
there, he decided after a few days to go on another trip around
the city, hoping it would help him come to some clarity. On this
second journey too however he saw a sight that upset him, a
middle-aged man with a severely distended abdomen, his shoulders drooping, his limbs thin and pale, grunting in pain as he
moved with the help of someone beside him. Siddhartha asked
the charioteer what had happened to the man, and the charioteer explained that the man was afflicted by sickness. The prince
asked whether sickness affected that man alone or whether it
was something that could happen to all people, and the charioteer replied that sickness had many forms and that anybody
could get sick, that there was no way to guarantee against it.
Once more Siddhartha fell silent. Asking to be taken back to the
palace, he stayed alone in his chambers for several days in a
state of despondency. The king grew furious that his orders
hadn't been followed to the letter, and hoping that a positive
experience might change the prince's mind, he commanded
that a different route be found, that it be decorated so as to be
even more beautiful than the first, and that any person whose
sight might in any way be upsetting to the prince be removed
from the area. He pleaded with his son to go on one more ex-
cursion, to which the prince agreed, but on this occasion too he
saw something he wasn't meant to see, he saw, on an adjacent
street, beyond the crowds that had gathered to see him, a motionless body being carried by a number of people in mourning. He asked the charioteer why the person was being carried
in this way, to which the charioteer replied, reluctantly, that the
person had died. The prince didn't know what death was, and
on being told that it was a state without consciousness, a state

in which a human was no different from a log or a stone, unable to see or hear or talk or feel, the prince suddenly became inconsolable. The cheering, smiling, laughing people who'd gathered by the road began to take on a sinister aspect, and looking around at them he began to feel they must either be insane or completely deluded, for how, otherwise, could they go about their lives unaffected by the fact that they would get old, that they would get sick, and that eventually they would die? Returning to the palace Siddhartha continued to reflect on what he'd seen, unable to take pleasure in anything he'd previously enjoyed, neither wife, son, consorts, nor friends, unable to see the life he'd been leading as anything but a farce. It was his inability to move on from these facts, according to the poem, that had eventually led the twenty-nine-year-old prince to leave the palace in secret one night, embarking on that long and famous journey that led, finally, after six years of homelessness, penance, self-mortification, and meditation, to liberation from the cycle of birth and death, from the misery and bitterness of the so-called real world.

Krishan had been greatly moved by the story of Siddhartha's disillusionment, which despite having heard so many times growing up he was only then fully considering, and dwelling on it now as he was borne toward Rani's funeral it occurred to him how similar, in a way, Siddhartha's disillusionment was to Rani's, how similar what he'd gone through must have been to the experiences of most people who'd lived through the end of the war. Just as Rani's life and the assumptions on which it was founded had been exploded over the course of the few short months that left both her sons dead, so too had Siddhartha's life and his assumptions that sickness, old age, and death did not exist, that the body and the world could go on living in harmony forever. Just as the end of the war had left Rani irretrievably traumatized, so that again and again images came to her of her two dead sons, the younger one especially, in flashbacks when she was awake and in nightmares when she was asleep, leaving her unable to return to ordinary life afterward, so too had Siddhartha been traumatized by what he'd seen on his three excursions, sights so fundamentally at odds with everything he'd come to believe over the course of his life that he simply could not go on as before. His youth, if Ashvaghosha's account was anything to go by, had been very different from the childhoods of ordinary people, since most people were, from their earliest days, continually exposed to old age, sickness, and death. Ordinary humans were, from the very beginning, slowly and gently exposed to these facts of life, which never subsequently strayed too far from their minds, and they learned to take pleasure in the world despite the contingent and transitory quality of its pleasures, to value small joys and happinesses in spite of the fact that they would not last forever. Siddhartha by contrast had been systematically and intentionally blinded to the existence of sickness, old age, and death, had never even considered the possibility that the pleasures he indulged in might one day dissipate or disappear, that the life he was leading might one day end. His sudden and vivid exposure to these facts over the course of a few short weeks could only have resulted in shock so great as to be traumatic, in the strict, medical sense of the word, for what else could have explained his desire to so abruptly leave behind his father, wife, son, friends, and lovers, to so mercilessly reject everything that constituted the world he knew? What else could have explained the years of rigid austerities and unfathomable deprivations, the violence he inflicted on himself in search of a life free from what he'd seen on his excursions, what else could have explained any of it except a pathological response to a profoundly shocking event, a condition that had been treated, in Rani's less fortunate case, by regimens of electroshock therapy that left her hands and feet in a state of constant spasm?

The train was slowing down, the clanging of the wheels on the tracks becoming more dispersed, and noticing the small huts and houses that lined the tracks, the weathered posters for various Tamil political candidates pasted on their corrugated steel walls, Krishan realized that they'd arrived at last in the Northern Province. The train made its way a short distance through the town and then into the station, grinding slowly to a stop as it passed the board labeled VAVUNIYA at the head of the platform. A few of the passengers still remaining in the carriage stood up—a young Tamil couple with a child, a middle-aged Muslim man, and two soldiers—and collecting their things they made their way out onto the platform, which was empty except for the stationmaster, a soldier, and three armed policemen. Looking out through the opposite window at the other platform, where a small group of people were waiting for the train headed south, Krishan noticed a large, freshly pasted billboard on the far end, its left half depicting a rough sea under dark clouds that seemed on the verge of erupting. Tossing and turning in the midst of the waves, seemingly on the point of being engulfed, was a small, rickety fishing boat, and in thick red Tamil letters, emblazoned across the center of the image, were the words THERE'S NO WAY: YOU WILL NEVER BE ABLE TO SET FOOT IN AUSTRALIA. The right half of the billboard consisted of a black background with dense white text that Krishan couldn't decipher at first, though as the train jerked back into motion and his carriage moved past the billboard he was able to make out a few of the lines, which stated that traffickers were trying to profit by cheating people who wanted to move to Australia, that Australia was no longer accepting people who tried to come to the country by boat, that boats attempting to reach the country would be steered back into deep waters by the Australian navy. He'd heard similar advertisements on Tamil radio stations and TV channels, usually aired in prime-time spots in the late evening and night, but this was the first billboard he'd seen and it was no accident, he knew, that it had been put up at Vavuniya, the first station in the Tamil part of the country. The Australian government had put tens of millions of dollars into such advertisements, not just in Sri Lanka but in other countries with large displaced populations like Iraq, Afghanistan, and Bangladesh, hoping to stem the tide of people from these countries who tried to make the long and arduous journey by boat. It was difficult to say whether the advertisements actually worked, for most of the people who made the journey chose to make it despite the exorbitant sums they had to pay the middlemen, knowing very well the danger of crossing thousands of miles of deep sea in dilapidated fishing boats, tightly packed for weeks with other asylum seekers in nearly uninhabitable conditions. Such people made the journey knowing their chances of reaching Australia were slim, that even if they did survive the boat trip they were likely to be kept in illegal offshore detention centers for years. The majority of them were people who'd lost everything during the war, people who, even if they hadn't been detained, bereaved, tortured, or raped, had seen untold amounts of violence, for whom life in their homeland had become more or less unbearable. It was true probably that severe trauma could never be escaped, that you carried it with you wherever you went, but trauma Krishan knew was also indelibly linked to the physical environments in which it was experienced, to specific sounds, images, languages, and times of day, as a result of which it was often impossible for people to continue living in the places they'd seen violence occur. It was often hard, he'd read somewhere, to convince a person who'd had a serious car accident to get back into a car, many such people preferring to take other modes of transport whenever they could from then on, and if this was the case with car accidents then how much harder must it have been to convince people to remain in places they'd been bombarded by shelling, places they'd come face-to-face with punctured bodies and severed limbs? Even if they were the only places they'd ever known, places their forebears had lived and that they themselves had never imagined leaving, how was it possible to convince such people not to risk their lives going elsewhere, not to attempt migrating to countries that seemed, in their minds, far removed from these sites of trauma, even if they knew they were likely to die in the process and even if they knew, in their heart of hearts, that most people in places like Australia and America and Europe would never let them live in their countries with full dignity?

It always made Krishan a little uncomfortable that he'd chosen to return while so many Tamils were willing to risk everything to leave, a choice that had only been possible, he knew, because of the fortune and privilege of his circumstances, the safe distance of his own life from the violence and poverty of the northeast. It was true that his father had been a casualty of one of the Tiger bombings in Colombo, that he had in this sense been deeply affected by the war, but the fact was that he'd grown up in comfort, in a house of his own far away from the actual fighting, that he'd never had to experience violence directly, neither gunshots, shelling, nor displacement, nothing more than casual racism here and there, threatening interrogations by police and soldiers on the street. The idea of doing social work in the northeast would have never even occurred to him, probably, had he not been so insulated from the traumas of the war, and in a way his departure after two years had only underscored how different his life was from those who'd spent their lives in the northeast, those for whom coming and going wasn't simply a matter of choice. Krishan looked at the scenes passing outside as they left the town, the outlines of the trees in the distance distorted by the intensity of the heat, and feeling a little restless he took out his phone and looked at the time. They were less than an hour from Kilinochchi and he wasn't sure what to do with himself, whether to try reading or listening to music, neither of which he felt like doing. He didn't want to remain seated, had been sitting for several hours and felt an urge to stand up, then realized that he hadn't yet smoked that day, that it would be nice to leave the carriage and have a cigarette now that he was finally in the north. He reached down and took out his lighter and pack from his bag, glanced around quickly to make sure no one happened to be walking through the carriage, then stood up and began making his way along the aisle, holding the seat backs for support till he passed out into the small corridor between the carriages. He waited a few seconds to make sure he was alone, then lighting a cigarette discreetly against the wall he pulled open the train door, latched it to the wall, and leaned outside, his face immediately assailed by a blast of hot, dry wind, his eyes by the penetrating, preternatural brightness of the day.

Just a stone's throw from the train he could see the A9 running in parallel with the tracks, veering sometimes closer and sometimes farther away, the air above its smooth black surface trembling from the heat of the tarmac. The highway was hardly a highway, consisting of only a single lane for each direction of traffic, but because it was the main road linking north and south it had assumed a kind of epic proportion in the minds of everyone who'd lived through the war. The southern section had been controlled by the government for most of the fighting, the northern section by the Tigers, each side manning their portion of the border with heavy fortifications and multiple checkpoints, so that for the better part of twenty-five years it had, like the train line, been completely inoperative. It had been reopened finally in 2009, just a few months after the defeat of the Tigers, the military quickly filling up the craters, demining the adjacent land, and repaving the road so it was ready for civilian use, though for a long time soldiers continued checking every single vehicle that crossed the border, going methodically through every single compartment and every single piece of luggage if the passengers were Tamil. The train line had taken much longer to be put back into operation, not only because all the stations on the northern section of the line had been bombed out, but also because every inch of track and every nut and bolt had been stripped away by the Tigers, who'd made use of the iron for weapons, bunkers, and anything else they required in their typically meticulous way. It had taken several years for the government to relay the track, and when the line was officially reopened the previous year it had been celebrated with great fanfare, the government using the occasion to symbolize how the entire island was now back under its control, a marker of their achievement as liberators of the country. That had been in 2014, toward the end of his time in the northeast, when he'd become so used to traveling by bus that he didn't even think to use the train, and looking at the highway from his slightly different vantage point now, Krishan found himself thinking of all the journeys he'd made between Colombo and Jaffna since returning to the island, the intense longing he'd felt, during those first months especially, as he gazed out from his bus window at these same unending landscapes of brush and palmyra, landscapes so flat and dry and unforgiveable that it seemed sometimes almost miraculous that so many generations had worked life and sustenance out of the earth.

It was hard to say what it was about the northeast that had drawn him there after so many years abroad, what it was that had taken root so deeply inside him that he abandoned the life he'd built for himself in Delhi in search of another one here. It was true that guilt had played some part, guilt for the relative ease of his life growing up, guilt for the fact that he'd spent so much of his twenties lost in academic texts, but there was also something in the sparse, desolate beauty of the region that had brought him here, he thought as he gazed out the train, something much stronger and more substantial than guilt. He'd spent so many hours looking at images of the northeastern countryside during his time in Delhi, not during his initial obsession with the war's final massacres but afterward, sensing in those images of sprawling fields and thick jungle something an-

cient and almost mythical, something that made him dream of
a possible fulfillment without knowing how or from what
source. Compelled by some need to dwell more on the origins
of the war, to understand the nature of the longings that had
led to such a devastating conclusion, he'd begun reading about
the earlier, more idealistic days of the separatist movement,
and it was the story of Kuttimani more than anything else, he
remembered now, that had captivated him at the time, that had
crystallized the longing to live in the northeast that was just
beginning to take hold of him. He'd known about Kuttimani
since childhood, about his role in the early days of the separatist struggle, his trial, incarceration, and subsequent murder, but
it was only during his time in Delhi that he'd actively tried to
find out more about the life of that early insurgent, about the
circumstances in which he'd grown up, the moods with which
he'd lived. He'd been unable to find even the most basic bio-
graphical information, not even his date or place of birth, and
the only material of value he'd found were a few scanned newspaper photographs, most of them taken during his trial or just
afterward. He could still see two of those images vividly in his
mind, both of them black-and-white, grainy and out of focus,
the first showing Kuttimani in the courtroom, probably immediately after the verdict had been pronounced, clean-shaven,
smartly dressed in a white shirt and sarong, handcuffed arms
raised above his head in a sign of victory despite the fact that he
was surrounded by policemen and had just been sentenced to
death. The second showed him leaving the courtroom after the
trial, his handcuffed arms held out in front of him, the side of
his handsome mouth curled into a smirk as he looked straight
into the camera with his squinting, sun-shaded eyes, his taller,

thinner, mustachioed comrade Thangathurai standing beside him, also looking at the camera, though with an expression that was noticeably less triumphant. In both images Kuttimani was fresh-faced and seemingly well in possession of himself, exuding a sense of calm, easy assurance, a bearing that had probably been achieved only with great effort, Krishan knew, for the newspaper article that contained the pictures also gave a long list of the tortures to which Kuttimani, Thangathurai, and Jegan, the third accomplice in the robbery, had been subject by police, a list that included, among other things, being stripped and beaten by batons and rifle butts, being forced to inhale the fumes of burning chili, having metal rods inserted into their anuses, and steel wire inserted into the urethral opening of their genitalia. It could only have been after much inner struggle that Kuttimani found the composure required to present himself in court the way he did, Krishan knew, to make the arguments and the famous last statement that were published the next day on the front pages of all the major newspapers, sending ripples from the south of the country all the way north.

The crime for which Kuttimani had been arrested, the robbery of eight million rupees from a People's Bank in Jaffna in March 1981, had not, in fact, been his first. In 1969, when he was probably in his early twenties, he'd formed, together with Thangathurai, an informal separatist organization that later became the Tamil Eelam Liberation Organization or TELO, an armed separatist group that funded most of its activity through the smuggling of contraband and the robbery of state or state-affiliated institutions. He'd been arrested by Indian police in 1973 while seeking a safe haven in Tamil Nadu, and after being deported at the request of Sri Lankan authorities had been imprisoned in his home country without trial till 1977, when he was finally released due to foreign pressure. He rejoined the insurgency, organized increasingly more daring attacks and robberies that culminated in the 1981 People's Bank robbery in Jaffna, leading to a vigorous manhunt by government authorities. He was arrested off the coast of Jaffna by the Sri Lankan navy only two weeks later, on a small motorboat trying to make his way with Thangathurai and Jegan to Tamil Nadu, where he'd been hoping to hide once more till the search for him died down. The trial, which took place at the Colombo High Court over a year later, was packed with journalists and members of the interested public, and was followed throughout the country with intense scrutiny. Kuttimani was charged with murder— there had, apparently, been people killed in the course of the robbery—and wanting no doubt to make an example of him to other separatists, the court had sentenced him to death. The judge asked whether he had any final words or requests that he wanted the court to hear before it was adjourned, and in response to this suggestion, according to the article, Kuttimani had proclaimed to the court that he was guilty of no crime whatsoever. He was an innocent person, taken into custody by the police and forced to sign a confession after months of unbearable torture. The court's verdict, he went on, which nobody in the country would find surprising, would only add new urgency to the separatist movement growing in the northeast, would only give new and more compelling reason for the establishment of the new state of Tamil Eelam. More and more Tamil youth would be arrested on false charges, and as this went on the movement for Tamil liberation taking hold in the northeast would only further be strengthened. He ended his speech by asking that he be hanged not in Colombo, where the trial was taking place, but in his ancestral village in Jaffna, that his vital organs be given to Tamils who needed them, and that his eyes in particular be donated to a young Tamil boy or girl who could not see, so that even if he himself never had the opportunity to see Tamil Eelam, as he put it, his eyes at least would one day have the chance.

Reading of Kuttimani's capture on one of the small boats that militant groups had used throughout the war to smuggle arms, money, and people between the northeast coast of Sri Lanka and the southern coast of India, Krishan had remembered another image he'd found on the internet, an undated color photograph taken somewhere on the northeast coast much later, probably at some point in the nineties. In the foreground of the image were two Tiger cadres standing at the edge of the beach, both barefoot, wearing shorts that left much of their thighs exposed, the shorter, thinner man on the left wearing a baggy button-up shirt, the taller, stockier man on the right wearing a camouflage T-shirt. Both of them were holding AK-47s, the man on the right with a magazine of bullets slung across his left shoulder, and both were looking out intently at the still, golden sea that stretched out from their feet. About thirty or forty feet from the shore a small motorboat sat quietly on the still water, inside it the small, blurred outlines of three or four seated men, while wading through the knee-high water, just disembarked from the boat, four more figures were making their way toward the shore. They were, most likely, returning from Tamil Nadu, where they'd gone either for some kind of military training, or to procure arms that they could smuggle back to the island. The two armed men standing barefoot on the edge of the shore had probably been stationed there to await their arrival, though they didn't seem to have much interest in the boat or in the men making their way back from it, such arrivals and departures probably being extremely routine. They seemed, instead, to be gazing to the northwest, across the enormity of the motionless sea, toward that line in the distance where the edge of the silently bright water became indistinguishable from the bright, cloudless horizon, a point so distant from their small section of beach that it could only have been on or near the Indian coast. It was while looking out at that same convergence of sea and horizon, Krishan couldn't help imagining, that Kuttimani had been arrested on his way to Tamil Nadu, and perhaps it was even because he'd been distracted by the sight of that distant meeting point that he'd let himself get caught. There was something so freeing or fulfilling about looking out across such distances, after all, such a feeling of freedom even in the act of stepping out under open sky, where one's eyes were no longer hemmed in by walls and roofs and could range, without constraint, over earth and sea. It was precisely for this reason, Krishan couldn't help feeling, that Kuttimani had asked for his eyes be given to a sightless child, so that they too might look into the horizon, so that they too might look across the distance at the land that belonged to them and the possibilities it contained. The freedom that Kuttimani desired, the freedom that perhaps all liberation movements sought, was not just the freedom that came when one could move freely over the land on which one's forbears lived, not just the freedom that came from being able to choose and be responsible for one's own life, but the freedom that came when one had access to a horizon, when one felt that the possible worlds that glimmered at its edges were within one's reach. It was only when looking at a horizon that one's eyes could move past all the obstacles that limited one's vision to the present situation, that one's eyes could range without limit to other times and other places, and perhaps this was all that freedom was, nothing more than the ability of the ciliary muscles in each eye—the finely calibrated muscles that contracted when focusing on objects close by and relaxed when focusing on objects far away—nothing more than the ability of these muscles to loosen and relax at will, allowing the things that existed in the distance, far beyond the place one actually was, to seem somehow within reach.

Kuttimani was moved, on being sentenced to death, to Welikada, the maximum-security prison built by the British in Colombo in 1841 and still, seventy years after their departure, the largest prison in the country. Krishan had never been inside Welikada, but he'd passed its imposing façade on Baseline Road plenty of times, the dominating white wall emblazoned with the crest of the Department of Prisons at the top, below it a long, beaten copper mural depicting the different stages of the rehabilitation of criminals. The mural began on the left with images of men committing crimes like murder and theft, followed to the right by downcast, penitent figures standing trial in orderly courtrooms, then by inmates engaging in manual labor of various sorts, laying bricks, painting, and shoveling, ending, finally, with scenes of joyful, sober individuals walking out of the prison under the watchful but caring eye of the guards. The mural, together with the large text printed below stating that PRISONERS ARE HUMANS, gave the impression that Welikada was a humane and progressive environment, an impression that Krishan always suspected to be false and that was discredited beyond doubt as he learned more about the massacre of Tamil prisoners there in July 1983. These massacres, which according to the government were simply the result of Sinhala prisoners getting out of hand, had taken place during the larger anti-Tamil pogrom that occurred in Colombo that month with the collusion of the government, leading to the destruction of eight thousand Tamil homes, five thousand Tamil shops, and the death, on some estimates, of up to three thousand Tamil people. The prison killings took place on two separate days in the midst of this pogrom, on the twenty-fifth of July and then again on the twenty-seventh, and were, according to the book Krishan read in the hope of learning more about Kuttimani's death, far from accidental or unplanned. Fifty-three Tamil inmates, all of them political prisoners, were killed, and the government story that the killings were the result of Sinhalese prisoners getting out of hand was, according to the authors of the book, patently false. No prison guard was killed or hurt during the violence, which almost certainly would have been the case if they had made any attempt to stop the Sinhala prisoners. Armed military personnel stationed within the prison grounds took no action to stop the killings either, apparently on orders from above, and after the attacks these same personnel refused to allow the still breathing Tamil prisoners to be taken to the hospital, which led eventually to them dying of their wounds. The conflicting evidence given by prison guards and officials made it clear, the authors of the book argued, that the killings were politically motivated at the highest levels.

Kuttimani had been housed, apparently, in a prison building

named the Chapel by the British because it was shaped like a cross, with four rectangular divisions on each floor and a central lobby on the ground floor. The seventy-four Tamil political prisoners held there had been jailed in three divisions of the ground floor, while the fourth division on the ground floor as well as all the upper floors housed Sinhala prisoners convicted of murder, rape, and other violent crimes. Kuttimani was held in an eight-by-eight cell together with his associates Thangathurai and Jegan, according to the book, and it was in this cell presumably that he spent the large part of his sixteen months in prison. Reading this detail Krishan couldn't help wondering how Kuttimani passed his time there with his two comrades, during all those long days and nights before their unscheduled killing. Probably they'd talked about news relating to the war, which must have come to them in bits and pieces through prison guards, and probably they'd discussed and debated the separatist movement and the political situation, not only among one another but also, during mealtimes and the recreation period, with the other Tamil prisoners, most of whom also belonged to separatist armed groups or political parties. The TELO were explicitly anti-ideological, in the sense that they had no specific ideas or proposals for what kind of country the people of the north and east would live in when the freedom struggle was finally won. Their first and only demand was for a Tamil homeland—all other matters would be considered after their homeland was won, they argued, since doing so beforehand would only be a distraction. Other groups, such as EROS or the PLOTE, were more strongly ideological, most of them socialist or Marxist, with strong anti-imperialist stances and distinct social and political visions of what the Tamil homeland would look like. These more abstract, intellectual articulations of the future were eventually destroyed by the Tamil Tigers when they annihilated or violently assimilated all of the other armed groups in the years that followed, less because of ideological differences—the Tigers too, like the TELO, believed that ideology was mostly a distraction—than simply to consolidate their position as the most powerful separatist group in the north. The prisoners couldn't have discussed politics all day, of course, especially since their news of what was happening in the world outside must have been limited, and Krishan wondered how Kuttimani must have spent the rest of his time in prison, whether he read, or wrote, or exercised, whether there was a window in his cell from which the sky could be seen. He liked to imagine Kuttimani looking out through a window, liked to imagine that he spent time looking into the distance even if there was no actual window, even if the cell contained no light, for even when you were fast asleep it was possible, Krishan knew, to dream of wide landscapes and endless roads that led all the way to the horizon, so that waking up it was as though you'd spent the last several hours in the outside world and not in a cramped cell with your eyes tightly shut.

What actually happened on the day Kuttimani was killed was unclear, but according to the book the attack of the twenty-fifth started around two in the afternoon, when some four hundred Sinhalese prisoners escaped their cells, no doubt with the help of some of the prison guards. Gathering in the lobby of the ground level they obtained the keys to all the Tamil cells, then attempted to enter the three sections of the ground level that housed the Tamil prisoners. Feeling a loyalty to the Tamil prisoners inside the section he guarded, one Sinhalese prison

guard apparently told the mob they would have to kill him to
enter, in response to which the mob left that noble guard unharmed and entered the other two Tamil sections, where the
guards in charge gave them free entry. It took the disorganized
mob some time before they were able to work out which keys
opened which cells, and this allowed the Tamil prisoners to organize some resistance to the attackers. The Sinhala prisoners
vastly outnumbered them, though, and were armed with weapons that, according to the text, could only have been procured
for them by the guards. Entering the cells one by one they cut
down and battered the occupants, leaving most of them dead
and the rest seriously wounded. The mob was no doubt aware
who Kuttimani was—accounts of what he'd said during his trial
the year before must have spread through the prison—for when
they entered the cell he shared with Thangathurai and Jegan,
the attackers made sure not to kill him immediately. It was re-
ported that after knocking the three occupants to the ground
several of the attackers had held Kuttimani fast on his knees,
while another used an implement of some kind, most likely a
knife but perhaps also a key, to gouge out, one after the other,
both of Kuttimani's eyes. The process must have taken some
time, Krishan knew, each eye must have been scored out slowly
and clumsily, losing its delicate integrity in the process rather
than being scooped out whole, and when the eyes were removed they had probably been crushed in the carver's hands or
trampled under his feet, for it was difficult to imagine the prisoners leaving them as they were.

Leaning out of the train door as the hot, dry wind buffeted
his face and the train wheels pounded heavily over the tracks
below, Krishan felt he could see, with stark clarity, the figure of

Kuttimani kneeling down in his grimy prison cell, two dark wounds in his head where previously his eyes had been. It was strange how sometimes scenes one has never witnessed could appear before the mind's eye more profoundly than memories from actual life, but looking out over the flat, arid landscape rushing before him, its far edges flickering in the distance like a mirage, the same landscape Kuttimani had no doubt imagined so many times from his cell, Krishan had the strange sensation that what he was seeing now was not exactly his own vision but the superimposition of Kuttimani's upon his own, the superimposition not just of Kuttimani's vision but the vision of all those many people from the northeast whose experiences and longings had been archived or imagined in his mind. He had the strange sensation that the images he was seeing were a product not just of the light entering his eyes from outside but of all the various images he'd come to associate with the northeast over the course of his life, the firsthand images from his childhood visits and his two years living there as an adult, the secondhand images from all the photographs he'd seen in books, newspapers, and websites, the images he'd constructed in his mind out of all the things he'd read and heard, idyllic images of rural life and horrific images of war, images depicting a life he might have lived had history been just a little different, the faint traces of these countless images all projected now over what his eyes actually saw as the train raced north. He could see the leafless thickets of brush rushing past in the foreground before him, the white-hot horizon melting into the cloudless sky in the background, could feel the thin steel floor vibrating beneath his feet and his shirt billowing in the wind, but standing there leaning out through the door of the train, knowing that soon he would be arriving in Kilinochchi and that soon he would be in Rani's village, attending the funeral of a person he still could not quite accept was dead, he couldn't help thinking, as the train hurtled closer toward his destination, that he'd traversed not any physical distance that day but rather some vast psychic distance inside him, that he'd been advancing not from the island's south to its north but from the south of his mind to its own distant northern reaches.

BURNING

8

IT WAS A little past four in the afternoon, the light softer now and more diffuse, the intensity of the day's heat beginning to wane, and standing by himself in a corner of the garden Krishan was observing the people gathered in Rani's house for the funeral, somewhat unnerved, after his long and meditative journey, by how quickly he'd found himself in this place so different from his point of origin, this setting that, despite conforming to all his abstract expectations, had nevertheless managed to catch him off guard. The sense of calm, peaceful self-containment he'd felt on the train had remained with him on the two quiet buses from Kilinochchi, and it had persisted too on his long walk from the bus stop, as he made his way slowly along the network of paths that ran through the noticeably deserted village. The properties on either side of the lanes were marked off by low fences of dried palm fronds thatched together with wire and rope, most of them fronted by small,

well-cultivated gardens, each with its own little vegetable plot
and an assortment of trees—drumstick, banana, coconut, curry
leaf, as well as others he couldn't identify. The houses themselves were simple and unadorned, the larger concrete ones
containing a kitchen and one or two rooms, the smaller ones
consisting of mud walls and thatched roofs and no more than a
single all-purpose hall. He'd taken his time noting and regarding everything he passed, as if he'd come for no other reason
than to discover what effect the surroundings had on the trajectory of his thoughts, and it was only as he turned into the lane
where Rani's house was located, as he heard the low, irregular
beat of funeral drums rising up from the end of the lane, that
he began to realize his journey was over, that he'd finally arrived at his destination. He wondered suddenly how he should
comport himself, what he should say to Rani's daughter when
they met, how he could give her his grandmother's money
without drawing attention to himself, questions he'd had the
whole day to consider but had avoided thinking about till then.
Approaching the house he saw first the band of drummers
standing just behind the palm-leaf fence, four men aloof from
everyone else in the garden, looking at one another intently as
they rapped the small, flat, beautifully constructed drums that
hung from their necks—members, he knew, of one of the most
marginalized castes in the northeast. In the garden behind them
a large crowd had already assembled, two or three hundred
people at least, almost all of them people from the village it
seemed, which explained perhaps why the village had felt so
quiet on his walk. Some of the attendees looked desolate or
forlorn, some merely bored, but most of them were talking in
low voices, as if using the gathering as an opportunity to dis-

cuss whatever matters were on their minds, the women wearing black, gray, or white saris, some of them in pale, unobtrusive colors, the men wearing mainly shirts and formal white sarongs. The band began to drum louder and at a faster tempo as he made his way toward the gate, giving, Krishan realized with discomfort, what was in effect a kind of announcement of his arrival. Walking through the garden he did his best to ignore the curious faces of the people as they turned and looked at him, all of them aware no doubt that he was not from the village, most of them probably able to tell from the way he was dressed, from his trousers and dark blue collarless shirt, that he wasn't from any of the neighboring villages either. The house was on the larger side of the houses he'd passed on his brief walk through the village, with white concrete walls, an untiled asbestos roof, and smooth red cement floors, and climbing up the two short steps to the veranda, where the crowd was more concentrated and nobody seemed to notice him, he took off his sandals, left them by the collection of footwear near the entrance, and went up to the threshold of the front door.

In the center of the room, elevated on a kind of low table or cot, was an open wooden casket overlaid with plastic lamination on its surfaces, and standing around the casket were a number of people, mainly women, some of them looking into the casket and whimpering or crying, a few quietly reciting hymns from small booklets they held in their hands, verses most likely from the *Sivapurānam*. Seated a little away on the floor in front of one of the walls was a priest, an array of fruit, coconuts, lamps, and other items spread out on banana leaves in front of him, and sitting cross-legged opposite him was a broad, muscular man of about thirty, wearing a white sarong and a white thread tied diagonally across his otherwise naked torso. The man was conducting the rites for the deceased, which meant, Krishan guessed, that he was Rani's son-in-law, the husband of Rani's daughter, the responsibility of performing the rites generally falling on a son-in-law if the deceased didn't have any sons. Krishan scanned the room for Rani's daughter, and his gaze soon came to rest on a woman whom several other people in the room were watching too, a woman in her mid- to late twenties standing by the head of the casket, her arms supported by a couple of older women as if they were worried she might faint. She had Rani's dark complexion but didn't quite resemble her on first glance, her build much less substantial, her face rounder and softer. She wasn't crying so much as out of breath, it seemed, her eyes not quite focused, as if she wasn't able to see clearly, and it was only when he noticed the two young girls holding on to her dress and looking somewhat lost, the only children present in the room, that Krishan realized the two girls must be Rani's granddaughters, that the woman they were holding must be Rani's daughter. Not knowing how to approach her Krishan remained at the threshold, wondering what to say, studying Rani's daughter till the older woman beside her noticed him standing there and gestured him toward them. He went up and introduced himself, looking first at the older woman and then at Rani's daughter, trying to diminish his stature and summon a look of grief on his face. This was the moment he'd feared most since learning about the death two days before, the moment Rani's relatives finally came face-to-face with him, looks of silent accusation on their faces, but registering who he was Rani's daughter only smiled sadly and welcomed him, her voice soft and plaintive, very different from how it had been on the phone. So you managed to make it, she said looking straight at him, you managed to find the house. I'm glad you were able to come. Turning to the two women she was standing next to she explained who he was, that it was at his house that her mother had been staying in Colombo, that it was his grandmother her mother had been looking after. Krishan looked at the women with an uncertain smile, searching their faces for any sign of resentment, for any sign that they, if not Rani's daughter, might hold him responsible for what had happened, but they too simply looked at him knowingly and warmly, as if to them he was merely one more mourner at the funeral, not the object of any ill will.

The older woman motioned him toward the casket, which he'd carefully avoided looking at till then, and drawing closer to it, slightly hesitant about looking directly at Rani, the first things Krishan noticed were the two oversize garlands draped over her chest, the way the plain white sari she was wearing blended in with the white satin interior of the casket. Her strangely pale, almost white hands were patiently folded over her waist, and her equally pale, unadorned feet were tied together by a thread that linked her two big toes. Taking in these details Krishan allowed himself to get a little closer, glancing at last toward the head of the casket at Rani's face, at the hair combed neatly back, at the eyes closed, the lips slightly pursed, the skin just as strangely pale as her hands and feet, coated, he realized, with several layers of talcum powder. Her face was expressionless, or rather wearing an expression that didn't seem exactly coherent, certainly not consonant with the mournful faces around her, and standing there with his hands by his sides Krishan was not sure what exactly he should be feeling or what exactly he should do. He was somehow moved, but he didn't feel any sadness or tears rising to his eyes, only a softer, tenderer version of the alienation he'd felt upon hearing the news two days before. Even if he no longer had difficulty remembering who Rani was and what she was like, even if he could remember all her mannerisms, her gruff but warm way of speaking, the sadness and longing she always carried with her, he struggled to connect the image of Rani in his mind with the body now lying in front of him, which seemed, with its ghostlike face, hands, and feet, with the unfamiliar white sari and strangely formal posture, to belong to someone he didn't know. He heard at that moment, coming from behind him, the sound of a woman wailing, and turning around saw that an older couple had entered the room. The woman held Rani's daughter's hands in her own for a moment, then pulled her hands away and began striking them against her temples, crying out that she could not believe Rani was gone, that first it had been her sons, then her husband, and now Rani herself. She repeated these statements rhythmically and without break, becoming even more strident as she left Rani's daughter and approached the casket, causing some of the women who were already standing beside it to begin crying louder themselves.

Krishan watched the scene for a while, surprised by the pitch of the woman's emotion, especially since Rani's daughter herself was so subdued, and decided that the woman must have been a close relative or perhaps an intimate friend. Turning to look at Rani's daughter, seeing that for a moment nobody was paying attention to her, he took from his shirt pocket the envelope his grandmother had given him and went up to her, leaning forward as he told her, almost in a whisper, that his grandmother had asked him to give it to her in order to help with the funeral expenses. Rani's daughter looked a little surprised, even though his mother had told her about the money the day before, then nodded her head in acknowledgment as she took the envelope. Looking away she hesitated for a second, then turning back and meeting his eyes she spoke to him again. My mother felt very close to your grandmother. She enjoyed staying in Colombo a lot, and would always talk about your family when she came back for visits. I don't know why she ever decided to leave, I kept telling her that she should go back, that that was what the doctor had said was best, but she was so stubborn about remaining here. She didn't want to stay in Colombo anymore, and she didn't want to go back to the hospital for treatment either. She said that the only thing she wanted was to stay at home with her granddaughters, that she didn't want to miss them growing up. My mother loved my two girls so much, even more than she loved her youngest son, I'm glad she was able to spend some time with them at least before she left us behind. Rani's daughter paused upon saying this, reflecting on what she'd said in the distinctive manner the bereaved sometimes have when talking to other people, appearing on the surface to be engaging in conversation when all the while speaking only to themselves. Krishan nodded and tried to smile, glanced at the girls who were now standing next to the priest and their father, observing the men with a mixture of interest and confusion. He was unsure what to say and waited to see whether Rani's daughter would say more, but smiling with an air of finality she turned and went into the adjacent room to put the envelope away. He waited there a little longer, hoping they might continue speaking when she returned, but by the time she did another family had entered the room and begun giving their condolences. Seeing no point to remaining inside, Krishan looked once more at the casket, touched his hands to its base, then slipped out to the garden and looked for an uncrowded place to stand, somewhere he could watch the proceedings unobserved and reflect on what he'd seen and heard.

He'd believed till then that he would be able to learn what happened to Rani by attending the funeral, that merely by studying her daughter's face he would be able to ascertain the nature of Rani's death, but seeing her daughter in person at last it was evident to him that his expectations had been misplaced, and not only because the constant stream of people coming in to give their condolences made conversation impossible. He'd expected, for some reason, to be able to obtain some kind of decisive affirmation or refutation of his suspicions, but the moment he heard Rani's daughter talking he realized that no unambiguous verdict was possible, that even if he waited till the funeral was over to talk to her the subject of suicide would never come up explicitly, that he would be left in the end with only his own interpretations of whatever she told him. He'd been relieved by the warmth and openness with which she'd received him, so different from the distant, mechanical tone of her voice on the phone, and he'd been relieved too by what she'd said about Rani's feelings toward Appamma, which meant his fears that Rani resented their life together in Colombo were unfounded, that she hadn't left because she disliked staying with them but for other, more significant reasons. She had said she wanted to spend time with her granddaughters, and this was no doubt true, but he got the sense from Rani's daughter's account that Rani had left more because she wanted to escape her mind and her mental condition than anything else, that she'd left in the same way that so many of those who are chronically depressed move from one place to another or back and forth between different places, hoping that a change of environment will make things better, though at the end of the day they were compelled to take their minds with them wherever they went, like movable, invisible prisons in which they were trapped. He'd been struck, too, by the palpable tone of regret in Rani's daughter's voice, as if her mother's decision to leave Colombo and stop therapy had led to the worsening of her condition and perhaps ultimately to her demise, as if her mother's depression and her death were connected in some significant way. This more than anything else made him wonder whether his suspicions about suicide might be right, but there was a good chance he was reading too much into the way Rani's daughter had spoken, he told himself, for there was often a certain kind of regret in the way the bereaved talked about how the people they'd lost had died, as if they believed that the death would not have come about if some small detail had been different, as if they believed that not only the more specific death but also the more general phenomenon of dying itself could have been avoided. There was an openness or vulnerability in Rani's daughter's bearing that felt incompatible with the possibility that Rani had committed suicide, for if she really did believe or suspect that her mother had killed herself she would have been a lot more guarded, he felt, would have spoken less freely about her mother, not only out of shame but out of fear that someone might guess what happened. Even if there had been concrete signs that Rani had killed herself it was clear her daughter was oblivious to them, that either she hadn't noticed the signs or, more likely, if there were such signs, that she'd intentionally averted her eyes from them. There was no sense, after all, in pursuing the possibility that her mother had committed suicide unless the facts were undeniable, and since there was no concrete evidence that this was the case, it was probably just easier to assume it had been an accident and leave the matter at that. In a way Krishan was grateful to be able to stop there, to learn that he would not be able to find out anything more, that he could let the issue go with the relative likelihood that Rani hadn't ended her own life. Even on the off chance that it had been suicide, he told himself, it was clear from what Rani's daughter had said that his family couldn't have been responsible, that they'd done their best to help her and that what she'd done to herself, if indeed she'd done anything, was the result of far more subterranean forces inside her, forces that had their genesis outside their lives.

Looking up from the patch of ground he was staring at Krishan saw that the crowd in the garden was getting larger, the buzz of low voices around him louder now and more sustained. New arrivals were continually trickling in, acknowledging the various people they saw as they walked toward the house, everyone knowing everyone, it seemed, which was in a sense what defined village life, the total absence of anonymity, nobody a stranger to anyone, even if not everyone was friends. Entering the house the new arrivals all went straight to Rani's daughter to give her their condolences, the women crying loudly and dramatically as they took her hands and then breaking out into loud waves of lamentation as they approached the casket, beating their chests, raising their hands up to the sky, speaking to Rani's dead body as if she were still alive. Coming back out to the veranda, wiping their tears away with their hands or their sleeves, a few of these women seemed to undergo a remarkable transformation, as if having left the presence of the body and the bereaved they were immediately able to regain the composure they'd lost while inside. Krishan had often heard his mother, who'd grown up in Jaffna and had always resented village life, disparaging the lamentations she claimed could be heard at every village funeral, not the lamentation of the bereaved, whose grief was of course usually sincere, but the lamentation of everybody else, the people who were much less affected by the death and who sometimes didn't even really know the deceased, people who, according to his mother, would come to the funeral whistling a tune or telling jokes, who would break out into histrionics in front of the body and then afterward, when no one was watching, go on with their lives as though nothing had happened. It was all just acting, his mother had said contemptuously of such women, a performance they put on to show everyone else how close they'd been to the deceased. It wasn't just the people who came to the funeral either, she went on, at some funerals the family of the deceased themselves hired people for the purpose of lamenting, just like they hired drummers and a priest, in order to show everyone how important their relative had been, how loved they were and how missed they would be. It had been hard for Krishan to actually understand what his mother meant at the time, never having been to a village funeral at that point, and because his mother was generally suspicious of emotion, preferring to cry in private if she had to cry at all, he'd dismissed what she said as simply another example of her general cynicism regarding the expression of emotion. Listening now to the crying and wailing of the new arrivals though, not all of whom could have been close relatives or friends, observing how coming back out to the veranda they returned so quickly to a state of equilibrium, he couldn't help wondering whether perhaps his mother had been right, especially since the only woman who didn't seem to be shedding any tears was Rani's daughter herself, the one person who should have been more affected than anybody else. Despite being in a state of visible distress and vulnerability Rani's daughter was not, Krishan could tell, completely beside herself like many of the other women were or were pretending to be, perhaps because she was too exhausted to really feel grief, because she was still processing everything that had happened, perhaps because there was no natural correspondence between the moments conventionally prescribed for grief and what the bereaved actually feels.

The man directing the funeral, a middle-aged man with a slight limp who was casually dressed in trousers and shirt, came out to the veranda and began calling out to everyone assembled in the garden, shouting that everybody who wanted to put rice into the deceased's mouth should come forward. Several people on the veranda and a few in the garden stood up and went into the house, filling up the already crowded front room, and Krishan too took a few steps forward, not to go inside but to get a better view of what was happening. He watched as one by one the close relatives and friends of the family went up to the casket, took a small handful of dry rice, and let the grains fall gently from their palms over Rani's mouth, an act whose meaning or significance he had never been quite able to understand. All he could think about as he watched was the irony of Rani being accorded the full set of funeral rituals, she who'd mentioned on more than one occasion during her time in Colombo how much she wished, instead of having to leave her youngest son by the side of the road for the flies, she'd been able to give him a proper funeral. She'd been unable to do not just the funeral, Krishan knew, but also any of the other ceremonies, certainly not the kaadaatru, which was supposed to come the day after the cremation, when the ashes were picked up from the cremation ground and taken home. Interned inside army camps, she probably hadn't been able to do the function that was supposed to take place on the fifth or seventh day after the cremation, the ettuchelavu, as it was called, when all the deceased's favorite foods were offered up symbolically to a garlanded photograph, and not having any of her son's ashes she wouldn't have been able to conduct the anthiyetti either, the ceremony in which the ashes were scattered into a river or a tank or the ocean, probably the most significant of all the postcremation rituals. The only ceremony she'd been able to perform was the annual death anniversary, the thuvasam, for which neither the body nor the ashes were necessary, only a photograph, a garland, and a priest. Rani had done the thuvasam for both her sons every year since leaving the camps, and in the previous two years she'd used the money she earned looking after Appamma to organize them with great lavishness, inviting everybody in the village and leaving Colombo more than a week in advance to undertake preparations. They'd been watching the news one evening in Appamma's room, Krishan remembered, listening to a report about a monthslong protest in a small village organized by the aged mothers of disappeared Tamil men, the women demanding that the government inves-

tigate the tens of thousands of Tamil people who'd vanished
without a trace during the war and immediately afterward.
They wanted some kind of verdict on their disappeared sons,
husbands, and brothers so they could finally have a measure of
peace, one of the women was telling the reporter, so that they
could conclusively learn what had happened to the people they
loved. Rani had turned to him after the segment was over and
told him, shaking her head, that she was grateful for having
seen her dead sons' bodies, for having managed to hold the
younger one in her arms for a few seconds, that she didn't know
what she would have done had either of them suddenly gone
missing one day, had she been forced to live in uncertainty
about whether they were alive or dead. When you didn't see
and hold the body of a dead child you couldn't understand that
they were gone, she told him, and unlike her the relatives of
people who'd gone missing were forced as a result to live their
lives in a kind of suspended state, unable to accept that their
sons or husbands or brothers were dead, knowing there was a
chance they might be alive in some unnamed cell somewhere,
though at the same time they were hesitant to give this possibility too much credence, afraid to believe in it given how many
unmarked graves they knew were scattered around the north
and east.

Krishan had always assumed that Hindus cremated the bodies of the dead and scattered their ashes as a kind of acknowledgment of the body's impermanence, of its vulnerability and
transience, and so it was strange for him now, watching as one
by one people dropped grains of rice over Rani's mouth, to
think that nevertheless the physical body played such a central
role in Hindu funerals, that it was given such prominence in all

the mourning rituals. It was acknowledged not just at the funeral, where the body was dressed up, caressed, and talked to
by the people who came to mourn, but also in the cremation
and the rituals that followed, first in the ash that was collected
in the urn after the body had been burned, the urn becoming a
kind of materially reduced body that was treated, even after the
cremation, with all the reverence due to the original body. Even
when the ash was dispersed over water thirty-one days later,
when this materially reduced body that had been held on to for
a month was given up, even then a kind of symbolic body was
retained in the physical object of the photograph, which was
garlanded and placed on a wall of the house, taken down every
year during the death anniversary and prayed to and offered
food, as if the image itself were capable of consumption and
digestion, the photograph becoming, in other words, not so
much a representation as a physical manifestation of the dead.
The process of letting go of a person was always done in gradual stages, from what he'd seen, from the actual body to a reduced body to a symbolic body that was always kept in the
house, an acknowledgment both of the difficulty of giving up
the body and also of the fact that the bodies of the ones we love
can never be fully renounced. And perhaps this was why the
symbolic acts of feeding were so important in the mourning
rituals, it occurred to him, in the pouring of rice over the mouth
of the deceased and in the offering of food to the photograph
of the deceased, for it wasn't surprising that in a culture in
which food and the activity of eating were so important, in a
culture in which feeding was one of the primary acts of care, in
which to ask whether somebody had eaten was to ask whether
they were well, in which the question of whom you can eat

with and whose food you can eat was a way of enforcing the boundaries between castes, that in such a culture the acts of serving and eating were also the physical processes that the bereaved found most difficult to part with, so that even after the body had stopped consuming and digesting food the bereaved continued to find solace in the act of feeding the deceased.

Standing there in the garden looking into the house Krishan thought of the cemeteries for fallen cadres that the Tigers had built all over the northeast, cemeteries that no longer existed and that harkened back in his mind to a time, only a few years before, when the northeast had been an entirely different place. The Tigers, though they consisted mostly of men and women who prayed in private to Hindu gods, had always buried their dead instead of cremating them, a practice inspired, Krishan had learned somewhere, by the significant population of Christian Tamils in the northeast. Cadres who died on campaigns that were successful in capturing new land were buried in new cemeteries constructed on the land they'd fallen fighting for, while the other dead were buried, symbolically if their bodies could not be recovered, in one of the several massive cemeteries already established across the north and the east. Krishan had never been to any of these cemeteries but he'd seen photographs and videos of them—vast, open spaces filled with endless rows of large horizontal stone tombs, identical except for the small engravings at their base indicating who rested there. The cemeteries, which were swept every day and kept open through the night for anyone to come and mourn their dead, were festooned on special occasions with the small red-and-yellow flags of the Tigers strung out high above the rows of tombs, and during Maaveerar Naal, the annual day for the remembrance of the war dead, masses upon masses of people would gather at these sites from all over Tiger-held territory to listen to speeches and cry over the sons, daughters, brothers, and sisters they'd lost, taking sorrowful pride in their sacrifices as they listened to Tiger songs of fearlessness and devotion blaring from loudspeakers, scenes of immeasurable pain and sadness that Krishan had never once seen in person but which were, somehow, etched into the back of his eyes. All those cemeteries, containing hundreds and thousands of dead fighters, had been razed to the ground by the army after the end of the war, their huge Chinese-made bulldozers mowing down graves indiscriminately, hardly a trace of them left anywhere in the northeast now, hardly a trace of any of those male and female cadres who'd died fighting in anonymity for a future that never materialized, not even of Rani's eldest son, who, Krishan realized now for the first time, must also have been buried in one of those cemeteries, must also have had his remains destroyed and removed from their place of rest.

It was not just the cemeteries that had been destroyed, naturally, for all the former Tiger offices, bases, and weapons depots had been destroyed too, all their signs, posters, and statues, after which the army had begun the labor of clearing rubble from bombed sites, of extracting the land mines buried all over the northeast, of relaying shelled-out roads and train tracks. Soon the only external signs that there'd once been a separatist movement and a war were the tents in which people still lived and the scars still inscribed on their bodies, the hairless skin on what remained of people's amputated arms and legs. The purpose of all the government's demolition and renovation in the northeast had, of course, been to erase any memory that might spur the Tamil population back toward militarism, and in this it had been more or less successful, for one hardly heard ordinary people talking about the Tigers in the northeast now, one hardly heard anyone giving them more than a passing thought. It was strange to consider, since for decades the Tigers had been the central fact of life in the northeast, but it also made sense to a degree, for memory requires cues from the environment to operate, can function only by means of associations between things in the present and things in the past, which meant that remembering became far harder when all the cues that an environment contained were systematically removed. Without the physical objects that allowed it to operate organically, memory had to be cultivated consciously and deliberately, and how could the average person in the northeast afford to actively cultivate their memory of a world now gone when there were so many more urgent concerns, how to make ends meet, how to rebuild their homes, how to educate their children, concerns that filled up all their mental space? The truth was that eventually most people would have ceased remembering the past anyway, even if all remaining traces of the Tigers had been left untouched, for the truth was that all monuments lose their meaning and significance with the passing of time, disappearing, like the statues and memorials in Colombo dedicated to the so-called independence struggle against the British, into the vast unseen and unconsidered background of everyday life. Deliberately or not the past was always being forgotten, in all places and among all peoples, a phenomenon that had less to do with the forces that seek to erase or rewrite history than simply the nature of time, with the precedence the present always seems to have over what has come before, the precedence not of the present moment, which we never seem to have access to, but of the present situation, which is always demanding our attention, always so forceful and vivid and overwhelming that as soon as one of its elements disappears we forget it ever existed. A shirt we wore every week for several years can be thrown away and then forgotten forever the week after, a table on which we ate two meals a day for a decade can be replaced and the strangeness of the new arrangement gone within a month, and even when something vital disappears, something our lives have centered on for years, even then we move on very quickly, very quickly adjusting to the new circumstances, so that within a few months or years the new way starts to seem like the way things have always been.

Forgetting was, of course, something we ourselves chose to do on purpose sometimes, as when after the end of a painful relationship we delete all traces of it that existed in our phones, attempting to excise it from our lives, and in this sense forgetting was not so different from remembering, an important and necessary part of life, just as central as remembering when it came to establishing an identity and orienting ourselves toward the future. And yet there was a crucial distinction, Krishan knew, between the forgetting that takes place as a result of our consent, which is a forgetting we need in order to reconcile our pasts and presents, and the forgetting that is imposed on us against our own will, which is so often a way of forcing us to accept a present in which we do not want to partake. Whenever forgetting was imposed in this way it would always give rise to people who insisted stubbornly on remembering, people who resisted not only the specific erasures of the past by those in power but also the more general erosion that would anyway

have been brought on by time, people who remained committed to commemorating the world taken away from them no
matter what happened, sharing stories and images and songs
and videos that they kept safe inside their heads and their hard
drives, trying to ensure that even if all the objective evidence
was taken away, even if there was no means in public spaces for
the communication of such histories, that their pasts would
continue to exist somewhere, somehow. Even if sharing what
happened during the war was painful, even if it was easier for
most people to pass over these wounds in silence, suppressing
their memories of the world they'd helped construct and the
violence that had destroyed it, even so people would remain
who insisted on remembering, some of them activists, artists,
and archivists who'd consciously chosen to do so but most of
them ordinary people who had no other choice, people like
Rani who, in the most basic sense, simply couldn't accept a
world without what they'd lost, people who'd lost their ability
to participate in the present and were thus compelled to live out
the rest of their lives in their memories and imaginations, to
build in their minds, like the temple constructed by Poosal, the
monuments and memorials they could not build in the world
outside. Perhaps this, it occurred to Krishan as he stood there in
the garden of the funeral house, was why Rani had seemed to
spend so much of her time in Colombo lost in thought, not
because she was sad or depressed but because she was busy
constructing in her mind a place where she could be reunited
with the sons she'd lost, a place she could occupy as an alternative to the world that bombarded her senses with its emptiness
every single day and night.

The sound of the lamentations was more or less continuous

now, rising out of the front room in waves and mingling with the drumming from the gate, the tempo and volume of which in turn had been increasing, the quicker, louder beat that announced new arrivals becoming almost indistinguishable from the beat that was rapped out in the interim. Looking up Krishan saw the funeral director come out to the veranda again, this time to say that it was the last chance to see the body, that they were about to close the casket, upon hearing which the people who'd been waiting in readiness in the veranda and the garden gave a collective stir, those in the garden moving toward the veranda, those on the veranda forming a line near the door so they could enter the house. Krishan made his way toward the house, which was more or less packed with people now, joining the haphazard line that went in through the front door. Those already inside were thronging around the body, jostling to get closer in the same way devotees jostled in temples to catch sight of the deity when the curtains were drawn, the men touching the casket with their hands, some of them crying and talking to the body but most of them stone-faced, the women stroking Rani's face and shoulders and arms, raising their hands to the sky and beating their chests as they wailed out loud. The lamentation was reaching a peak, all the women crying in unison, their voices rising and falling so loudly and rhythmically that at moments it seemed even to eclipse the drums, whose sole function now was to provide accompaniment to their voices, to give the music of collective lamentation a beat on which it could fall back. Overwhelmed by the scene around him, so different from the staid funerals he'd witnessed in Colombo, Krishan caught sight of Rani's daughter as he edged deeper into the sea of mourners. She was standing be-

hind the head of the casket and no longer fully in control of
herself, her feet not quite steady, supported by the two women
who were standing beside her earlier, sobbing loudly as she
touched her mother's face. This was the last time she would see
her mother, only men being allowed to accompany the body to
the cremation ground, and goaded perhaps by this knowledge,
by the intensity of the drums and the wailing of all the women,
she too had begun to speak to the body, to cry and lament with
the other women, though what she was saying was lost among
all the other voices rising and falling in the room. Krishan still
couldn't tell how genuine most of the lamentation was but it
occurred to him, as he was pushed toward the center of the
room, his feet trampling and trampled by the feet of the others
crowded around him, the heat of their bodies and their breathing pressing in against him, that perhaps he was wrong to think
of lamentation in terms of sincerity or insincerity, that perhaps
the crying and wailing and sobbing all around him was intended
not as an expression of emotion but as a kind of service offered
to the bereaved, a performance in some sense but a performance that, together with the drums and the rituals, was meant
only to help the bereaved with their own lamentation, to ease
out, like the calm rhythmic words and firm kneading hands of
a midwife during a difficult birth, the tears that the bereaved so
often found impossible to bring out by themselves. It was difficult after all to understand what a death meant, even for those
who will be affected most vitally by the loss, it was difficult to
really accept a death, to really let go of oneself and in doing so
begin letting go of the other, and perhaps the custom of lamentation was meant above all to help the bereaved in this process,
the friends and relatives and community of the bereaved trying

to help the bereaved cry by crying themselves, even if they did not feel the same pain. Nearing the casket Krishan was seeing Rani's body for the second time now, her powdered face, the grains of rice that had fallen from her mouth onto the white satin of the casket, her pale hands clasped together over her waist. He was unable to cry, unable to produce anything more than the welling in his eyes, but caught up in the density of people around him, in their pushing and pulling and jostling, in the wailing and lamenting and the sound of the drums, he now felt totally immersed in what was happening, a participant in this process, whatever it was, rather than a spectator, capable of feeling fully the force of what was happening, as if something inside him too was being channeled by everything around him, being called to the surface of his mind. He brought his hands together and touched Rani's shoulder lightly, brought his hands to his eyes and blessed himself with her, touched her neck and forehead and blessed himself again, and understanding now that it was really Rani lying in front of him he stood there in front of the casket looking at her till the pushing of people behind him compelled him to move, to shuffle around the casket and make his way back out to the garden.

Outside there was an air of anticipation, the drums beating with a feverish intensity, the four drummers still standing in the same place behind the fence, immersed in the rhythm of their drumming. More and more of the people who'd gone inside the house returned outside, the funeral director calling more impatiently now for people to leave the front room as he tried to clear a space around the casket. Krishan watched as the two women supporting Rani's daughter, who was still standing by the head of the casket, drew her back a little, as the director and

his assistant carefully lifted the lid of the casket and then lowered it over the body. The two of them came out, went to the
side of the house, where a bier consisting of two wooden poles
was leaning against the wall, the two main poles held crosswise
by several sticks that were bound by rope and covered by a
patchwork of dried palm fronds. The two of them carried the
bier around the side of the house and placed it on the ground a
few feet in front of the veranda steps, the director trying to
shout above the wails and the drums for everyone to give them
space. He signaled to his assistant, who went back inside and,
together with four or five other men, heaved the casket up. The
director leading the way, clearing the path in front of them,
they brought the casket out through the door to the veranda,
moving slowly and vigilantly, doing their best to keep the casket
stable, Rani's daughter coming out behind them together with
all the women who'd been inside from the beginning, all of
them beating their hands against their chests, their wailing loud
and unabating. The men moved with the casket down the veranda steps and into the garden, shouting at one another over
all the noise to coordinate their movements, then cautiously,
almost delicately, they lowered the casket down onto the bier.
Everybody in the garden crowded around this central point despite the repeated cautionings of the director, watching as the
men began to secure the casket to the bier with rope. The
drummers had already made their way out through the garden
gate, Krishan saw, were beating their drums out on the lane,
and Rani's daughter's husband, who was carrying a large and
seemingly heavy clay pot on his right shoulder, followed them
out without expression. The funeral director shouted for the
people around the bier to give them space, and the casket now

loaded firmly onto the bier, the men gave a count of three and heaved the bier up onto their shoulders in a single motion, two men in front, two behind, and two on each of the sides. The lamentation reached a crescendo, a chorus of mainly female voices rising up into the air, and shepherded through the garden by the director, the bier was carried in stops and starts toward the gate, the crowd following them as they went. Struggling a little at the narrow gate the men carried the bier out into the lane, the women in the crowd following them only up to the fence, raising their arms to the sky and continuing to wail, the men following the body out through the gate, forming a cortege that Krishan too joined as the body began to move away from the house. Turning back Krishan saw Rani's daughter standing in front of the fence, no longer crying or wailing, entirely silent, chest heaving, struggling for breath it seemed as she watched them, her figure becoming smaller and more spectral as they moved farther and farther from the house, till they turned a corner and she was lost to sight. The procession continued at a slow but even pace, led in the front by Rani's son-in-law, who carried the clay pot on his shoulder in silence, followed by the bier and the rest of the all-male procession, some of whose members dropped out as they passed their homes, the rest continuing to walk soundlessly behind the body. They made their way slowly through the village, not toward the main road where he'd gotten off the bus but farther and farther away from all links to the outside world, through narrow, winding, unpaved lanes that opened out, eventually, into a sprawling landscape of grass and brush. They scarcely seemed to advance as they walked through this vastness, making no discernible progress against the palmyra trees that stood solemnly in the distance, their tall figures turning into silhouettes as the sun began tracing the visible portion of its descent, as the afternoon moved toward its climax and the golden-yellow light began enfolding the land around them, as Rani began making her last, silent journey into the distance beyond.

9

THEIR PROGRESS REMAINED slow, subject to the burden of the body, the wide and gently rolling landscape ahead becoming gradually more verdant, swathed by grasses, plants, and shrubs that burst forth in undisciplined abandon, by clusters of trees weighed down by the density of their branches and leaves. Except for a cyclist who passed by in the opposite direction, easing to a stop as he neared the procession and then pulling over beside the path, there was little sign of human life as they made their way, little movement around them except for the small, weightless white butterflies that flitted in and out of the vegetation as though in slow motion. Krishan had traveled for seven hours from Colombo by train, for three hours from Kilinochchi town to the village on two separate buses, had felt upon arriving at Rani's house that he'd traveled as far interior as possible within the northeast, but having made his way now to the far side of the village and out into this unexpected space,

walking along this unpaved path miles from any main road, he
couldn't help feeling he was entering a sphere of vast remote-
ness, a place undiscoverable on any map and untouched by any
written history, a place that felt, all the same, somehow familiar, as though he'd walked through it in a dream or a previous
life. He was still at the back of the procession, the men in front
of him, maybe twenty or thirty in all, moving silently and patiently, their gazes directed at the ground in front of them or at
the path ahead, the drummers rapping their drums quietly behind the body, their accompaniment serving only to amplify
the silence surrounding them. Inside the small, contained space
of Rani's house and the neatly fenced-off boundaries of the garden he had been overwhelmed by all the emotion, by the clamor
of the lamentation and the drumming, the sight of the body
and the people thronging all around it, but moving out in the
open now, the late afternoon sky stretching out before them,
these feelings seemed small and almost petty, as though forced
into a wider relief, into a contrast with the world's expansiveness that dissolved them into nothingness, so that deprived of
the shared emotion that had united him with everyone else during the funeral he was returning now to his own thoughts once
more, remembering once more his own identity.

In the distance ahead the land seemed to gradually flatten,
the area to the left of the path becoming a vast glimmering
surface that reflected the pale gold of the sky. The butterflies
became scarcer, the quicker, more mercurial movement of
dragonflies taking their place, and as they drew closer the glimmering surface resolved into what was actually an immense
lake, its near banks covered with ferns and tall grass, its distant
banks too far to make out, merging silently with what looked

like hills or cloud on the horizon. It was hard to say whether the lake had formed naturally or whether it was one of the man-made tanks constructed centuries ago by old kings and chieftains, tanks that had been around so long that they were now an intrinsic part of the ecology, but studying it as he continued walking, the water calm and waveless, lapping softly and peacefully upon its banks, the feeling grew in Krishan that he'd been to this place before, that he'd walked across this same path and sat there by the banks of this same lake. There couldn't have been many bodies of water this size in the northeast, he knew, and taking out his phone he tried to see if he could find the place on Google Maps, which was unhelpful since there was, he saw, no signal on his phone. He wondered whether it was possible he'd passed it on one of the visits he'd made to the district back when he was based in Jaffna, but he knew for certain that he'd never been to Rani's village before, and couldn't remember having spent much time in the general vicinity before either. He could ask one of the men in the procession for the name of the lake, but none of them seemed to be paying it any attention and it would have been out of place to ask in any case, he felt, especially when everyone seemed so lost in their own thoughts. His gaze continued to return to the lake obsessively, as if at a face he'd come across somewhere but for some reason could not place, and it was only when he noticed a few reeds projecting out of the shallows that something clicked in his mind and everything seemed to resolve, when he realized with slight disbelief that the lake was familiar to him not because he'd been there before but because he'd seen it before on the internet, in a scene from a documentary he'd watched several years before in Delhi. It was a documentary he'd rewatched two or three times and which he'd been fixated on for several months afterward, which he'd stumbled across on YouTube not long after his obsession with Kuttimani, in that period when his attention had shifted from the traumas at the end of the war to the longings at its beginning. The film, whose name he could no longer remember, was not much more than an hour long, and though it had been made by a filmmaker from Denmark or Norway or one of those other northern European countries that were hard to distinguish, it had been devoid of the false benevolence common to so many British and European documents of violence and suffering in former colonies, devoid of the knowingness or righteousness so easily conjured up in such materials. The film's narrative centered around the life of a twenty-four-year-old woman named Dharshika, who he could still vividly recall, a woman who was, at the time of filming, an active member of the Black Tigers. The Black Tigers were the elite, much feared division of the Tigers that specialized in carefully planned and meticulously executed suicide missions— from assassinations of political figures to bombings in public spaces to small but devastating attacks on Sri Lankan army and navy bases—and it had been clear, watching Dharshika talk and move over the course of the documentary, that there was indeed something elite about her too. It was if she had in some way been divinely ordained for her role, not just because of the severe beauty of her appearance, her sharp, almost haughty features and darkly lustrous skin, but also because of the penetrating steeliness of her gaze and the certainty of her posture, the conviction with which she spoke about the brutality of the Sri Lankan government and her readiness to fight and die to protect her people. There'd been thousands of women like her but it was hard not to wonder, listening to her as she spoke, how such a person was possible and how she'd come to be, what experiences and what inner affinities had led her down this path so different from those taken by other men and women her age, a path that was headed so clearly toward death and the total extinction of consciousness it brought but that she followed, nevertheless, with such ease and confidence, as though she couldn't wait to reach its end.

According to her mother, whose estranged relationship with her daughter formed, Krishan recalled, one of the central subjects of the documentary, Dharshika had only been two years old when war broke out in Jaffna. Their family had lived in the midst of the fighting from its very earliest days, the most banal activities of their ordinary lives filled with great risk, sudden mêlées between the army and the Tigers often forcing them to stop what they were doing and run to take shelter. Even when there was no fighting there was the constant presence of soldiers who patrolled the villages, who would use security checkpoints as an excuse to harass and inappropriately touch girls and young women, as a result of which the movement of females outside their homes had to be severely restricted. As a young girl Dharshika had been extremely close to the aged priest of the nearby church, her mother told the camera, always sitting next to him during mass and prayers, assisting him in whatever ways he needed. It had been her daughter's goal from a young age to join the order as a nun, she added plaintively, so she could spend the rest of her life devoted to Mother Mary. Standing in front of the bombed-out ruins of this church in the next scene, asked by the filmmakers about this lost period of her childhood, Dharshika spoke at length about how the violence she'd seen had changed the course of her plans, recalling in particular an incident in which the army had shelled the church while civilians were sheltering there during the fighting, leaving behind a slew of bodies on the floor next to the fallen cross. On the verge of breaking down as she talked about these childhood memories, she managed to hold herself together for the length of the segment, wiping away a tear with the palm of her hand as if swatting away a fly before going on to criticize the Christian notion of turning the other cheek, asking how a God who cared about justice could let such things happen in his own house. These objections had led Dharshika to turn her devotion away from God and toward the movement and its Supreme Leader, but they hadn't, interestingly, been enough to turn her away from Mother Mary, and she still returned to the church grounds whenever she could, she told the camera matter-of-factly, where she would sit in front of the lone statue of the Mother that still remained and speak her heart out for hours at a time.

All of these experiences had no doubt played a role in her decision to join the Tigers, but it was above all the death of her father, her mother made clear, that led Dharshika to run away from home when she was still a young girl. Her father had been a peon at the post office in Jaffna town, and he'd been killed along with twenty-four other people by an aerial bomb that the army had dropped one morning in the center of town, opposite the main bus depot. Some children were able to bear the pain and grief that came as a result of such events, Dharshika's mother explained, while others lacked the capacity to return to ordinary life afterward. Her daughter belonged to the second category, and on an afternoon not long after the one-year anniversary of her father's death, at the age of about twelve or thirteen, she'd secretly left home. In what capacity she initially joined the Tigers was unclear from the documentary—she might simply have been a resident in one of the many orphanages they ran, or worked as a volunteer in one of their many nonmilitary organizations, or she might have joined as a recruit straightaway and been sent away to some secret location for basic training. What is clear is that at some point in her later teenage years she ended up joining one of the Tiger's all-women combat units, that she was selected eventually for one of the few highly coveted positions available in the Black Tigers. Speaking with a mixture of grief and pride at their family home, Dharshika's mother explained with a tinge of embarrassment that she'd had very little contact with her daughter since she left at that young age, that she saw Dharshika only once in a while, when her duties permitted it, and even then only for very short periods of time. She'd heard that her daughter had done well in the Tigers, that her courage and talent had earned her the respect of the other cadres and her superiors in the organization, but she herself had no idea whether her daughter was the same person she used to be, how her character had changed and to what degree, had no idea even whether she continued to pray. Dharshika herself, interviewed presumably somewhere close to her base, spoke of her mother without sentimentality, as though she were talking about a distant relative who'd died years before, and listening to her Krishan had wondered whether some kind of rift had developed between Dharshika and her mother in the year following her father's death, whether the daughter had formed some kind of resentment against the mother who'd been forced to raise her and her siblings alone after their father's death.

This refusal to show any sentimentality, it became clear, was part of a more general toughness that Dharshika seemed keen to present in front of the camera, a toughness that was mirrored to some degree by her best friend Puhal, the other main subject of the documentary, but underscored at the same time by their differences. Puhal was twenty-four and in the same unit as Dharshika, the same height but of slenderer build, and somewhat softer in her way of speaking and moving. She too seemed keen to emphasize her toughness, but she generally took more time responding to the questions she was asked and was often hesitant in the answers she gave, her conviction undercut by a willingness to reflect on her vulnerability in ways that Dharshika seemed unable or unwilling. The two of them had spent every day together for seven years, and their comfort and intimacy with each other was clear from the brief glimpses the documentary gave of their shared daily lives. In one scene the two women, both advanced belts in karate, sparred against each other in the early morning, ending their session with a set of three-finger push-ups that they performed in parallel and at the exact same speed, while in another Puhal stood behind Dharshika and combed out the latter's beautifully rough, unruly hair, straightening it out and plaiting it into two neat braids with an almost maternal tenderness and familiarity. In the interviews they did together they seemed to enjoy playing off each other, Dharshika's bravado against Puhal's thoughtfulness, as in a scene in which Dharshika joked about the US government gifting them an American tank that had been sold to the Sri Lankan army and then captured by the Tigers in battle, in response to which Puhal chided her as though she were a child, scolded her for making light of the losses that had been suffered in the course of winning the tank. In one of the scenes Krishan had been most struck by, the two women took turns discussing the modus operandi of the Black Tigers, whose missions, Puhal explained, involved taking out a major target with the use of very small, highly trained groups of cadres instead of relying on large numbers as the regular Tiger units did. They would be given their target months in advance of the mission, and for months their training would revolve around the specificities of that mission—its particular location, the season and time of day, and the nature of its target, military, political, or civilian. They were sent in with Claymore mines strapped around their chests, which they used either to destroy their targets along with themselves or, if they'd destroyed their targets by other means, to blow themselves up at the end of the mission so as not to be captured, which would of course have meant being subject to torture by government forces. Each member of the unit was always extremely eager to be selected for the next mission, Dharshika told the interviewer, each one of them begging and pleading to be selected, for which reason a kind of lottery system was used to choose teams, so that nobody could complain about being unfairly overlooked. No Black Tiger had ever returned alive from a mission, successful or not, and none of them went in with any expectation that they would return from their missions alive. You tended to stop caring about death after joining the Black Tigers, Puhal explained, learned gradually to take the inevitability of your own death for granted. This was the case for all Tigers, of course, but what distinguished Black Tiger cadres from ordinary cadres was that whereas ordinary Tigers could die at any moment, depending on the vicissitudes of battle, Black Tigers knew months before they died the exact location, moment, and method by which they would die, a death for which they trained for months once their mission was assigned and which they planned and visualized endlessly in the lead-up to that final moment. Krishan had been struck by the tone with which Puhal made this remark, as though she felt it was one of the virtues of being a Black Tiger that your death was totally in your own hands. There was an element of bravado perhaps in this remark, but it was clear that Puhal truly did find some solace in the thought that death could be planned and controlled—that this phenomenon that had been so omnipresent throughout their lives, that could strike at any time and was therefore a constant source of uncertainty and anxiety, could be something you chose rather than something imposed from the outside. There was something in the way both women spoke about their training and their future mission that made him feel that they not only had no fear of dying but were in fact looking forward to it, that they were in a sense even impatient for it, as though they felt they would, upon dying, be reborn into the nation for which they'd just died, as though they saw the nation for which they were fighting as a kind of heaven, as though death, for them, was not the end of real life but its beginning.

The scene that took place at the lake they were now passing, which had remained fixed in Krishan's memory as the climax of the documentary, began with Dharshika and Puhal sitting together on its banks in full military fatigues, looking out over the water and trying to make out whether it was mountains or cloud that lay on the lake's far side. The interviewer had just asked them, presumably, whether they thought much about the battles they'd fought in, for nodding her head at the camera Dharshika said with a smile that scenes of battle played in her mind every time she closed her eyes. She often dreamed of being in battle too, she went on, snapping off a leaf from one of the plants in front of her and beginning to shred it into little pieces, would often have dreams of seeing the enemy approach and trying to shoot but having her gun get stuck, or of shooting enemy soldiers but having no effect on their progress, the soldiers continuing to march zombielike toward her despite all the rounds she emptied on them. These were just dreams, of course, she added after a brief pause, drawing out a tiny glass vial that hung like a pendant from a string around her neck, in reality they knew they would never be captured, on account of the cyanide they carried with them wherever they went. No matter what happened they could always bite down on the capsule and end their lives if they were about to be captured, though if by chance they bit into the vial while they were asleep and dreaming, she said, glancing at Puhal and laughing, then that would be that, they would simply never wake up. Puhal then described how the capsule had to be used in the middle of battle or a mission, explaining that you had to bite into the vial with your teeth so the cracked glass would cut into your tongue, causing the cyanide to enter your bloodstream and kill you immediately. Even if you'd been wounded and were too weak to properly bite down, all you had to do was smash the vial and let a few drops of the cyanide drip onto your wounds, and this would be sufficient to obtain the desired effect. They talked as if the cyanide capsules were heirlooms that had been passed down generation after generation with these exact instructions, long-cherished reminders of their forbears and identities, and listening to the reverence with which they spoke on the subject Krishan had had the sense that they were, already in that moment of filming, talking to the camera as though from some other realm.

The two women were then asked what friendship meant to them, for Puhal turned her head away from the camera and looked shyly at Dharshika, a slightly embarrassed smile on her face, causing Dharshika in turn to laugh. It was clear from their smiles that the two friends hadn't discussed their relationship with each other explicitly before, perhaps because it was more natural for such matters to be negotiated through gestures rather than words, perhaps because the impending approach of their deaths in the form of an as yet unknown mission made discussions of their relationship seem futile. Friendship for them, the two cadres told the camera, their expressions quickly turning serious, meant sharing in each other's emotional lives. It meant sharing in each other's happinesses and sadnesses, and it meant helping and supporting each other in whatever practical ways they could, though they were of course prepared to separate, they hastened to add, if one of them had to be transferred to another location. The discussion then turned from friendship to the subject of betrayal, the gravest offense a cadre could commit, one that the Tigers punished with execution, Krishan knew, even when there was little certainty about the allegation. The two women tried to justify the harshness of the punishment, explaining that the Tigers were fighting for the good of the people, that if a single traitor could, by sharing military information, put the entire cause in jeopardy, then it

was better the traitor be shot than the movement and the people be endangered. Looking at the interviewer Dharshika then
added, apropos of nothing it seemed, that if someone were to
tell her that Puhal had betrayed the cause, if the accusation
were to be firmly proven, that she herself wouldn't hesitate to
shoot her best friend. A look of uncertainty passed shadowlike
across her face as she said this, as though she herself was surprised by what had just come out of her mouth, and falling silent she looked away from the camera, as if she'd spoken too
quickly and needed more time to consider the hypothetical
situation on which she'd just pronounced. She looked down at
the reeds in front of her, then turned back toward the camera a
second later and nodded her head gravely, as if to confirm that
her initial instinct had indeed been correct, that she would indeed kill Puhal if she betrayed the cause. Puhal, who'd been
looking out over the water all that while, turned and regarded
Dharshika, who raised her head and looked into the distance to
avoid her gaze. There was a period of long silence, in which
only the gentle sound of the water lapping against the banks
and the faint buzzing of dragonflies in the background could be
heard, Dharshika continuing to pluck bits of leaf from the
plants in front of her, examining them distractedly in her hand,
shredding them, and letting them fall. Puhal then began to
speak, breaking the silence with her own take on what Dharshika had said. Everything they did eventually made its way to
the Leader, she said—if they did something good the Leader
would hear about it, if they did something bad the Leader
would hear about it, and if they committed an act of betrayal
the Leader would hear about that too. If the Leader verified
that Dharshika had indeed committed an act of betrayal, then

most likely he would have somebody else execute her, but if for whatever reason it was she who had to do the job, then she too would shoot Dharshika, just as she was ordered. Puhal gave a small but triumphant smile as she said this, as though proud to show that she too was willing to kill her best friend for the sake of the cause, then rubbing the tip of her nose she immediately furrowed her eyebrows and looked away, an expression of irritation on her face, though it was hard to say whether her anger was directed at the interviewer recording the scene, at Dharshika for first so brazenly claiming that she would not hesitate to kill her, or at herself for responding in kind. The two women fell silent again, Puhal looking out over the water, Dharshika dissecting another leaf in her hands, and the film then cut to a wide landscape shot of the Vanni, of two large, seemingly unused buildings in the distance, surrounded on all sides by dense vegetation, the two women standing side by side in a corner of the screen, guns strapped tightly across their shoulders.

Krishan had been struck by that scene the first time he saw it, by the way it so vividly captured Dharshika and Puhal's relationship and situation, something simultaneously so moving, challenging, and disconcerting about how these two women had abandoned everything to join the Tigers, their homes and villages, families and friends, about how they'd formed, in exile from their previous lives, such an intimate bond, and how, despite waking together almost every day for seven years, they were ready to give each other up for the cause they'd joined, even to kill each other if the need arose. The two of them were no longer alive, Krishan knew, they'd died most likely within a few years of filming those scenes, probably in one of the increasingly desperate suicide missions the Tigers had ordered toward the end of the war or while defending the rapidly shrinking land still under Tiger control. It was strange to think that he might now be walking past the very same lake that these two women had once looked across, walking on the very same earth that they might have trod upon all those years before, and it was strange to think how different he himself was now from the person he'd been when he'd come across those scenes for the first time, to think how far he'd felt from the northeast during his time living and studying in Delhi, as if it was a place from which he'd been exiled and as if, with the end of the war and the destruction of the world that had existed there, it was a place for which his yearning could never be fulfilled. He'd been seeing Anjum for about two months at the time, and he could still remember now the urgency with which he'd wanted to share the film with her afterward, his eagerness to show her some glimpse of that destroyed world he felt to be a part of himself, his certainty that she would be impressed to learn that this was the lineage from which he came, even if he didn't fully agree with everything that all the other members of this lineage had done. He'd told her about the film the next time they met and they'd agreed to watch it together, but this had turned out to be more difficult to accomplish than expected, for Anjum was rarely in Delhi during the weekends and rarely able to meet more than once a week even when she was in town. They were spending entire days together when they did see each other by that point, and there was of course always time available in the literal sense of the word, but all they could seem to do when they were in proximity to each other was gaze at and be gazed at by each other, consume and be consumed by each other, so that even when he remembered the film he hesitated to bring it up, worrying that watching a film was too mundane an activity to do together, that sitting together but not paying attention to each other would fail to do justice to what they felt for each other.

It was for this reason probably that when he and Anjum did finally watch the documentary, the first and only film they watched together, it was toward the end of their time in Bombay, toward the end of that trip that was the first occasion in four or five months that they spent continuous time with each other, in which the urgency for transcendence that they'd previously felt gave way to the possibility of other, more gentle ways of being together. They were staying in the room of a friend of Anjum's who was out of town, and after the initial awkwardness and uncertainty of the train journey they'd spent the first couple of days much as they would have in Delhi, smoking, talking, and sleeping together, occasionally going outside but even then not very far, the only difference being that this time there was a totally different city in the background, a city by the sea of immense wealth and poverty, a city that seemed, even more than Delhi, like a veil or a mirage or an illusion that surrounded them. It became clear soon enough that they could not spend the entire trip this way, that being together for an extended period of time meant they would need to pay attention to all the various human and animal needs they more or less ignored in Delhi. They needed, first of all, to eat, and since they couldn't afford to always eat out they'd had to plan their meals, to buy meat and vegetables and cook together. Their sleeping patterns too became more regular, no longer a capitulation to fatigue as it had been earlier, for if they didn't sleep in the night they wouldn't be able to see the city during the day, which was ostensibly part of why they'd come to Bombay to begin with. Anjum had a few friends in the city with whom she was supposed to spend time, people she'd gotten to know over the years through her activist work, and so they appeared together in social contexts for the first time as well. He'd been surprised by how charismatic Anjum could be in the presence of others, how friendly and lighthearted, qualities he'd intuited during their initial, public encounter, but which he'd somehow forgotten about in the time since. She continually asked her friends questions about their thoughts and opinions, their habits and routines, thoughtful, thorough, and disarming questions that came from a generous curiosity about other lives but were also, he sensed, part of a strategy that allowed her to avoid sharing too much of herself. He noticed that she was careful not to say or do anything that would allow anyone to perceive them as a couple, and though these moments troubled him he forgot about them with relative ease, reassured by how close they were otherwise becoming on the trip, by how much more open and accessible Anjum seemed to him now. He'd become familiar with so many of her invisible patterns and rhythms, with all those tendencies of being that were revealed only when one spent extended time with another person—the variation of mood in accordance with time of day, energy, digestion, and environment—and he'd begun, for the first time, to glimpse what a more substantial relationship between them might look like, what it would be like to actually share a life with Anjum. A calm and tender domesticity began to emerge as they cooked and ate together, went on long walks together and met other people together, the rapture and otherworldliness of their time in Delhi transformed, during their three weeks together, into a gentle and patient coexistence with their surroundings, washed by waves of desire that never ceased flowing, but that no longer made it impossible to participate in the outside world. He had known from previous relationships how quickly desire began to dissipate when two people became used to each other, how quickly the hope of transcendence with which infatuation begins was replaced by mere comfort and security, the safety of habit and routine, but he realized during their short time in Bombay that domesticity didn't have to signify the domestication of desire, that it could mean not its dullening and deadening but its deepening and widening, habit becoming something that fortified and buttressed desire without at the same time stifling it, like a glass case that protects the delicate flame of a candle while being open enough to let in the oxygen needed to keep the flame burning.

It was as they were rolling a joint on the afternoon of their penultimate day in Bombay, their last full day in the city, that the idea of watching the documentary came up again and they decided to finally watch it together. Drawing the curtains, placing the laptop on the bed between them, they lit the joint and let the video play, watched the scenes unfolding on the screen before them in a deepening trance. They sat there watching in silence till the very end, listening to the music that played as the credits rolled, and when the video at last came to an end Anjum closed the laptop gently and they both remained unmoving for a while, reluctant to speak or look at each other in the same way that when a film ended at the cinema and the lights came on, there was a moment in which you were reluctant to make eye contact with the person beside you, as if to do so would be to acknowledge the transience of the world in which you'd just been immersed. He asked whether she'd liked the film and she nodded that she had, that she too had been moved by it and could see what had attracted him so much to it, after which they said little else about the film, deciding in a kind of tacit agreement to remain in their thoughts a little more, to let the impression it had made linger inside them a bit longer. Outside the sky was already turning into the lavender gold of early evening, it was getting late, they realized, and they would have to leave the flat soon. They'd planned to spend their last night walking the length of Marine Drive, the long C-shaped road that ran along the sharply curved southwestern coast of the island city, a road that shared the same name as the road in Colombo near which Krishan had grown up, but that was so much more immense that no comparison was possible. They got ready and took the local train down as far south as possible, crushed into each other by the constant press of people in the carriage, then walked from the station down to the southernmost tip of Marine Drive. The sun had just gone down but the concrete was still exhaling heat as they began to make their way up the length of the broad pavement, cars rushing by on the road to their right, tall apartment buildings reaching up into the monumental sky behind them, the water breaking gently against the man-made rocks to their left, the boundlessness of the ocean stretching out into the distance beyond. They talked about various things, what things exactly he could no longer remember now, their gazes directed above the countless people they passed, commuters, students, walkers, joggers, and couples, and it was only when they'd covered about half the length of the promenade that the documentary came up again in conversation, when deciding to sit down and smoke on the concrete ledge that gave onto the sea they began to talk about the dynamic between the two cadres, the nature of the friendship that clearly meant so much to each of them but that both had taken such pains to disavow.

She couldn't stop thinking, Anjum told him as they looked out at the darkening sky, about the scene by the lake, the scene in which Dharshika and Puhal had claimed to be willing to kill each other for the sake of the movement. Dharshika would not have made such a cruel statement unless she'd actively wanted to wound Puhal in some way, she felt, unless she'd held some secret resentment against her friend that she wished to punish her for. It was the kind of deep, unspoken resentment that was only possible between people who loved each other intensely and yet sensed the possibility of being hurt by each other, between people who needed each other and were yet unable to fully acknowledge this need to each other for fear of becoming vulnerable. It was a form of cruelty common in families and close friendships, where people are so dependent on each other but also so hemmed in and restricted by each other, and it was a form of cruelty that was an intrinsic part of the dynamic between lovers too. Watching the two cadres interact she'd wondered whether there might not be something deeper hidden behind their friendship, between the brasher, more assertive Dharshika and the somewhat more approachable Puhal, there was something almost erotic, she couldn't help feeling, in the alternating boldness and shyness with which their eyes continually met, their gazes continually moving toward each other and then away. Anjum said all this more or less at once, as a clear, fully formed thought that she articulated, as was her wont, only after having dwelt on it by herself, and surprised by the suggestion, which he would never have otherwise considered, Krishan asked her whether she thought the two cadres had been lovers, adding that he thought it unlikely given how rigidly disciplinarian life for Tiger cadres was supposed to be. Anjum shrugged in a slightly indifferent way, as though the veracity of her interpretation was not really what mattered, then turned and looked out at the sea, rotating the ring on her middle finger absentmindedly. The documentary had reminded her, she went on after a moment, about a collection of old Buddhist poems she'd recently read, a collection of poems written between the third and sixth centuries B.C. by Buddhist nuns from all over the subcontinent, collected, translated into Pali, and passed down in the tradition as a single work. The poems were written across the social spectrum, by oppressed-caste women and upper-caste women, by serving women and prominent ladies, all of them evincing the same veneration for the Buddha and for the liberation that came with following his doctrine of radical detachment. Several of the poems depicted the situations that led to the conversion of their authors in surprising detail, many of them single women who'd joined monastic life as a way of escaping the compulsion to marry men they had no interest in, many of them married women who'd sought escape from the drudgeries of domestic labor and the unwanted sexual demands of their husbands, from what would now be called marital rape. Some had wanted freedom from the sexual violence casually inflicted on them by upper-caste men, while some had wanted freedom from the violent heat of their own high libidos and uncontrollable sexual urges, a coolness they found in Buddhism. Many of the women, Anjum added, had also joined the order as a way of coping with grief, with the untimely death of a son or daughter or brother or sister, the Buddha's teachings on death providing the only consolation that really made sense of all their suffering. All of these elder nuns had, in other words, two thousand five hundred years before, left their homes and relatives in order to find, through the monastic order, liberation from the societies in which they'd been born, and she couldn't help thinking about the parallels with Dharshika and Puhal, with all the other women who'd left their families to join the Tigers. Like the Buddhist nuns, they too had given up attachment to their bodies in response to the traumas they'd experienced, and like the nuns they too had joined a movement for liberation, a movement founded and led, like Buddhism, by a man, a movement that to their minds promised not only the possibility of freedom from the Sri Lankan state but also real and immediate freedom from their own society's expectations and oppressions.

There was some truth to the comparison Anjum was making, Krishan knew, for he'd watched interviews where female cadres talked about how joining the Tigers had helped them escape from certain of the patriarchal tendencies of Tamil society, had read in various places about the fact that many of them had experienced one form of violence or another at the hands of men in occupying forces, that even the Black Tiger cadre who'd assassinated the Indian prime minister in 1991 had been raped as a young girl by Indian soldiers stationed in Jaffna. There was something in the authority with which Anjum spoke though that seemed to suggest more, as though she perceived herself to be more closely connected to Puhal and Dharshika than he was, as though, Krishan couldn't help feeling, she was trying in some way to appropriate what he'd wanted to share with her of himself. The sentiment bothered him but it wasn't without basis either, he knew, not merely because of the possibility that Dharshika and Puhal might, like her, have sought something beyond heterosexuality, but more importantly because they, like her and unlike him, had the conviction to follow a path that involved abandoning the ordinary world, the strength to cut off ties with family and society in order to devote themselves fully and absolutely to a cause. Krishan thought of how Anjum had avoided touching him in the presence of her friends, how she'd introduced him as a friend from Delhi, things she hadn't seemed to do with any explicit intent or purpose but that had served, nevertheless, to remind him in those moments that he could not take their relationship for granted, that soon she would be moving away and that their time together would soon be coming to an end. He'd known these things already, of course, they had after all been the source of all the anxiety he'd experienced since meeting Anjum, but in a way he'd been evading these facts over the previous three weeks, he realized, in a way he'd allowed the comfort and familiarity that had developed between them to shield himself from their implications. It was this subject that Anjum was trying to broach now by likening herself to Dharshika and Puhal, Krishan realized, as he looked at the thoughtful, almost brooding expression on her face, not explicitly, since that was not Anjum's way, but lightly and gracefully, hoping he would be perceptive enough to understand what she was doing without the heaviness of having to tell him directly. It was their last evening in Bombay and she was trying, gently, to remind him that she was different from him, that her own path in the world had already been staked out and that he would need to find his own, and it was at this moment, turning and looking out over the darkly shifting sea, that he finally felt the inevitability of their parting of ways coming home to him, a kind of sudden, silent shift taking place in the geology of his mind, a fact he responded to not with anxiety now or desperation, as he had in the past, but with the silent conviction that he too had a path ahead of him, that he too had a history and a destiny of his own. It had been at that moment, sitting beside Anjum with the ocean before them and the city of Bombay to their backs, having spent all his adulthood, almost seven years at that point, living in India, that the thought first came to him of returning to the country of his birth, of leaving behind his graduate studies and his plans of being an academic, of devoting himself to working in the northeast, a thought that had no doubt been preparing itself in his mind for some time, encouraged by his obsession with the war but also by his time with Anjum, the model she'd provided for a life governed by the vision of another world. He felt a kind of sadness come over him, not so much the sadness of separation from Anjum as the sadness of being separated from a life he'd become familiar with and comfortable in, but stronger than this sadness was the sense of possibility he suddenly felt rising through his body, the sense of possibility that came with extinction of the self and submission to higher powers, from the prospect of leaving behind all the difficulties of loving someone who couldn't be with him and devoting himself instead to the project of a new world, a world that would give him the same sense of liberation he felt with Anjum but without the sadness and the desperation, a world that would take him away from this person he loved but would also, somehow, bring them closer.

The two of them finished their cigarettes quietly, each of them lost in their own thoughts, then resumed walking down Marine Drive, slowly and in silence. Even though nothing exactly had happened, even though their conversation about the film had been abstract and unrelated to their relationship, it was as if each of them sensed that some turning point had been reached. It was as if the logic that had begun to unfold five months ago, when their eyes first made contact, was coming finally to its end, and it was in response to this feeling, perhaps, that they held hands for the first time as they walked, clasping each other not firmly or with fullness of contact, not giving each other promises they could not keep, but loosely and tenderly, only their little fingers intertwined. It was dark now, the pavement lit by the sodium glow of the tall streetlamps on the road to their right, and stretching out to their left the water glimmered in the warm night, the city's reflected intensities fluctuating on its surface. To their right, curving outward with the coastline into the distance ahead, high-rises rose up to form the skyline, the first of endless lines of buildings that comprised the island of Bombay, buildings that contained within their small compartments tens of millions suffering and striving people from all across the country, a condensation of human life so dense and so rich that it was impossible to believe such a place existed till one saw it with one's own eyes. It was as though, as they walked together holding hands that night, they were being presented with a crystallization of two contradictory possibilities of liberation that existence on earth offered, the possibility, on the one hand, that one felt whenever one came across an immense number of people living in a single place, the possibility of finding among all those millions a per-

son or people with whom one could be happy, and the possibility, on the other, that was felt whenever one looked into the
endless, lightless reaches of the night sea, the possibility of liberation that was associated with oblivion, with the cutting of
ties and voyaging out into the unknown. Krishan held Anjum's
hand a little more tightly, and looking at her as she looked back
at him, her tall, graceful form silhouetted by the silver-yellow
halo of the city behind her, she appeared to him just as she'd
appeared the first day they met, just as she'd appeared that
night on the train with the countryside rushing past behind her,
with that combination of sadness, longing, and conviction that
he would, he'd felt with certainty that moment, never forget.
He continued gazing at her, at the severity of her profile and
the vulnerability of her gaze, and it was as though he could feel
the sight of her penetrating his eyes in real time, burning itself
delicately into the film of his retinas, forming an image that
would remain imprinted in the back of his eyes like a shadow or
like tracing paper over everything he saw subsequently. And
maybe it was for this reason, it had occurred to him at that moment, that eyesight weakened with the passing of the years, not
because of old age or disease, not because of the deterioration
of the cornea or the lenses or the finely tuned muscles that controlled them but because, rather, of the accumulation of a few
such images over the course of one's brief sojourn on earth,
images of great beauty that pierced the eyes and superimposed
themselves over everything one saw afterward, making it harder
over time to see and pay attention to the outside world, though
perhaps, it occurred to him now, four years later in the country
of his birth, walking at the back of the procession bearing
Rani's body for cremation, Rani who'd seen so much that she

had never been able to forget, perhaps he'd been naïve back then, perhaps it was not just images of beauty that clouded one's vision over time but images of violence too, those moments of violence that for some people were just as much a part of life as the moments of beauty, both kinds of image appearing when we least expected it and both continuing to haunt us thereafter, both of which marked and branded us, limiting how far we were subsequently able to see.

10

THEY HAD LEFT the lake behind some time ago, the vegetation along the road less exuberant as they moved farther from the water, merging into the dustier, browner landscapes of tangled brush and gnarled trees that had dominated the scenery from station to village. They'd been walking for maybe half an hour and he could feel the moisture trickling down his back and sides, his body beginning to feel heavier and more cumbersome despite having no part to play in shouldering the bier. Krishan knew that cremation grounds were generally located some distance outside villages, a fact that had to do with the supposed impurity of funeral rites and of those compelled to base their livelihoods upon them, but he wondered now whether the distance between village and cremation ground might also be related to the process of grieving, whether it might also be meant to give the relatives who carried the pot and bore the body a more vivid sense of the materiality of what was being lost. He continued moving at the same slow, even pace, trying to calculate how far they had come from the village, to keep track of the path they were taking so he could make his way back alone if needed, and it was some time before he made out, coming up on the right, a large plot of land bounded by crumbling gray cinder-block walls, the sprawling land inside visible through a collapsed section of wall, overrun by brush and weeds. The four drummers, still playing lightly at the head of the procession, entered the plot of land on reaching the gate, followed by the casket-bearers, and Krishan realized that it was this walled-off plot of land, hardly distinguishable from the landscape surrounding it, that functioned as the village's cremation ground. He'd never been to a cremation ground in the northeast before, only in Colombo, where in addition to a kind of pavilion for cremations there were usually also large sections containing Muslim and Christian tombstones, physical graves that gave those sites the atmosphere of being populated. The ground they were entering now felt strangely empty in comparison, devoid of anything human, only the section near the center of the ground cleared of vegetation, the only permanent structure there a small cement platform that was level with the ground. Four thick iron bars were anchored into the rectangular platform at its corners, and it was within the confines of these iron bars that the pyre had been prepared, a number of dry, unevenly hewn pieces of wood stacked between them to a height of two or three feet. A small distance away several items had been laid out on the ground in readiness for the cremation, another small pile of wood, a dried palmyra leaf, a sack of hay, and a bottle of kerosene along with a few smaller items. The funeral director helped guide the casket to the center of the ground so the men carrying it could lower it onto the pyre, several other members of the procession joining as they let the front of the casket down and then slid the rest forward till its weight was entirely supported by the pyre. The drummers drew off to a side to continue drumming lightly, as unconcerned with the proceedings as they'd been at the funeral house, and the rest of the men in the procession gathered on one side, the closer relatives nearer to the pyre and the others farther back. Krishan watched as the director unfastened the lid of the casket and Rani's body was revealed once more to the light of day, her face still ghostly pale, her eyes still closed, her body still laden with garlands of flowers. With the help of his assistant he began taking the garlands off Rani's body, the still fresh flowers probably an impediment to the burning, lifting them up one by one with both hands and putting them carefully down on the ground a short distance away. Taking a large, curved, sicklelike knife the director severed the thread tying Rani's big toes together, separated her feet from each other, then unfolded her hands and separated those too, this too presumably to aid the burning. From the small pile on the ground he began to carry pieces of wood one by one to the casket, placing them gently, almost reverentially, upon Rani's body, the assistant helping him till her body was mostly concealed, so that looking at the casket it was hard to say whether the purpose of the additional wood was to help with the body's burning or to shield spectators from the sight of it disintegrating under the flames, from the disturbing scene of human turning into mineral right before their eyes.

The director called to Rani's son-in-law, who was standing a few feet away from the pyre observing the proceedings, the clay pot still on his left shoulder, and he made his way dutifully toward the head of the casket. The director gave him the torch he'd been carrying, a short stick of sandalwood that had already burned halfway down, and taking it in his right hand Rani's son-in-law held it behind his back with the smoldering end pointing away from his body. The director took the curved knife in his hand and stood just behind the son-in-law, who, like a man about to be shaved at a barbershop, remained where he was with almost nervous stillness. Gripping the knife not by the handle but by the blade itself, the director marked a spot near the base of the clay pot and struck at it sharply with the point of the knife, making a small, precise crack in the pot out of which water began to trickle. The drummers immediately began playing louder and more intensely, and in accordance with the director's instructions Rani's son-in-law began walking counterclockwise around the casket, solemnly and cautiously, the pot on his left shoulder and the torch in his right hand. The director followed close behind him, using his right hand to guide the trickling water away from the casket, slapping it as it fell in a gesture whose significance Krishan didn't quite under-stand. He stopped Rani's son-in-law at the head of the casket after one circumambulation, and taking the knife in his hand tapped sharply a second time at the back of the pot, this time a little farther down, creating a second hole so that the stream of water became a little broader, wetting the path that Rani's son-in-law now took for a second time around the body. Krishan had registered the son-in-law's physical presence in passing at the funeral house, but he was struck by his handsomeness as he moved now in the softness of the evening light, by his dark, muscular upper body, bare except for the white thread strung across his torso, the broadness of his chest and shoulders. The entirety of his back, he noticed, was marked by scars, making his stoic, graceful bearing even more impressive as he moved, and studying them as the pot was struck a third time and he began his third revolution, Krishan wondered whether perhaps they'd been inflicted by the army after the end of the war, which would have made sense, he knew, since Rani's son-in-law would have been in his early twenties at the time, and regardless of their affiliation with the Tigers most men that age would have been treated with suspicion. When he finished the third round the director stopped him at the head of the casket, turning him around so he was facing away from the body, then instructed him to throw down the pot and light the pyre without turning to look. Rani's son-in-law hesitated for a moment, as though he'd developed an attachment to the pot he'd carried with him all the way from the funeral house, then threw it down in front of him and watched as it shattered with a heavy thunk upon contact with the ground, the exploded water spilling onto the dry earth before him. Still looking away from the body, he reached toward the casket uncertainly with the smoldering torch, groping till he made contact and then letting the torch fall into the pyre. The pyre remained unlit, which was of course the standard course of things, the lighting of the pyre by the male relative usually nothing more than a symbolic act, and ushering Rani's son-in-law quickly to the other side of the casket, the director cut the thread around his torso and deposited it in the casket by Rani's feet. He opened a small packet of camphor tablets, deposited a few of the tablets on the ground by the foot of the pyre, then handed Rani's son-in-law a matchbox. Crouching down in front of the camphor tablets Rani's son-in-law lit a match and set the camphor alight, then getting on his stomach and stretching out his body on the dusty earth in front of the flame, prostrated himself before Rani one last time. He stood up slowly, still taking care not to turn his face toward the body, then turned around and began walking away from the pyre, back toward the entrance of the cremation ground. There was shuffling among the men behind him, and turning Krishan saw that several of them too had begun heading for the entrance. It was some kind of defilement to watch the body burning, he knew, but he didn't want to abandon Rani before the pyre began to burn, it didn't make sense having come all the way, and looking around, seeing that a few of the men were still standing there with hands behind their backs, no intention of leaving till the actual lighting took place, he turned his gaze back to the scene before him.

The director was taking out bales of hay from the sack beside the pyre, inserting them one by one into the gaps and crevices between the wood piled above and below the body, rendering Rani completely invisible. He began tearing out the white satin lining on the inside of the coffin lid, revealing the bare wood beneath, then picking up the dried palmyra leaf and taking the long stem in both hands, thrust the fan of the leaf inside till it was lodged inside the stack of wood. He lit a match and brought it to the part of the leaf that was now inside the pyre, lighting the fan at a few different points and then blowing in order to encourage the fledgling flames. Krishan had heard the news of Rani's death two days prior, had seen and touched her lifeless body just two hours before, but it was only now, watching the director trying to light the pyre, that he truly began to register that Rani would soon be gone, that she was, in fact, already gone. It was only now that he was realizing what it meant for her body to burn, what it meant for a fire to build in the hay and the wood, for it to spread to the casket and to the surface of Rani's body before entering, finally, inside her. Her hair would be the first to burn, he knew, the wild and unruly hair of her head that had been combed and domesticated after her death, followed by her eyelashes, her armpit hair, and the hair on her arms and legs, then by the softer, tenderer parts of her exterior, her lips, her eyes, and her skin, which would probably melt before they burned. The director had managed to consolidate a small fire beneath the casket, the fan of the leaf and the bales of hay burning in unison, the individual stalks blackening and curling as fire ran through them, and though the flames hadn't yet spread to the wood, let alone begun touching the casket, Krishan could sense within his own body what he knew would soon be occurring to Rani's. He thought about the burning of her eyes, so fragile and delicately constituted, thought about the melting of the eyelids, the dissolution of the iris and the lens into the simmering water of the tear glands, thought about the retina curling up and with it all the images that had been imprinted there over the course of Rani's lifetime, images of beauty and violence that had been superimposed over everything she saw. The fire was spreading slowly and evenly below the casket, crackling as it burnt up the hay and the shavings on the surface of the wood, spitting out embers as it ate its way through the fan of the palmyra leaf, and Krishan thought of how, if there still remained in Rani's body any trace of memory or consciousness, this too would soon be extinguished. He wondered whether this was what Rani had, during all her time in Colombo, secretly desired, the complete dissolution of all her thoughts and feelings, the extinction of consciousness that she could never hope to achieve through sleep the way most people did, that she hadn't been able to achieve through the mind-numbing quantity of sleeping pills she took or any of her other medications either. It was an extinction she'd tried and failed to obtain through shock therapy, through the general anesthetic she took and the electricity that was passed through her brain immediately afterward, an extinction she'd tried and failed to obtain through her various attempts at self-harm as well, hoping perhaps that severe physical pain, which had the effect of reducing all consciousness to the site of injury or laceration, of reducing the world to a point on the body's surface, leaving nothing else available for thought or consideration, would allow her to forget her other, deeper and less tangible pain.

It no longer mattered whether Rani's death had been planned or accidental, Krishan understood now, there didn't need to be a sharp line between these two kinds of death, a meticulous plan wasn't necessary for a death to have been intended. All it took sometimes was a vague desire for self-destruction in order for a person to become just a little more careless when crossing the road or leaning out of the train, to become just a little less vigilant when lighting a firecracker or fixing a hole in the roof, all it took sometimes was a silent half-wish for oblivion in order for the line between accidental death and planned death to be blurred, for death to become something the deceased would, eventually, be pushed toward. The idea of Rani being driven toward such a death seemed more and more plausible to him now, even if he had no evidence except the regret in her daughter's voice when she'd spoken of wishing that Rani had never left Colombo, even if her daughter herself seemed untouched by the possibility that her mother had wanted to die. Rani had lived for six years since the loss of her two sons, had been unable to recover despite her best efforts and the best efforts of everyone who knew her, and it made sense, after all that effort and all that time, if death, the total and irrevocable cessation of consciousness, had seemed to her in some instinctual, primordial way like the only way to achieve the extinction she sought. Thinking about the possibility no longer made him feel guilty, his brief interaction with her daughter at the funeral house having made it clear that Rani's death was not something he or his mother or grandmother could have prevented, not something they had caused or been responsible for. Rani's fate had been sealed long before their paths came together, on that day before the end of the war when a shard of shrapnel had sliced through her younger son, as though a fragment from that same shell had pierced her too that day, entering her not through her skin but her eyes, a small but insidious fragment that had entered her pupils like a needle and gradually made its way deeper inside her body over the years, eventually becoming the cause of her death too. What he felt was not so much guilt as a kind of amazement that he'd shared a home with such a person to begin with, that their lives, so different in quality and tenor, had somehow run in parallel, that Rani had been part of their lives for so long without him being able to foresee what was now so obvious, the inevitable endpoint of the trajectory along which she'd been silently advancing, though perhaps such trajectories only became visible when everything was over and it was already too late, perhaps they only began to seem inevitable or necessary in retrospect, once they'd already been incorporated into a new, more sober conception of reality.

Watching as the wood beneath the casket began to catch fire, the fire beginning to spread from the center of the pyre as the long stem of the palmyra leaf slowly burned through, Krishan remembered a conversation he'd had with Rani on New Year's Day, back when he was still living and working in the northeast. He'd returned to Colombo for the occasion and had planned to go out, less because he cared about New Year than from a desire to get intoxicated with friends after the sobriety of the previous months in Jaffna, drawn by the appeal of being out among people his own age in a state of heightened receptivity, the slim but enticing possibility of meeting someone new he always felt in such situations. The plan was to have dinner and drinks with a few friends before going out later to a house party they'd been invited to, and he'd gone that evening to his grandmother's room to say good night a little earlier than usual. Appamma and Rani had just finished eating and were watching the news with absorption, listening as the presenter discussed the various preparations for the night that had been undertaken throughout Colombo, while in the background of the studio, behind the presenter, flakes of digital snow were soundlessly falling, an embellishment that felt especially absurd given the drought that had been afflicting the country that year. The screen cut to clips of the president and prime minister wishing all Sri Lankans the best for the new year, snippets of their speeches dubbed into Tamil by the station, then to scenes of fireworks and celebrations from Sydney, Tokyo, and Beijing, where the New Year had already begun. Appamma had asked him what his plans for the night were, what time he was plan-

ning to come back, and he told her for what must have been the
third or fourth time that day that he wasn't sure, that it would
probably be late depending on what his friends wanted to do.
He'd asked Rani whether people celebrated New Year's in the
north, more for the sake of making conversation than to really
find out, knowing that for most people in the north the New
Year began not in January but the middle of April, in accordance with the Tamil calendar. Rani responded that people acknowledged the day, since it was a government holiday, but that
nobody she knew really celebrated it, not at least in the way it
seemed to be celebrated in Colombo. It occurred to Krishan as
she said this that Rani might like to go and see the fireworks at
Galle Face that night, that she might enjoy experiencing this
aspect of Colombo that she wouldn't otherwise have the chance
to see. Rani didn't generally like leaving the house, he knew, but
Galle Face for some reason was always heavily frequented by
Muslim and Tamil families and she would feel safe there, especially if he was with her too. He knew it would complicate his
plans for the night, but not bothering to think the matter
through he asked whether she wanted to join him, saying he
could come back home shortly before midnight to pick her up
and then bring her back once everything was over. She would
get to see all the fireworks, he went on, there would be a big
display, she probably hadn't seen anything like it before, and it
was only on saying this that he realized that being in Galle Face
could actually be triggering for her, that the sound of laughing,
shouting Sinhalese voices and the sudden, chaotic explosions of
firecrackers going off around them might remind her of the
end of the war. Rani smiled to show she appreciated the offer
but said that she couldn't, that she and Appamma were plan-

ning to watch a film that night. He looked at Appamma with surprise as if to ask whether this was true, to which Appamma had nodded her head and told him that yes, they'd made their own plans, that he wasn't the only one with something to do. They were airing a special film for New Year's, Rani explained, a new Vijay film that would play at midnight, the kind of film you would otherwise have to go to the cinema to see. Krishan shook his head in mock disapproval, as though he was jealous of being left out of their plans, then smiling stood up and kissed each of them good night, relieved that his offer had been turned down but warmed, at the same time, by the fact that Rani and Appamma had made their own plans for the New Year.

He'd gone out to dinner with his friends as planned, had drunk and smoked weed at one of their homes before heading out to the party, the kind of party he would be unlikely to meet anyone interesting or thoughtful, he'd known beforehand, but which he was nevertheless keen to attend, too drawn by the possibility of flirtation or intimacy to be put off by its more obnoxious elements. He could no longer remember any of the specific details of the night, the flat had been loud, smoky, and crowded, populated mainly by English-speaking people in their twenties and thirties, liberal people who said liberal things but became uncomfortable whenever identity or tradition was foregrounded too strongly. Everyone was drinking, smoking, and talking, and as midnight approached the party migrated to the roof to watch the fireworks, remaining there for a while after the fireworks had peaked and then making their way back down, everyone looser and more familiar with each other for having shared the intimate moment of transition. The music became louder, the movement and interaction more lively,

more people beginning to dance as their drunkenness deep-
ened, a few people arriving after having spent midnight at other
parties, the ashtrays slowly filling up and the empty bottles and
cups accumulating. When, around four-thirty in the morning,
the energy of the party began dwindling and people began fil-
tering out, first the couples and then everyone else in little
groups, Krishan did his best not to give way to the sense of
disappointment he always felt at the end of such events, when
it began to dawn on him that the promises with which the night
had started were failing to come to fruition. He and the two
friends of his who were still at the party were heavily intoxicated, had been smoking joint after joint through the night, and
not yet wanting to return home but knowing they'd be over-
staying their welcome if they remained much longer, had decided to smoke one last joint and go to Galle Face, where they
could talk for as long as they liked and where there might still
be people. They managed to find a three-wheeler after wandering the roads for a while, and were relieved when they arrived
to see that the place was still lively, the long, wide lawn far less
crowded than earlier in the night no doubt but still full of activity, mainly groups of boys and young men dancing obliviously
to the clashing music that sounded from different speakers,
though there were also, surprisingly, a large number of families, mothers and fathers, babies, children, and grandparents sitting peacefully on mats they'd brought from home, some of
them talking as they sipped on cups of tea or coffee, others
stretched out and fast asleep. The grass was full of the debris of
the night, spilled food, ice cream wrappers, empty plastic bottles, and the burnt remnants of firecrackers, but managing after
a while to find a section that was relatively untouched, the three

of them sat down in a small circle and made themselves comfortable. They lit cigarettes and talked under the wide, starless
sky, the salt breeze of the sea cool on their tired skin as the
darkness gradually let up, the crowd becoming sparser as the
sun came up quietly behind them. Increasingly weighed down
by their intoxication and from having spent the entire night
talking, their conversation soon petered out, each of them losing themselves in their own heavy, swaying thoughts as they
looked out over the calm January sea that was making itself
visible beneath the pale dawn light.

He had known it was time to make his way home, his throat
was parched from smoking one cigarette after another, there
was nothing he could possibly obtain by staying up longer, but
feeling a kind of restlessness at the thought of leaving, a reluctance to admit that the night was coming to an end, he'd per-
suaded his friends to stay just a little longer, citing the length of
their friendship and the fact that he would soon be returning to
the northeast. It was normal of course to be reluctant to go
home when you were inebriated and unfulfilled, not just on
New Year's but whenever you were out and about, but thinking
of that night at Galle Face now Krishan wondered why it had
always been so difficult for him to end such nights unless he
was absolutely exhausted, till going home was no longer a
choice but a necessity. It didn't simply happen when he was out
with other people, he knew, he found it hard to go to bed at a
reasonable hour even when sober in his room, some part of
him always resistant to going to sleep, as though going to bed
was a kind of concession or surrender, as though by staying up
something might happen that would justify having lived
through the day. In Delhi, where for the most part he'd had no

fixed schedule, he'd frequently found himself trapped in cycles of going to bed later and later every night, waking up later and later every morning, cycles he would attempt to correct by forcing himself at last to wake up early one morning, hoping he would fall asleep early the next evening out of sheer fatigue, cycles that repeated themselves no matter how hard he tried to maintain a consistent schedule. The pattern had been broken to some degree during his time in the northeast, where work was often so physically exhausting that he came home looking forward to sleep, but it had resurfaced once more upon moving back to Colombo, where despite having to get up early for work he went to bed late almost every night, losing sleep almost every day of the week and then compensating for the loss over the weekend. He often wondered about people who managed to keep regular hours of sleep with little effort or discipline, people who went to bed at the same time each night as though naturally in sync with the revolutions of earth, sun, and moon, as though the movement of their bodies was in some kind of inner harmony or alignment with those of the solar system. It was as though the desire that drew one out into the world each morning in the hope of some small fulfillment or some profound discovery was counterbalanced, for each person, by the disappointment and struggle that moving through the world entailed, as though by the end of each day most people's longing was equaled or exceeded by the fatigue the world produced, so that at a certain moment each evening they became content to stop searching and return to the comfort of their homes, to yield finally to sleep and the concession to reality it involved. It was as though for most of his life he'd been driven by a longing that was somehow stronger or more insistent than that of most people he knew, by a desire that had to meet more resistance than average before it could be vanquished, as though his body was adapted not to a twenty-four-hour day but a twenty-five- or twenty-six-hour day, so that what he and others like him needed, he couldn't help feeling, was nothing so much as a world of vaster circumference, a world whose movement through space could do justice to the longing he felt inside him.

By the time he'd said goodbye to his friends it had been seven or seven-thirty in the morning, the new year already well under way, and entering the house quietly he'd gone straight to his room, not wanting to alert his mother to his presence in such an unkempt state. He'd peeled off his clothes, full of the stale, damp odor of cigarette smoke, then stepped directly under the shower, letting the cool water wash over his hair and body. Turning off the tap he'd heard the sound of Appamma's door opening and closing outside, of Rani announcing to his grandmother that she'd brought up their tea, and knowing that if he went to bed he wouldn't wake till afternoon, that it would be nice to wish the two of them while it was still early morning, he dried himself off, put on a pair of fresh clothes, and went to their room. The two of them were sipping their tea in silence, Rani on her chair, Appamma at the edge of the bed, and kissing each of them on both cheeks he wished them a Happy New Year. Appamma was under the impression he'd just woken up, that he'd come home early the previous night, and after explaining that he'd just returned and hadn't yet gone to bed he asked how the film had been, whether they'd stayed up to watch the whole thing. Rani had looked at Appamma with a teasing smile, then told him that his grandmother had fallen asleep five minutes after the film started. Appamma immediately interjected, a mixture of embarrassment and indignation on her face, insisting that she'd been tired all of the previous day, that she'd hardly slept the previous night, that she didn't like watching all these new Indian films and that seeing the introductory part was enough for her to know that she was better off going to bed. He asked Rani if she too had gone to bed without watching the film, knowing she might have felt let down by Appamma's withdrawal from their plan, but Rani shook her head with a smile, told him she'd switched off the lights and stayed up to watch the film anyway, the volume turned off so not to wake his grandmother. With the volume turned down or with the volume turned all the way off, he'd asked, taking her last statement to be an exaggeration, to which Rani confirmed that she had indeed watched the entire thing without sound, shrugging as though there was nothing surprising in this. He asked how she'd managed to watch without being able to understand the dialogue, not quite believing she'd spent two and a half hours in front of a soundless screen, and she replied that it hadn't been too difficult to follow, that you could tell the emotions of the characters simply by looking at the expressions on their faces.

Krishan had talked to Rani and Appamma a few minutes more, had gone to wish his mother for the new year, then returned to his room, where despite the tiredness in his eyes and the lightness in the back of his head he was unable to fall asleep at once. Lying on his back with his eyes closed he thought about what Rani had said, the image fixed in his mind of her staying up by herself in that silent room, surrounded by darkness except for the images moving on the screen and the flickering light it cast on the walls. There'd been a similar occasion a few months earlier, when entering Appamma's room he'd found Rani sitting by herself in front of the TV, the sound blaring this time as some unrealistically dramatic scene, a kidnapping or assault, unfolded before her on the screen. He'd watched beside her for a while and then asked what had happened, what was the cause of the scene's exaggerated violence, in response to which Rani had looked at him with slight confusion for a moment before telling him, embarrassment on her face, that she wasn't exactly sure, giving him some vague explanation of the scene that didn't quite make sense. She'd been sitting there staring at the TV, he'd realized, without actually paying attention to what was happening, had been watching the screen as if it were showing her a sequence of images and sounds without meaning or connection to each other. Every time he saw Rani watching TV since then he'd wondered whether she was actually paying attention, and the fact she'd been able to watch an entire film without sound the previous night confirmed these suspicions to him now, for there was no way she could have followed the film without knowing what the actors were saying, especially since she wouldn't have been able to hear the music, which such films relied upon so heavily to set up the emotional valence of a scene, to tell the audience whether they should be sad or hopeful or anxious or fearful. She couldn't have had any sense of the plot, any sense of why something was happening and what consequences it would have for the characters, and if Rani really was content to watch a film this way then it must have meant that its logic and meaning were in some way irrelevant to her, that she was watching it without wanting or being able to inhabit it the way a spectator normally did. The sense of hearing was vital to the sense of participating in a situation, after all, and to watch a film without listening to it was to experience it at a remove, to observe the moving colors and shapes the way you might observe the patterns of passing clouds or the ripples on the surface of a lake. We can direct our gazes toward what lies in the distance whenever we want, toward things that have nothing to do with us and lack the power to affect us, but usually we can hear only what is in our vicinity and has the potential to affect us, so that sound, unlike sight, was associated with the physical presence of a thing and the possibility of interaction with it. It was for this reason perhaps that ghosts and spirits and phantoms were so often depicted as silent presences in films and books, as beings we can glimpse but cannot hear, that can watch but cannot speak, as though to signify that while these beings are in some way present to us they cannot participate in our world, no longer have the power to act and affect us, just as we ourselves are present in some way to them but cannot engage in the world to which they have been cast. What it was like to live in this way, to see but never hear, to be seen but never heard, Krishan did not know, but standing there as the fire grew beneath the casket he couldn't help feeling that this was what Rani's life had been like since the end of the war, physically located in a world that was shorn of the people she loved and unable therefore to participate in it, her mode of existence more akin to that of ghosts than humans, even if she'd existed in a body that possessed weight and could move physically through space, even if she'd remained capable of love and pain, laughter and generosity, even if the life inside her had been undeniable to anyone who saw her.

Krishan watched, mesmerized, as the fire engulfed more and more of the pyre, the wood inside crackling and bursting in response to the heat, the flames beginning to lick the bottom of the casket, the smoke beginning to rise up in thick, dark clouds. The director was still adding occasional handfuls of hay to different parts of the pyre, using his knife to prod and nudge the wood inside, but he too was more of a spectator now than a participant, watching the fire as it began to burn of its own volition, as though conscious of its own existence and the need to keep itself alive. The man standing beside him turned and began walking back toward the entrance, and looking around Krishan saw that nobody else from the procession remained now but him, that except for the funeral director and his assistant he was the only person left standing before the pyre. He too would have to leave soon, he knew, the intensity of the light in the sky was waning, it must have been five o'clock or later, and he didn't want to make his way back to the village in the dark. He remained standing there transfixed as the fire spread to the foot of the casket, as the wooden panels that formed its sides began to smolder and smoke, as the wood above Rani's feet began to catch flame. Picking up the end of the still burning stem of the palmyra leaf, the director drew the stem out from below the casket and inserted it into the wood above the body. He picked up the bottle of kerosene and sprinkled the oil over the wood, as though impatient for the casket to begin burning, took whatever hay was left in the sack and inserted it wherever he could. Rani was being exposed to the flames directly for the first time, Krishan could tell, and though her body hadn't started burning yet, though in any case it was concealed from sight, he felt he could hear the fire nearing her, hissing and sputtering as it spread. Listening to these sounds he suddenly felt anxious—it bothered him that Rani remained si-

lent as the flames surrounded her body, that he himself stood
there doing nothing, even though there was nothing he could
do—and making eye contact briefly with the director, he took a
first step back. He wondered whether to make some gesture of
obeisance to Rani, but not wanting to seem foolish he turned
and began to walk, moving slowly and deliberately back across
the ground. He began feeling calmer as the sound of the burning receded into the distance, as though what was happening
behind him, no longer audible, was happening in another sphere
or medium, and it was only when he reached the entrance,
drawn by some lingering curiosity, that he turned to look back
once more.

The pyre, much smaller in the distance, was burning densely
and brightly in the center of the ground, deep amber-orange in
the early twilight, its smoke wafting up and dissipating into the
air. Beyond the walls of the ground the pale blue horizon had
taken on a gray hue, its vastness interrupted here and there by
the palmyra trees dotting the landscape, and looking into this
vastness Krishan felt, coming over him, the strange sense that
there was nowhere left for him to go. His gaze moving between
the soundlessly burning pyre and the landscape of brush and
bramble that spread out on all sides he wondered what had
brought him to this place so far removed from the world he
knew, what forces had led him to leave the life he'd created for
himself in India, to come to this place he'd never actually lived,
this place that had hardly figured in his life growing up. He
wondered what movements of fate had led to his seemingly accidental encounter with Rani in the hospital ward, to her arrival
in their home just a few months later, to her unexpected death
two days before and his attendance now at her cremation, un-

able to shake off the sense that his presence in this scene of desolation had been decided somewhere long before, that something inside him had been driving him toward it long before the end of the war, something more than just guilt, something like freedom, even if he could not say what exactly freedom was. The specific path a life took was often decided in ways that were easy to discern, it was true, in the situation into which one was born, one's race and gender and caste, in all the desires, aspirations, and narratives that one came thereafter to identify with, but people also carried deeper, more clandestine trajectories inside their bodies, their origins often unknown or accidental, their modes of operation invisible to the eye, trajectories which were sometimes strong enough to push people in certain directions despite everything that took place on the surface of their lives. It was such a trajectory, set in motion by the things they'd seen, that had led so many young men and women to join the separatist movements decades ago, it was such a trajectory that had led Rani and so many people like her to their accidental or intentional deaths in the years after the war, and it was such a trajectory, Krishan now felt, that had led him too, in his own quiet and unremarkable way, to this cremation ground at the end of the world. His own path through life had been decided when he was much younger, not long after the death of his father perhaps, though what came to mind now was not so much his father's death as a period several years later, his final months of school and the long, aimless months he'd spent waiting for exam results, those endless days and weeks filled with yearning for a life he couldn't articulate and didn't know where to find. The cease-fire had been breaking down at the time and the war in the northeast was beginning to resume in full force, as a result of which his mother rarely let him or his brother leave the house by themselves, overly anxious that they would be stopped and interrogated, taken away by soldiers or policemen, overly fearful she might lose a son after having already lost her husband. He'd begun feeling trapped having to spend all that empty time within the walls of their small home, and although he hadn't understood it at the time it had probably been this sense of entrapment, this loss of freedom, that led him to pass so much time on their roof in those months, climbing up on the balcony railing and then onto the gentle slope, lying there for hours at a stretch in the nights while his brother, mother, and grandmother slept, listening to music while gazing up at the ocean of blue suspended above, at the silvery translucence of the clouds that he'd always felt were carrying messages to him from afar, thinking as he lay there, in that naïve and moving way of adolescents, how large and unknown the world was, how much it seemed to contain.

It had been in those months of waiting probably that he'd first become aware of the absence inside him, the longing for a life that existed beyond the boundaries of the Colombo and Sri Lanka he knew, an absence that he hadn't felt as an absence so much as a kind of willingness to be drawn elsewhere, an absence that had made him, paradoxically, more present to the world around him, more delicately aware of its surfaces and textures and moods. He'd not had any sense, back then, of what it was that life could offer, hadn't yet known what it would be like to live in another place, to live by himself and be responsible for his own decisions, to kiss, have sex, or be in love, to make a home for himself somewhere or to move from place to place. He hadn't yet experienced the objects of any of his desires, whether people or places or situations, his desires at the time no more than images in his mind, abstract objects possessing meanings he couldn't glean, things to which he attached significance without knowing why. What he'd felt at the time was not so much desire as a kind of yearning, for though both desire and yearning were states of incompleteness, states involving a strong, sometimes overwhelming need for something outside one's life, what was called desire always had a concrete object, a notion of what was necessary to eliminate the absence one felt inside, whereas to have what was often called yearning was to feel this absence and yet not know what one sought. To desire, in a sense, was to know or think one knew what one wanted, to know or think one knew the paths by which it might be reached, even if those paths turned out to be too difficult to follow, even if the things they led to, the things one desired, turned out not to provide the liberation one thought. To yearn on the other hand was to be lost, to lack bearings in the world because one did not know what one was seeking or where it could be found, so that unable to distract oneself, by frenetic activity or single-minded pursuit, from the painful sense of lack, one's only consolation was to look out across vast distances, as if surely somewhere in the expansiveness of the horizon, across space and sea and sky, some possibility was contained that could make life self-sufficient and devoid of need, some possibility that could bring an end to time. That such a possibility didn't exist he was now old enough to know, but it was a yearning of this kind that had led him here, he felt as he gazed at the pyre burning soundlessly at the center of the ground, that had led him along all the many paths he'd taken and brought him here at last to Rani's burning body—Rani, whose

vividly painful longing contained both the particularity of desire and the directionlessness of yearning, the knowledge of
what exactly she needed and the knowledge that it could no
longer be found—as though to tell him that any attempt to cure
or solve absence would lead, sooner or later, only to death and
the extinction of thought.

The evening was gathering over the landscape, and standing
there at the entrance to the cremation ground Krishan gazed
for a last time at the brilliant red glow of the pyre, all of it alight
now, the wood and the casket and most likely the body inside
too, all of it burning brightly in the lifeless gray light of the
evening. It would take several more hours for the burning to
be complete, he knew, the human body contained a lot of material, not just flesh and bones and organs but feelings and visions, memories and expectations, prophecies and dreams, all
of which would take time to burn, to be reduced to the sooth-
ing uniformity of ash. It was these ashes that Rani's son-in-law
would pick up the next day, which would be kept for a month in
their home and then dispersed afterward over a body of water,
perhaps over the sea on the northern or eastern coast, perhaps
over the lake they'd passed on the way to the ground, in either
case dissipating, eventually, into the long wide arc of the world.
Eventually nothing would remain of Rani's body, eventually
nothing would remain of what she'd thought or felt or seen or
heard, though watching as the flames flickered in the distance,
shooting out embers into the void, Krishan no longer felt any
particular sadness at the thought of Rani's body being reduced,
perhaps because he could no longer hear the actual sound of
the burning, perhaps because he understood now that Rani had
already left the world. He watched as the scarlet glow of the

fire grew brighter in the darkening evening, as the air around it warped with strange clarity in the intensity of the heat, watched as the substantiality of a human life was transmuted, like a mirage or hallucination or vision, into thick clouds of smoke billowing up into the sky, thinning as they rose and then disappearing into the evening, a message from this world to another that would never be received.

ACKNOWLEDGMENTS

THIS NOVEL WAS a more collaborative effort than my first novel, and would not have found its present form if not for the generosity of many people: my editors P.E. at Hogarth and L.B. at Granta; J.B., R.R., and the rest of the team at Hogarth; my agent A.S. at ICM; my sister and first reader A.A.; my long-time mentor P.K.; and my dear friends A.G., A.T., B.M., C.E., G.K., H.B., J.R., L.S., M.L., O.N., S.K., T.M., T.T., and V.S. My thanks also to *The Paris Review* for excerpting part of the novel in their fall 2019 issue.

The text incorporates a number of works of translation and documentary: the version of Poosal's story from the *Periya Purānam* in the first chapter is based on a translation from the Tamil in David Shulman's *Imagining the Real;* the version of *The Cloud Messenger* told in the fourth chapter is based on James Mallinson's translation from the Sanskrit; the version of the *Life of the Buddha* told in the seventh chapter is based on a translation from the Sanskrit by Patrick Olivelle; the story of Kutti-mani's death told in the seventh chapter is based on Rajan Hoole's account in *The Arrogance of Power: Myths, Decadence, and Murder;* the documentary described in chapter nine is Beate Arnestad and Morten Daae's *My Daughter the Terrorist;* the account in chapter nine of Buddhist women's poetry is based on a translation from the Pali by Charles Hallisey.

This book is for my mother and father.

ABOUT THE TYPE

This book was set in Dante, a typeface designed by Giovanni Mardersteig (1892–1977). Conceived as a private type for the Officina Bodoni in Verona, Italy, Dante was originally cut only for hand composition by Charles Malin, the famous Parisian punch cutter, between 1946 and 1952. Its first use was in an edition of Boccaccio's *Trattatello in laude di Dante* that appeared in 1954. The Monotype Corporation's version of Dante followed in 1957. Though modeled on the Aldine type used for Pietro Cardinal Bembo's treatise *De Aetna* in 1495, Dante is a thoroughly modern interpretation of that venerable face.

Keep in touch with
Granta Books:

Visit granta.com to discover more.

GRANTA

Also by Anuk Arudpragasam and available from Granta Books
www.granta.com

THE STORY OF A BRIEF MARRIAGE

WINNER OF THE DSC PRIZE FOR
SOUTH ASIAN LITERATURE

SHORTLISTED FOR THE DYLAN THOMAS PRIZE
AND THE INTERNATIONALER LITERATURPREIS

'Extraordinary . . . hypnotic' *Mail on Sunday*

'A strange, profound, mini-masterpiece' *Financial Times*

'*The Story of a Brief Marriage* is written with subtlety, tact and
intelligence. Every image in the book, including the most
desolate, is rendered with precision and an aura of pure truth
and tenderness. It is a great achievement, one of the best books
I have read in years' Colm Tóibín

Dinesh and Ganga meet and marry in the final days of the Sri
Lankan civil war. For years their lives have been pared back to the
essentials: eat, sleep, survive. Now, as the army draws ever closer,
they begin to explore their new and unexpected connection – a
fragile light to keep the war at bay.

'Astonishing' Lisa McInerney, *Irish Independent*

'Brave . . . Brilliant . . . This is a book that makes one kneel
before the elegance of the human spirit and the yearning that is
at the essence of every life' *New York Times*

'Very seldom in a reading life does a novel alter your sense not
only of literature but of the world. This extraordinary debut
is of that class . . . an exquisite, unbearably moving work of art
equally alive to brutality and tenderness. Anuk Arudpragasam has
written a great book. I will never forget it' Garth Greenwell